WHAT THE RAKE REMEMBERS

Agents of Change, 4

AMY QUINTON

CONTENTS

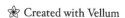 Created with Vellum

What the Rake Remembers

England 1814: He is a known rake recovering from life-threatening injuries. She is a survivor from his past, forged by men like him. Who could've predicted there might be problems along the way?

Theirs was a forbidden love...

Agent for the Crown, Ciarán Kelly, is an Irishman who loves women. *All* women. Big, small, buxom, slender, blonde, ginger, rich, poor—their features matter not. Fortunately, he was born with a silver tongue, enough wit and charisma to rival Claude Duvall, and an air of mystery, necessary to be an effective spy. In short, women love him. But after being branded a traitor and tortured by the very villains he's vowed to destroy, he's lost his memory and is left with only one person in the world he can—and must—depend upon...and she despises the very air he breathes.

No matter, he is:

- Confidently optimistic—she'll come around.
- Smooth-talking—beneficial when he makes her angry. And he will make her angry.
- And brilliant—useful, if only he could remember...

And he isn't:

- Impatient—There's always time. See also confidently optimistic above.
- Or afraid—of being in love. He's been there before. Maybe.

Frederica Glyndŵr has matured since her father erased her from the family tree, tossing her to the streets of London with nothing more than her wits to aid her survival. What started out as a horrific journey towards female enslavement has ended up being the best possible thing to happen to her. She's learned to be a fighter, a thief, a stealthy observer, and a surprising revelation to any villain who happens along —they love to underestimate her. Everything is finally perfect. Until a disappointment from her past invades her life once more, threatening to expose her secrets. She's ready for a reckoning, but never forgiveness...too bad he has no memory of their past.

No matter, she is always:

- Prepared—a life lesson; she will never be caught ill-equipped again.
- And capable—she's proven *that* to herself time and again.

And she isn't:

- Sloppy—with the men they're after, this could mean the difference between life and death.
- Patient—normally not a positive trait, but time is of the essence. Bad men are coming.
- Or in love...or won't be if she could only retrieve her heart from the man who stole it.

As the enemy closes in and Kelly's mind begins to heal, he discovers just how deep his betrayal goes.

Can true love prevail over such sins?

Frederica can't speak for some sins, but she's damn sure it can't survive all secrets...

Acknowledgments

I would like to thank Jessica Cale for the beautiful cover and fine editorial work; I am forever grateful we met.

I would like to also thank Angela Mizell, for the hours and hours and HOURS spent dissecting Kelly and Freddie, for thinking through REASONS, for plotting, plotting and PLOTTING again, and for the superior editorial work. Thank you so much. I adore being your best friend. LOL

Thank you!

For my family...thank you for your patience. I love you.

And for Angela Mizell...here's your favorite Agent of Change. I hope you adore him.

Prologue

England, 1814: Somewhere Along the River Mersey

Ciarán Kelly felt fluid, boneless. The constant pain he'd endured for the past fortnight was gone. In its place was a peaceful numbness; he wanted nothing more than to just float away on this newfound tide of pleasant harmony. He felt neither cold nor hot. There was no smell. No sound. Nothing to taste. He couldn't sense his broken fingers. Nor his battered legs or cracked ribs. His burned torso no longer throbbed. The scratches along his back uttered not a peep. Hell, he couldn't even feel his cock.

Tsk...the poor ladies...

Well, at least his humor was still intact.

He squinted, or so he thought, and found his eyes were working as well as his wit.

Maybe.

Everything appeared to be tinged pink as if the world lay cloaked beneath a veil of watery, rosy silk—dancing silk, for everything around him seemed to be moving in a decadent rhythm, undulating as if every living thing floated upon a never-ending line of waves. One after another, up and down, then, back up once more. It was a slow, peaceful pace and calming, like a leisurely waltz.

He was ever the poet.

Kelly squinted (or at least he thought he did) as something in the distance caught his eye. A woman? Real or an illusion, he knew not. Closer and closer her image drew near, her hips and shoulders swaying with the swells. She moved ever so slowly, and his impatience to know more about her threatened to get the best of him, ruining his newfound sense of peace.

When at last, the woman appeared before him, finally into view though just out of reach, his heart surged proving that it, too, remained unspoiled; though as always, never whole.

For in the center of this strange, new world...was *her*: Lady Frederica Uriana Patience Althea Dawe.

She'd died seven years ago though he thought of her every single day of his life.

Ah, Freddie...

He wished he could chuckle, or simply smile for that matter, for she'd hated being called Freddie.

Instead, he contended himself to simply watch as she, too, rolled with the rise and swell of the waves. Her luscious curves swayed to and fro. He wanted to believe she danced just for him, that she beckoned him near. He wanted desperately to answer her siren's call—to grasp her, hold her, and kiss every loving inch of her. Ah, what he wouldn't give for one more kiss...

"Mmmm..."

Had he arms, he would reach out and seize her and this time, never let her go.

All too soon, her apparition dissolved into nothingness, and in its place, was an intense pain, the likes of which he'd not recently endured, beginning with an insistent throbbing in his shoulder.

No!

He shied away from the discomfort and searched in vain for Freddie. Where was she? He wanted her back, dammit.

Yet despite his desperate desire to do so, he could not find her, her likeness replaced by blackness and the slow return of pure agony. Besides, he begged for the impossible.

"Aaaaaarg..." He cried out with a fresh surge of pain.

Dammit. Someone was...moving him?

A sharp ache shot through his left leg, and his cracked ribs joined in protest with the rest of his body, voicing their complaints in no uncertain terms.

Ungh... Umpf...

At once, every bone in his body, broken or otherwise, made its presence known. He shivered now as if he'd been lying on a blanket of snow for days; yes, he was cold, so cold. He noted a broken arm, at least two broken fingers, several cracked ribs, a broken and clogged nose, and more bruises than he could have ever imagined. His lips were swollen and split, his lungs hurt, and he could taste the salty tang of sea water on his tongue, could feel the sea itself lapping against one side of his face, then flooding his mouth on a rush. He spat. Even that hurt.

Though the pain of his injuries was immense and the sea water both a nuisance and a threat, instinct kicked in and he forced himself to reach out with his senses—to try to understand what was happening.

He was being hefted and pulled now; one strong hand gripped his arm above the elbow. His head dropped back as he was lifted, then something hard dug into his side, yet also dipped beneath his weight. One of his cracked ribs screamed once again; and again, he shoved aside the agony.

Was he being pulled onto a boat?

Someone tugged on him, harder, and he slid further over the solid edge, which dug into his hip now.

Damn! He wanted desperately to reach out and shoot whoever was trying to move him. It fucking hurt!

"Unnnn..." His warning to cease and desist didn't quite come out as forcefully as he'd intended.

A muffled voice grunted, and he felt himself being pulled with one final show of strength; then he was tumbling, landing on something flat and wet but solid, his legs and arms akimbo.

"Argh!" He screamed, but with his clogged ears it seemed as if he'd barely uttered a sound.

Someone grabbed at his arms, pushed on his chest, then pulled the hair off his face. There was a pause, then a chuckle. "Well, lookie what we have here. I bet someone would pay a pretty penny for the likes of you."

"Mmmm..." Was the extent of his cutting reply.

The old man, for the voice was that of an aging codger, shifted him once more, his body settling more firmly in what he was sure now was the bottom of a small fishing vessel.

Then...nothing.

He heard the unmistakable sounds of oars being positioned, then a small splash as they dug into the water. With a lurch, the vessel shot forward.

Kelly tried opening his eyes, but they burned and opened to no more than slits. Still, he searched through the grime encrusting his lashes and lids for the source of his troubles, for the man who'd spoken —the bastard responsible for disrupting his memories of *her*.

His gaze latched onto the craggy features of a rough sort of cove; not the kind of man one would find at a London ball, but he didn't have an unkind face, either. Kelly could just make out the general shape of the old cuff's features between the dim glow of a half moon and his own slitted eyes. His face was weathered and lined, probably from a life spent on the sea. His nose was large and bulbous, his eyes deep-set beneath heavy white brows. He wore a knitted cap, but from beneath the edges was a veritable forest of white hair, flapping in the breeze.

The man glanced down, and his coarse face split into a grin only broken by a sparse collection of rotting teeth. "Evenin' Gov'nah. Welcome to Runcorn." Then, he laughed.

For a fleeting moment, Kelly tried to sit up, but pain exploded through his body. He collapsed, falling towards oblivion once more.

Kelly smiled. *No matter*; he would see *her* there...he always did.

And when he woke, he would burn the Society for the Purification of England to the fucking ground.

Chapter One

Two Days Later: Castell Ddu, Dinas Powys, Wales

"I have a new mission for you, a matter of some urgency," warned Owain Glyndŵr.

Lady Frederica Glyndŵr née Dawe couldn't subdue her smirk over that comment as she flicked her long braid over one shoulder and strode across the great hall of Castell Ddu, her long stride eating up the considerable distance to the dais in a matter of seconds. They weren't really married in truth, though they pretended to be when the occasion called for it. She'd been all too happy to shed her maiden name after Father had dumped her in the stews of St. Giles and had relished reinventing herself as Frederica Glyndŵr.

Besides, the name Glyndŵr, in Wales at any rate, opened many doors which would otherwise be barred to her.

Today, Frederica wore her habitual men's trousers, which she sported most days, for they allowed her a freedom of movement one couldn't hope to achieve while wearing a traditional lady's dress and corset—a particularly useful thing when practicing her swordsmanship.

She approached her sometimes husband, sometimes protector, sometimes boss, Owain—or more formally, Lord Rhodri Owain Perce

Bewlyn Glyndŵr—as he lounged upon his ebony throne, one leg tossed casually over the arm.

Truly. His literal throne. And yes, it stood there tall and ornate with carved wood and velvet cushions, all of it black—the velvet, the wood —blacker than the night sky.

As was his habit, Owain toyed with the rings on one hand. He radiated a sense of calm with his relaxed pose, though she knew for certain his hawkish eyes missed nothing.

Frederica stopped before the short dais and crossed her arms. "Urgency you say? Do tell, Your Grace..."

Owain sneered at the honorific, and Frederica laughed for she knew how it rankled him when she called him Your Grace. In truth, he was the 8th Duke of Powys and a descendant of one of the lost princes of Wales before England began proclaiming that title for their own kings way back in 1301. The duchy was a newly bestowed title, one from a previously extinct line, gifted to Owain by Prinny himself. If the Prince Regent only knew the truth...

"Very funny." He followed with a scowl.

Frederica shook her head, then pursed her lips. "Go on, then. What urgent matter requires my attention—er...my unique set of skills, as you say."

He snorted. "Unique." Owain glanced away, a frown marring his brow. "There's a person of some importance who needs your specific brand of assistance."

"Friend or foe?"

Owain took his time to respond, his gaze on some unseen point in the distance, whilst drumming his beringed fingers on the arm of his throne. He took a deep breath and faced her once more. "We'll call him a friend. For now."

Frederica pointed her finger at him. "I'm NOT babysitting some—"

Owain held up one hand, a lacy sleeve dropped down revealing long, elegant fingers, a flash of his silvery rings, and the edge of a tattoo on his forearm. "I need you to bring him here. As soon as feasibly possible; he's gravely injured—"

She swallowed. "'Tis a shame. Nevertheless—"

Owain leaned forward then, his expression fierce, his palms together as if in prayer. "I'm not entirely certain he'll survive."

Frederica lifted her chin—one last stand of mutiny—and recrossed her arms. "The Society for the Purification of England has been growing bolder. They're in Liverpool this week, openly blackmailing and strong-arming the local aristocracy, pressuring those lords to vote against the upcoming immigration bill. Clearly, it's not enough that they've *murdered* to achieve their aims."

There were more important battles to be won in this war against the Secret (not so secret) Society for the Purification of England. Owain *knew* this. Those men, powerful men of the aristocracy, used whatever means necessary to achieve their goal: to rid England's shores of any who were not purely English. At the moment, their main target was the Irish, but it wouldn't be long before they broadened their reach to include the Scots—and the Welsh.

They were the entire reason behind how she'd lost *everything*—

She would see the entire organization brought down and the bastards behind it all hung, or she would die trying.

"If you know all this, then you've heard about the *HMS Nightingale*?" he continued.

She nodded. "I have. It exploded. Possibly, the Duke of Stonebridge and his agents were involved, but—"

"The Society held a prisoner on board, a man of some import to everyone..."

"I understood there were no survivors."

"I have it on good authority he's been fished from the River Mersey."

"But—"

"Frederica," He barked. Then added with solemnity; his gaze direct. "Trust me. I—*we*—need him to survive." But then, he sat back with a smile she understood all too well and was far worse a sight than his gravity. "You'll thank me—later."

'Later.' The most frightening word in the English language when uttered by a man such as the Duke of Powys, especially while wearing *that* sort of smile on his face.

And then, there was the matter of trust...

Frederica sighed and unconsciously reached up to squeeze her locket, sliding the golden oval along its chain, while she shuffled her boots through the rushes on the stone floor. It was either that or hit something, preferably Owain. She sighed. "Where is he?"

"England."

Frederica's head snapped up. *Of course.* She glared at Owain.

His smile widened, then he lifted his left hand, gesturing with a folded piece of paper that jutted out from between the middle knuckles of two long fingers. Frederica stepped forward and snatched it from him, unfolding it as Owain picked up a glass of whisky with his freed hand and said, "Our quarry was last spotted leaving a small fishing village on the River Mersey. He was surrounded by a bevy of rough looking men."

"Runcorn?"

Owain shrugged and took a sip of whisky, then gestured with the hand holding his tumbler. "That note is from our man in Blackpool, George."

The note contained dates, number of men. Frederica snorted. "A bevy? Sounds like four men plus our mark." She crumpled the paper. "George could handle that in his sleep." She walked over to the fireplace and tossed the note into the flames.

Owain chuckled and slid the tip of one finger around the rim of his glass. "Indeed, as could you. But we need this man alive, working for our side, and we need it to happen yesterday. He has information vital to our cause."

Of course, he does. Frederica turned her back on the fire and approached Owain. "So, the directive is..."

Owain set down his glass and abruptly stood, then stepped off the dais. He spoke as he strode toward her. "Bring him to me—"

She paused and lifted her brow in question. "—using whatever means necessary?"

Owain stopped beside her and considered her a moment too long, then as he strode away, he murmured. "Somehow, I don't think that will be required."

She called to his retreating back, "He'll need time and a safe place to convalesce before he's ready to make the journey to Wales."

Owain glanced over his shoulder. "I have every confidence you can sort it all out. But if needed, there is a little place in Runcorn—"

"Oh? Not one of yours then?"

"Not one of the *duke's*. Rather, this particular property belongs to Viscount Sharpe."

"Ah. I see..."

Viscount Sharpe. Yes, *that* told her everything she needed to know.

Although when dealing with a man like Owain, one could never be entirely sure. She'd have to be prepared...for anything.

Chapter Two

Ciarán Kelly came to as the restraints were being tightened around his ankles. On instinct, he sat up swinging. His ribs screamed in protest, but he swallowed back the pain and fought like a man possessed.

Not again.

One ruffian fell to the stone floor when Kelly's uppercut connected with the man's jaw. Kelly eyed the unconscious man while reaching for the first strap. He managed to undo the restraint just as another ruffian made it across the room. He dispatched that one as easily as the first and within seconds, had the second leather shackle off his other ankle.

He shoved off the table and landed with a wince and an oath. "Shite."

Fuck, that hurt.

He twisted his head and gritted his teeth, willing away the pain, then stood and took stock of the room he was in. It appeared to be some sort of cell made out of what looked like a cave, probably underground for there were holes high above that allowed in some light and a small, but steady trickle of water, which rolled down the stone wall and splattered onto the floor before sinking into the earth.

He wore no shoes; what clothes he donned—only trousers, which hung too low on his lean hips, and a shirt—were shredded and filthy. His ribs were definitely cracked, and his feet stung as if he had cuts on the bottom.

And by the feel of things, his right knee was three times its normal size.

He quickly searched the two ruffians and was only rewarded with a small knife for his troubles. He'd used larger knives to *eat* with, but it was better than being totally unarmed. Maybe.

He shuffled across the room in record time, considering, but stopped short as the largest man he'd ever seen in his life ducked his head through the doorway and stepped inside the cell.

Kelly slid to a halt with a wince of discomfort and smiled to hide his grimace. The man was certainly large, but he didn't seem the sort to hurt a soul.

However, Kelly wasn't one to underestimate anyone, not even gentle-looking giants.

Kelly bent his knees at the ready and tossed his knife from one hand to the other. "I don't want to hurt you, *mo chara*, but I'm leaving this place, so I will if I must."

The giant darted a look to Kelly's butter knife, then smiled as if he were amused. "You funny, little man. Johnnie like."

At over six foot, Kelly wasn't, by any stretch, a little man but compared to *this* man. Well, everything was relative, he supposed.

Kelly sidestepped, *just*, as Johnnie lunged and attempted to sideswipe him with one meaty fist. Kelly felt a brush of air across his cheek as said fist sailed pass, missing him by mere inches. Had the giant's fist connected, Kelly was sure he'd have been knocked headfirst into next Tuesday.

Kelly retaliated with a right hook, and though he'd knocked the second ruffian out with the same throw, this time, his punch barely registered on his opponent's face. Kelly winced, sure he'd just busted a knuckle or two in the process while the giant felt the equivalent of a butterfly's kiss.

Kelly tossed his knife to the ground, knowing it was more hindrance than help and changed tactics. Kelly smiled and said, "Seeing as how we're headed to a draw...," the giant snorted. "Why don't we join forces? I could use a man like you on my side. Together, we could rout the villains, save the country, get the girl. What do you say, big man?"

Kelly saw the man's 'no' cross his face before he'd even said a word, so though Kelly hated to do it, he decided to take advantage of the pause. Without warning, he charged, shoulder down, and using every bit of strength at his disposal, shoved Johnnie into the wall. It was like tackling a bull, but it worked, and the man briefly lost his balance. *'Briefly'* being the concern in all that. But it was enough, and Kelly bolted for the door.

Johnnie didn't stay down long, and he was fast for a man his size, with a long reach. He caught the edge of Kelly's shirt with one meaty fist before Kelly had cleared the room.

Kelly ripped the thing in two, it was barely held together any longer anyway, shoved out of it, and raced up the stone stairs, bare-chested, one hand holding up his trousers lest he lose those, too.

He burst through the door at the top of the stairs into a peculiarly clean, one-room box of a shack with strange, white curtains. But he didn't stay long to admire the peculiarity of it all. He was out the front door in seconds and racing across a field toward the treeline. For the first time in weeks, freedom lay within his grasp, and the thought gave him a renewed burst of energy. He was going to make it.

The torture was behind him.

No sooner had those words tumbled across his thoughts, when a searing burst of pain shot up from his left leg, and he went down hard. Kelly rolled, and after he stopped, glanced over his shoulder only to discover a large knife embedded deep in the back of his left thigh. *I dtigh diabhail!* That was going to need a stitch or two.

He looked up and locked eyes with the man who, presumably, threw the knife.

Lord Fulton winced. "Ooh. That looks like it hurts."

Kelly glared at the man and spat. "Fuck you."

Lord Fulton squatted and tapped the end of his knife. Kelly fought back a scream.

The bastard said, "Lucky for you. I was aiming for your back."

Kelly was not surprised Lord Fulton would be the type to stab a man in the back.

Kelly narrowed his eyes. He was sweating from his run and from holding back the bite of agony, but rather before succumbing, he bit out, "Lucky for me, you have terrible aim." And with one swipe of his injured leg, he knocked Lord Fulton to his arse.

It was the last thing he did before passing out cold from the agony.

Chapter Three

Days and Days and Days on Horseback Later: Followed By What Felt Like Hours and Hours and Hours Inside the Wee Cock: Two Miles Outside Runcorn, England...

rederica settled in beside George, a black man with a deadly aim and a keen wit and one of her two partners on this misadventure, and mumbled, "This has got to be the right place."

Several clues made it certain her observation was justified:

1: The Wee Cock lay far off the beaten path—and should probably be condemned.

Frederica shifted in her seat, noting that her trousers seem to adhere themselves to the bench, and mumbled, "I don't suppose the owner has ever heard of a mop? Or a rag?"

George eyed his mug, then snorted before taking a swig of ale.

Aye. The Wee Cock was a dark and filthy place that looked to predate the birth of Good Queen Bess by at least a hundred years, and it clearly hadn't seen the swipe of a cloth or the sweep of a broom since the last century, at the very least. Worse, the exposed beams holding up the floors above were bowed in the middle to the point that most of the men had to duck to pass through the center of the room, and the entire building listed thirty degrees to the west, enough that Frederica eyed the ceiling with a strong measure of uncertainty.

Surely, it would hold for one more night.

Better still, the outer walls all but invited in the night air through generous gaps, offering the patrons a fragmented view to the great outdoors (which, on a positive note, helped with the view and the smell.). What plaster remained, loosely holding it all together, had long ago lost its snowy luster, appearing yellowed and brown and thick with grime through a combination of age, soot, and smoke.

The few candles dotting the walls and tables were tallow, of course, and stunk nearly as much as the stranger sitting on her other side, who at that moment, let out an offensive, meaty belch.

Frederica took a sip of her own ale, stifling the urge to shudder, and glanced past George and over to the bar to her left, where three men stood at one end speaking in hushed tones. She glanced down, pretending to search the inner pocket of her coat, and muttered, "The blokes at the end of the bar look promising."

George put his mug to his lips as if to drink, and said, "Aye, yesterday the big one was mouthing off about a big reward coming his way. If he's not careful, he'll be mugged afore the week is through."

Freddie once more darted a look over to the men. One, average-sized and puffing on a cigar, reclined against the wall, leg bent, the sight somewhat hilarious to her mind seeing as how the entire building leaned in his direction. The other two stood at the bar, one rather large, the other quite small.

Federica lifted her ale. "I've decided to call the mouthy, barrel-chested man Busty." From the corner of her eye, she saw George shake his head, and she smiled. "The leaner, smaller man who darts his head about constantly, shall be Birdie."

While obviously trying hard to suppress a smile, George asked, "And the one leaning against the wall?"

She tapped her finger on the edge of her mug. "Hmm. Haven't settled on that one yet."

She stole a glance once again and noted Birdie and Busty speaking rapidly, talking over each other, then in synchronized fashion, they downed their mugs of ale before simultaneously wiping the froth from their mouths with their sleeves.

She sighed and glanced back to her own mug. Aye, they were in the right place. Considering the location and the state of the building, no one in their right mind, or *up to any good*, would choose to spend their spare time here, which led her to point number two in support of her theory:

2: The regulars were not dressed for tea with Prinny.

More to the point, their clothes wouldn't have looked out of place in the lowest stews of London—she'd know, for she'd called the place home once upon a time.

Poor quality material, worn and ill-fitting and as dirty as the benches upon which they all sat, hung from narrowed shoulders curled over mugs of ale. Only a few women peppered the room, none of them there in any capacity related to maid of all work, and all of them wearing the haunted look of the desperate she'd seen on countless faces before, including her own.

There were certainly no children present, or at least, none she'd seen.

Likely, the men—and the women, for that matter—would do anything for coin, a sad state of affairs to be sure, and the sight tore at her heart, for once upon a time, she'd been one of them—desperate and forlorn and nearly without hope.

Unfortunately, that sort of desperation was useful if one were plotting nefarious deeds.

On this particular eve, most of the patrons, and there were only a handful in total, were drunk or well on their way, and the five that weren't obviously in either condition, stood largely out of place. Three they'd already remarked upon. And the other two, besides the men on her team, of course, well—

As if reading her thoughts, George said, "Do you see the two men at the far table?"

Now, it was Frederica's turn to snort. Frederica nodded. "Even my mother, bless her, couldn't miss those two."

Aye, those two men led her to point number three, in support of her summation:

3: The two men sitting together at a table in the far-right corner worked for the government.

Frederica tossed the officials her winningest smile, then toasted them with her mug of ale. They simultaneously adjusted their dark, perfectly tied cravats and looked away, noses stiff in the air. Freddie snorted and rolled her eyes, then muttered to George. "Amateurs."

George chuckled. But really, at least the men on her team blended with the crowd.

Still, the government men's presence here was curious. Considering her mission to take down the Society for the Purification of England had led her here, those men likely reported to the Duke of Stonebridge, who was *officially* tasked with taking down the Society. "Surely if Stonebridge thought this place was important, he wouldn't have sent *these* two characters?"

George shrugged. "Perhaps, they'd gotten lucky?

Frederica frowned. "Eh, perhaps."

She glanced back to the men in question and winked, catching them off guard before they startled away again. She stifled a smile and took another sip of ale.

Oh, they wouldn't actually *do* anything to her; she could thank Owain for that.

But their interference here could ruin everything, nonetheless.

Freddie glanced over to her teammate, Griffin, who entertained a woman on his lap but didn't miss Freddie's pointed look. He darted a glance to the corner, then back, dipping his head in acknowledgement, telling her he'd keep a close eye on the two officials.

Just then, the three men at the end of the bar broke apart. One left out the front, and the other two, Busty and Birdie, threaded their way across the room, ducking in the middle, and headed towards the back. Freddie pulled her cap down low, and after observing the two men disappear around the corner, stood.

As she stepped over the bench, she bent low, and in George's ear, whispered. "If I'm not back in twenty-five minutes, come and find me."

FREDERICA STEPPED THROUGH AN OPEN DOORWAY ON THE FAR SIDE of the stairs and into a narrow hall with a ceiling so low, she could touch it with the tips of her fingers if she so desired. She crept forward, careful not to make a sound, her eyes locked on what appeared to be an opening in the wall further down from whence a source of light flickered continuously, spilling out and into the hallway ahead.

As she approached, she could hear the low resonance of a deep voice, then the much lighter tones of a higher one. She paused just before the opening; pulled in a slow breath; counted one, two, three; and dared a peek into the room, confident she could always outrun them if need be.

The two men from the bar were at the far end of a small room and were situated around a square table only just large enough for two. Lucky for her, both men stood with their backs to the open door. In seconds, Freddie catalogued the room and dove behind a fortuitous stack of barrels to the right where she came to a kneel, prepared to settle in and listen. She squeezed her locket and offered up a quick prayer when no shouts ensued, signaling she'd been seen.

"I can't believe he's still alive," said the deeper of the two voices. Busty.

"Right? Considering the state he's in," came the other—Birdie.

"Near ta dead, and still I thought we'd never take him down."

"Aye. Wiley, fast." Busty rubbed his jaw. "Hugh broke every finger on the man's right hand, and still, he managed to knock me flat with one cross to the side of me head."

"Looked like it hurt."

"Well, of course it hurt, you moron." Busty cuffed Birdie.

"Ow!"

For a moment, Frederica thought they were literally going to break out in fisticuffs, and she prayed they'd keep their wits, minimal though they were, about them.

But after a few minutes of glaring and silent male posturing, Birdie, one hand cupped over his ear, continued, "Wouldn't want to meet him alone, even with him practically dead on his feet."

"Aye. You got that right. Don't think he'll have such a pretty face no more, either tha's fer sure..."

Both men chuckled, and Frederica rolled her eyes.

Birdie said, "I hear tell the ladies'll be in quite a state. Heard he's a real smooth talker, though, a prime rake."

"Yeah. He's gonna need that silver tongue, too, if'n his looks are gone. Suppose he'd still have those famous eyes what look like silver coins, though."

The hair on Frederica's arms stood on end, and she stole a quick breath as her stomach tumbled to her feet. She'd known a man with silver eyes like that. A long time ago. A real charmer, too. She'd spent the first few days of the seven years since she'd last seen him, wishing for his return. And the rest of that time, devising all the ways she would eviscerate him if he ever did. He was—

No. Frederica shook her head, cutting off that though. Owain would *never*.

Never.

He knew better.

"Could you imagine having such success with the ladybirds?" asked Birdie.

More laughing.

"Oh, how the mighty have fallen." Busty replied.

Probably just another wealthy rake, thought Freddie.

She hoped.

Freddie spotted something move out of the corner of her eye, and her breath caught at the sight of a large rat in the corner, creeping ever closer to her position behind the barrels.

"Wonder if he'll survive?" asked Birdie.

"Don' know, but I suppose the boss'll be happy either way. Makes no difference in the end how it's done, so long as it's done, eh?"

Bloody hell. Give her snakes, spiders, wolves, even a pair of incompetent ruffians, noblemen...anything. But not *rats*. The sight of their beady eyes, shining back in the candlelight... Frederica shuddered. And let's not forget the darting movement of their bodies, the twitching whiskers—which she couldn't truly see at the moment, but she didn't really need to, the image was all too familiar and forever seared in her brain.

She'd slept on the ground in the stews of London for long enough, the rats crawling over her food, her meager belongings—*her.*

"Can't believe we finally got 'im," stated Birdie, "He's a right wily one and strong, too, for his size. 'E put up one 'ell of a fight even with his injuries—even got away from ole' Johnnie fer a spell."

Long tails sliding across her skin—a clawed foot upon her lip—

"Aye. Not for long, though, eh? Wouldn't wanna cross that one in prime condition, no way."

"Not iffin he was coming at me, but ta watch him tangling with someone else, now that'd be a sight, fer sure—"

"I'd lay money on the rake."

More laughing.

"Naw—"

"'Onestly can't believe 'e's still alive..."

"Seemed somewhat off his noggin last time, though..."

Frederica suppressed the rising panic, swallowed back a surge of bile, and watched, helplessly, as the rat continued to stalk forward, and she ruthlessly willed it to turn around and just leave, for Christ sakes. She waved her hand in its direction, flapping wildly, silently shooing it away, to no avail. She pulled the hat from her head and waved that, too.

Nothing.

The room seemed to grow darker, and her panic escalated as the rat stood up, resting on its hind quarters, its ratty tiny fingers clutched together as if plotting her demise—death by plague. She imagined its nose twitching even harder now as it took stock of her, probing her for weaknesses. Knowing, most likely, that *it* was her Achilles heel and fully prepared to use that knowledge to its advantage—

But then all of the sudden, the rat turned about and scurried away in the opposite direction.

Frederica collapsed back against the wall and let out a quick breath of relief. *Thank God.*

And it was at that the precise moment, she noticed the room had gone strangely quiet. Too quiet. No voices; no shifting of feet. No laughing and ribbing or talking of rogues who'd lost their rakishness.

Startled, she glanced up—directly into four large, but no less beady, shifty eyes.

She blew the hair away from her face, then plastered on a smile and waved as she drew to a stand.

Neither Birdie nor Busty returned her friendly greeting. Both men crossed their arms, and Birdie said, "Heard enough, little lady?"

Chapter Four

She was going to *kill* Owain for this.

It was Frederica's last thought before she was shoved out the back door, into the muddy swamp posing as the rear courtyard to the Wee Cock.

She caught her balance after three precarious steps, then spun to face her opponent, the dark-haired ruffian she'd named Birdie who'd, unfortunately, caught her eavesdropping on his private, definitely-not-on-the-positive-side-of-legal, topic of conversation about the prisoner they held.

The prisoner she still planned to abduct for herself at the first opportunity.

God, she hoped he was worth it, whoever he was.

Frederica slammed the door on that thought and smiled, widening her stance in preparation—thank God for men's trousers—then gestured the ruffian closer. "Well then, sweetie, here we are. Let's see what you've brought for me."

Yes, her mistake had cost her, damn rat, and now, here she was, standing in the freezing rain, her boots buried in icy muck, facing down a man bent on maltreatment. Fortunately, he wasn't much larger than she. His partner, Busty, had gone to fetch this *Johnnie*.

Birdie returned her smile and laughed, confident he could handle a mere *woman*. "Aye, you wish to play, little lady?"

It was a mistake they always made—underestimating her.

He approached at his leisure, cocky and utterly unwary, while she stood her ground and did her level best to ignore the icy rivulets of water finding its way beneath her cravat and trailing down her back.

When he was within arm's reach, Frederica lunged for his shoulders and dragged him down as she slammed her knee into his nose with a satisfying crunch. A quick adjustment had the toe of her boot following suit, landing squarely between the man's bollocks.

Birdie tumbled to the ground with a most gratifying groan, all of it over in a matter of seconds.

Frederica smiled and mentally dusted her hands, but only had a moment to appreciate her handiwork, before she was grabbed from behind, two large, hairy arms crossing her chest.

Sigh. This was not how she envisioned this afternoon playing out, which consisted of time well spent before a warm bowl of stew, some tea, and perhaps, if she were lucky, a book.

A thick voice admonished, "Hold still, little one. Johnnie here doesn't want to hurt ye."

Frederica swallowed back a chuckle and tried wriggling from his grasp. "Then, let. Me. Go." Her words were more strained than she'd prefer as she fought to break his hold.

Johnnie chuckled. "I would, ma'am, but someone wants to see ye."

Frederica planted her feet and shoved backwards against his chest, but alas, physics worked against her in this; the giant beast of a man didn't budge an inch. Worse, her feet struggled to find purchase in the slippery mud.

"Well, I don't want to see him—" Frederica charged forward and got nowhere for her efforts.

Too tall for her to bust his nose, too heavy for her to move, she was in quite the pickle. Something stronger than tea would be called for before this day was through.

And where the hell was the rest of her team? Surely, it'd been longer than twenty-five minutes?

Resigned that she wouldn't win this battle and that her team would come to her aid—*eventually*—Frederica tried a different tactic. "Johnnie. Is that your name?" She glanced up and over her shoulder, confirming what she suspected... The man, though large and strong, was no hardened criminal; more of a gentle giant.

He dipped his head in affirmation and would've pulled at his forelock, but then seemed to recall what he was supposed to be doing and squeezed her tighter. She winced as a breath of air exploded out of her.

"Sorry," he mumbled and loosened his hold the tiniest bit.

She shrugged, or tried to, and replied, "Don't mention it."

Could this situation be any more bizarre?

Suddenly, the back door to the Wee Cock swung open, slamming into the outer wall and capturing their attention, and another man stepped out into the evening chill, the rain having tapered off to a fine mist.

Not one of hers, dammit.

God, if life had taught her anything over the past seven years, it was that waiting for a man was bound to end in disappointment.

Frederica sighed and eyed the newcomer warily while telling Johnnie, "I'll pay you double whatever he's paying you if you'll come work for me." And she meant it. God, how she meant it.

She heard the smile in his voice as Johnnie replied, "That's awfully nice little one, but I can't. He's—"

The new man interrupted their negotiations, his voice rippling with derision. "Now, now, Lurch. Is that anyway to treat a *lady*."

Freddie and her captor froze, then Johnnie squeezed her tightly, and Frederica tried in vain to shake the plastered, wet hair out of her face while eyeing the new arrival down the length of her nose.

He was a handsome man and well out-fitted, possibly in his late-forties. Johnnie's presumed boss approached with a measured stride, though she found the sound of muck sucking at his boots and dogging his every step amusing, and she swallowed back a laugh as he stumbled twice lest this entire scenario go from bad to worse before her team arrived. But really, so much for his commanding entrance.

"Johnnie," she tried again, while eyeing the approaching boss, "Are you sure? The pay is better. Plus, there's grand adventures, noble causes, justice...and don't forget the barmaids and ale. Besides *I*, would never treat you so abominably."

Johnnie laughed and squeezed her again, this time almost affectionately. "Aw, you're funny little one...and nice. Aye, Johnnie sure."

Frederica shook her head, resigned, still never letting the *boss* out of her sight. In the dim glow of twilight, she could see his eyes were dark and shifty beneath perfectly shaped brows—quite a juxtaposition of male beauty and an undesirable soul.

She lifted her chin and glared down her nose despite her disadvantaged position; she hadn't missed the sarcastic bent to his tone when he'd called her lady.

"And you are?" she asked in her haughtiest voice.

His lips stretched wide into a toothy, distrustful grin, his teeth perfectly even. "You may call me master."

He winked, and she envisioned settling her elbow in his eye socket at some point before retiring for the night. The idea certainly had merit.

A small whimper interrupted their exchange, and everyone glanced over to the dark-haired ruffian, *Birdie*, rolling on the ground, his hands still clutching his nose and privates. Frederica allowed a small smile at the reminder of her handiwork.

Boss man returned his attention to her, and Frederica looked him over, paused at his crotch, then smirked and decided right then and there to call him Little Dick. An apt moniker indeed for a man cavorting about The Wee Cock Inn...

Frederica pursed her lips. "No, I don't think I shall."

Pain exploded in her cheek as the back of his hand met her face, forcing her head to the side. Johnnie let out a low whimper but held tight. In a strange way, she appreciated the strength of his hold. She turned back to face Little Dick with exaggerated slowness, then locked eyes with the blackguard.

Never, let them see you cry.

Ten seconds passed, if that.

Little Dick glanced away first and said, "You will learn your place soon enough." Looking over her shoulder, he added, "Throw her in with *him*. And make sure she's secured."

"But Lord F—" came Johnnie's worried voice.

Little Dick lost the edge of his composure and slashed one hand through the air. "Just do it."

The action drew her attention to the large signet ring on his thumb, and Frederica stifled a knowing smile. *The Society. Perfect. She'd been confident but seeing concrete validation she and her team were on the right track was well received.*

Johnnie muttered, "But the barn—"

"Lurch!" Little Dick roared.

"Aye, milord."

So Little Dick was a lord, interesting but not unexpected.

Little Dick returned his attention to her and raised a thumb to her lip; unwelcome lust sprang to life in his eyes. She snapped her teeth at the tip of his finger, prepared to bite off the end if needs must, but he jerked his hand away, clearly startled.

She smiled even as he said, "Don't forget to gag her. It wouldn't do to draw unwanted attention."

A whine and a snivel once more sounded from the ground, reminding them all there was a third man down, and as Little Dick walked away, he tossed back, "And take care to guard your cock and balls."

A new voice echoed out in the darkness. "You can stop right there, milord."

Little Dick froze mid-stride, then raised both hands in the air.

Out of the shadows stepped a young, blond man, a long dueling pistol cocked and pointed at the general area of Little Dick's black heart.

It was Griffin, one of hers. *Finally.*

"Release the lady. Now," commanded Griffin.

Another pistol was cocked, the sound coming from somewhere behind Frederica. George, most likely.

Little Dick cursed, but said, "Do it."

Johnnie released her with an audible sigh of relief, and Frederica wasted no time; she marched across the courtyard and rounded on the blackguard who'd smacked her. She crooked her finger and said, "Come on. Just you and me."

He snorted and shook his head, then sprang for her, trying to press his advantage using the element of surprise, the coward. But she was too quick for the cocky bastard. Frederica spun, elbowed him in the eye—*it felt good*—then using her leg, momentum, and the appropriate application of leverage, shoved him onto his back and into the mud with a thoroughly satisfying splat.

Frederica stood over him and offered him an exaggerated wink. "You can call *me* master—while you're telling *your* superiors precisely how I stole your prisoner right out from under your nose."

She made sure to grind her heel into his groin as she walked over him to leave, while calling to George and Griffin, "Take care of the loose ends, find whatever keys we need to release the prisoner, and let's go."

Frederica paused and partially turned. "Johnnie, the offer still stands—" She held out her hand.

Everyone looked at Johnnie, even Little Dick tilted his head back from his position on the ground, his hand covering his left eye.

Johnnie stood, ringing his hands in indecision, glancing back and forth between Freddie and his boss. Frederica smiled, *his previous boss*.

Johnnie looked close to tears when he said, "Sorry, little brother."

Little Dick began sputtering in outrage, his face red as he screamed, "Johnnie, don't you dare! I'll put you in the rack for days for this. Days! This time without your—"

Frederica punched Little Dick in the mouth, furnishing him with a split lip to coordinate with his blackening eye.

Little Dick spat then yelled to her retreating back. "Bitch! What the hell do you want with Ciarán Kelly anyway?"

Chapter Five

It wasn't their first meeting, but for the first time, they were alone, and though this time, his charm was well within his control, finally, *inside*, Kelly was as giddy as a debutante at her first ball. He tried his best to hide that his hands were practically shaking with anticipation, but somehow, he suspected she knew. It was in the way her eyes twinkled when she looked at him, and the smile she tried to hide by glancing away.

Or perhaps, she was just as unsteady as he.

God, she was remarkable. Kind to every person she met, regardless of their station in life. Regardless of occupation or background. She didn't treat him as less for being Irish, or for not holding a title. She genuinely wanted to know him—the man behind the 'pretty face.' He appreciated it all more than he could say.

And every time she appeared—every single time—she took his breath away. Her red hair was a beacon in a dreary world, her fair skin as fresh as newly fallen snow. Her green eyes were both flirtatious and daring yet held a confidence and trust he felt honored to behold.

And her laugh. God, when he heard her laugh, he wanted nothing more than to make her laugh every single moment of every day for the rest of their lives.

She was a gift from heaven; he simply knew it. Like he knew the scars on his *hand; or, he chuckled, the dimple in her cheek that appeared when she was being mischievous.*

He stopped under the shade of an old English oak and lifted her face with a crooked knuckle. He daren't use the tips of his fingers, for he'd never be able to stop himself from becoming lost in the feel of her soft, creamy skin.

He counted the freckles dotting her nose, loving every single one of them.

She swatted his hand away. "What are you doing, Kelly?"

"Counting your lovely freckles?"

She gasped in mock outrage but struggled to hide her grin. "A lady doesn't have freckles."

He leaned in for a closer look. "Far be it for me to argue with a lady," He mouthed additional words as if counting once again. "but you have twelve marks of beauty proclaiming you the loveliest lass in all the land..."

He tilted her chin once again. "And I should like to kiss each and every one."

Her breath caught, her humor fading into something far more serious.

She ran her hands up his chest, the bold act hinting at the woman of strength she often kept hidden behind her genuine, youthful naïveté.

He sucked in a sharp intake of breath.

For certain, he wanted to kiss her, more than he wanted his next breath, but more importantly, he wanted her to understand his intentions.

"Freddie..."

"Yes, Kelly."

"I—I realize my reputation isn't all it should be..."

She pressed a finger to her lip. "You mean, that you're a Rake of the First Order, a womanizer—a scoundrel."

He felt himself blush. Blush! "Well—I—" He dragged a hand through his hair. For the second time in his life, words failed him. This was too important to bungle.

She pressed her hands to his chest. "Kelly, I'm only joking. Sure, you have the reputation of a man who knows his way around a woman," She blushed as she said those words. "But I like to think I am a good judge of character and can see the man behind the mask he presents to the rest of the world—and can judge his worth on my own."

See? Truly, a gift.

He opened his mouth to say something witty, he was sure, but she interrupted him. "I'm here to save you, Kelly."

"Get away from her, you filthy Irish bastard!" someone, a man, shouted.

"Kelly... Kelly!" Frederica screamed, her face twisted in terror.

Suddenly, her image faded, and he reached for her, but his hands met nothing but air. Everything darkened and turned cold, yet inside, he was on fire. What was happening? Where did she go?

Worse, not only had she faded away, but he found himself unable to recall her name. How was that possible? It was like, not only had she disappeared, but his entire memory of her was fading alongside her physical disappearance.

Suddenly, he found he couldn't even recall the color of her hair, her eyes. What had they been doing?

And just like that Kelly jerked awake, the movement making his arms scream in protest, his bloody knees once more scraping across the stone floor beneath where he hung, his arms above his head, suspended like a marionette with strings of iron chain.

Had he been dreaming? He couldn't recall, but the hair on his arms lifted, and the back of his neck prickled a warning. He darted a glance to his cell door.

Someone was coming.

Chapter Six

The Barn—A Misnomer to Be Sure

Frederica stood in front of the cellar door for what must have been two minutes but felt more like twenty, hyper-aware of the wooden planks, iron hinges, and every whorl and dip and crack making up the solid barrier before her. She allowed her hand to hover over the latch, fully aware she was stalling.

Thank, God, George, Griffin, and Johnnie were standing guard *outside*.

Two knots positioned at eye level made it appear as if a face glared back at her, like a brown-eyed old crone, both battle-hardened and wise, and Freddie let out a nervous laugh. "Ah, *Morrighan*. I don't see your familiar crow?"

Freddie glanced over her shoulder, looking about for the mythical bird, then shook her head. *I'm speaking to a door.*

She lifted her face to the damp, cool breeze that fluttered the nearby curtains before skating across her skin, raising gooseflesh across her arms despite the long sleeves she wore. She smelled the fresh scents of grass and hay and a subtle undertone of old dust and leather and a more recent application of lemon and linseed oil on the air.

It was amazing how one became so very sensitive to the world around them when preparing to come face to face with one's past.

On top of that, she felt achy and bruised, already tired from the altercation at the Wee Cock. God, even her toes hurt.

The room she stood in was basically a people-sized box with holes: four walls, a roof line reminiscent of a barn, two openings for windows, the front door, and *this* door off the back, which Griffin had learned led to a dungeon. No furniture; no guards, no divided off rooms, not even a fireplace or a cupboard or a table could be seen.

But it had curtains, strangely enough, and it was old but clean, the floors swept, the drapery white.

A part of her wanted nothing more than to bolt from this odd little room and leave this wretched place, telling Owain precisely where he could stuff his missions and games, his manipulations. His damn lies.

Yes, his lies, for there was no way on this Earth Owain didn't know precisely who he'd been sending her to find. And very deliberately withheld that information, with good reason.

'Thank me later?' Fuck you, Owain.

But she was stronger than that; besides, she would walk through the fires of hell itself to bring down the Society and all who were a part of it. Murderers and thieves masquerading as gentlemen, the lot of them. All of them maneuvering to rid England's shores of anyone who wasn't pureblooded English. She snorted. Pureblooded being a relative term.

Good thing, she was prepared to journey through fire and brimstone to bring *them* down, too. Because right now, as she prepared to open this door and face whatever—*him*—was behind it, she could feel the flames of hell practically licking her boots.

Frederica drew in a deep breath, then stretched her neck, twisting her head left, then right, before drawing back her shoulders. She flexed the fingers of her right hand, then gripped the latch and wrenched open the door.

The torch she carried wavered, then steadied, revealing a small landing and a set of stairs leading down into a dark abyss. Stones forming a tunnel of sorts closed in on either side. She thrust her torch forward and glanced down.

Twelve steps to the floor below. Three steps to the cell door beyond.

Past Frederica would have hesitated further, perhaps bitten her lip, unsure how to proceed. Or raced ahead, heedless of danger, to rescue her One True Love. *Bleh.*

She was no longer that innocent, youthful girl who saw her future in the twinkle of a silver-eyed rogue.

Determined, Frederica blew out a quick breath and crossed the threshold, prepared for a reckoning.

The past was here, and she would greet *him* head on.

The stone stairs were well-worn and almost slick, rubbed smooth from generations of booted heels, and descended into darkness, an abyss that threatened to swallow her whole. Still, she carried on, her fingers skating along the stones making up the walls surrounding her, the rough texture abrading her fingers and forcing her to focus on the here and now.

The air grew musty and damp as she descended, and the wind died a quick death, everything becoming still and stale and foul, so foul. Her stomach lurched, and she had to swallow back bile.

The smell of death hung heavy on the air.

She reached the landing and paused, listening. The only sound was the steady drip of water coming from somewhere ahead. No moans; no chains rattling; not a snore or a wheeze. Utter silence punctuated with a *drip. Drip. Drip.*

Her only choice was to move forward, toward the floor to ceiling bars making up *his* cell.

As she approached, her eyes darted everywhere, but she could see nothing or no one, yet the hairs on her arms lifted, and she knew without question he was here. Somewhere.

She fumbled for the key in the satchel she wore across her chest, and using the light of her torch, fitted it to the appropriate hole in a small, barred cell door. The lock turned with some difficulty, the metal tumblers creaking loudly in the near dark, but then an audible click sounded as she reached the stop. She stole another breath, then pushed the door in, and it groaned in protest but gave way easily enough.

Frederica stepped through the doorway, which opened up into a much larger room, the general shape of a good-sized cave at least thirty feet across but with a low ceiling. She paused a few steps in where a brazier, round and on iron legs, stood guard in the center of the room, waiting to be lit. She touched her torch to the wood, and it ignited immediately. She sniffed the air and detected a hint of whale oil, among other things.

Slowly, she lifted her head, her eyes following the edges of the room. To her left stood a high table, at least six foot in length, affixed with long leather straps, their brass buckles gleaming in the firelight. Wicked looking tools were strewn about the surface and hung haphazardly from the nearby wall, and at once, Frederica knew they sat ready and waiting to commit unspeakable acts of torture upon a body. She swallowed and carried on her search, ultimately landing on the far corner to her right.

She'd taken three steps toward him before she'd even recognized she'd moved.

He knelt on the floor, knees spread, head bent, arms outstretched and raised and chained to the walls.

He was completely naked; his body slick and black and bloody and so very *broken*.

Still, the hard lines and cut curves of every muscle in his arms, his chest, his thighs, stood out in stark relief, pulled taut in their fight against his unnatural pose; they were a shockingly formidable presentation of strength, despite the obvious signs of abuse, the flush of fever in his cheeks, and the thick chains holding him in check.

His cock, though flaccid at the moment, hung long and low, the tip just grazing the floor beneath him, and she jerked her gaze away, angry she'd even noticed.

His black hair, stringy and long, hung down in front of his face, but from between the jagged lengths of dirty strands, two steady, quick-silver eyes cut straight through every layer of protection that surrounded her black heart, and it tumbled over, the traitorous organ.

But it was not in control.

Frederica sucked in a steadying breath of air and said, "Hello, Ciarán."

With his voice deep and rumbling and his all too familiar Irish brogue glaringly evident, Kelly grunted out, "Who the fuck are ye?"

Chapter Seven

Well, *that was wholly unexpected.*

Though she supposed she'd changed quite a bit over the course of seven years.

Freddie glanced over the man before her, her gaze once more touching on all the familiar places—the hard muscles of his chest, his carved thighs—

He chuckled, and her eyes snapped to his. The left corner of his mouth hitched up in a rakish grin, entirely visible and mind-bendingly powerful even through all the swelling and bruising, the rogue, and Freddie rolled her eyes.

Some things definitely *hadn't* changed.

"Here to proclaim my fate, *Bain sídhe?*"

His words were slurred. Sure, he was awake, though perhaps he was a touch delirious.

Freddie dipped her head, her eyes following the path of the chains binding him, and said, "In a manner of speaking."

She strode over to the nearby wall, and scanned a small, wooden wheel, much like a miniature ship's wheel, which was embedded on an axle driven into the stone. Turn the wheel, clockwise, and the chains around Kelly's neck and wrists would lower, allowing for some slack. Turn the wheel, anti-clockwise—

Freddie grimaced, then placed her torch in a hanger on the wall and gripped the wheel with both hands. She tossed a glance over her shoulder and smiled. "Be forewarned, Kelly. This is going to hurt."

Using all her strength, she bent her knees, put her shoulders into the effort, and nudged the wheel to the right.

Cue the screaming.

Half an hour later, sweat dripped into her eyes, and her hands were blistered and sticky and shaking, for the wheel had never been oiled and was difficult to turn, but at last, Kelly was prostrate on the floor, though his hands arms were still lifted overhead, the chains binding his wrists not fully extending like the one around his neck had been. Blessedly, he'd passed out after one turn of the wheel. *After the screaming.*

She could have called for her team, for aid, but for some reason, she'd wanted—no needed—to do this on her own.

Beneath the flickering flame of dim torchlight, Frederica perused the tortured form of Ciarán Kelly, and though she hadn't seen him in nigh on seven years before finding him here in this dirty, dank cell running deep beneath this backcountry cottage, the Barn, they'd called it, she could recall with startling clarity his expressive, steely eyes—how they would flash beneath thick, black lashes when he was angry. Or when he was being mischievous or playful, teasing a naïve young woman with stars in her eyes.

When he was *aroused*.

Frederica closed her eyes. *Damn you, Owain. Damn you for sending me here. And damn you, Ciarán. For, everything.*

Almost, everything.

Freddie spun around, marched out the cell, and from the bottom of the cellar stairs, called up, "George, Griffin. Get down here."

She returned and busied herself stoking the fire. She threw in her torch and began feeding the flames with random implements of torture, though most wouldn't actually burn, but if felt good all the same.

And every single moment, she was fully aware of precisely *who* lay on the floor not ten feet away.

Frederica reached deep inside, pulling on her inner strength, and forced herself to recall the life lessons she'd acquired while surviving the streets of London, while surviving Owain, while *eradicating* unwanted memories of a dashing, Irish rogue.

This Irish rogue.

Frederica allowed those recollections to wash over her, embracing those warnings, which over seven years had formed her—hardened her —saved her, and recited her personal affirmations:

Trust only yourself.

Bury the past.

Never let them see you cry.

Frederica glanced over to Kelly's inert figure, forced dispassion drawing her lips into a tight frown.

Ciarán. Kelly. A man known for his silver eyes and jet-black hair, broad shoulders and long sculpted legs. A rogue who whispered terms of endearment with a silvered tongue and a deep, Irish brogue that rumbled over one's skin like a heated caress.

He was every woman's dream and every husband's nightmare.

Good God look at him now.

Frederica claimed another breath, then allowed the air to escape in a controlled slide from between her parted lips.

Her mission, her life now, was everything.

Kelly was not.

The sound of booted feet clamoring down the worn steps reached her ears, and Freddie straightened her spine. Eventually, both men shuffled into the dank room, their faces grim, and she was convinced the two of them accurately read the tension that hung thick in the air.

Who knew how much Owain had told them...

Frederica nodded toward the chains binding Kelly's wrists. "D'you have the key?" This she asked of George, who nodded his head while he fished around in the pocket of his greatcoat, eventually producing a medium-sized, iron skeleton key.

Upon his quirked brow, Frederica said, "Yes, go on," and George set about unlocking the iron band around Kelly's left wrist.

Frederica leaned against the wall and crossed her arms, watching as the men set to the task. The first band opened with an audible click, and she found herself once more stretching her neck to relieve the sudden tightness in her shoulders. George lowered Kelly's arm to the floor, and everyone paused when an answering grunt shot forth from Kelly. But after that, he remained still, and if it were not for the visible signs of his chest rising and lowering with each breath, they'd have thought him passed from this plane of existence.

George whistled a slow breath and tossed the key to Griffin, who reached to unlock the other wrist.

"Mmm... Freddie..." The words unquestionably from Kelly.

Everyone froze a second time, and it was as if time itself halted, the utter silence left in its absence was deafening, as if the entire world held its breath in wait.

All eyes were trained on Kelly's chest, which marched on in a steady cadence, up, down, up, down—so strong for a man so abused. Yet no more words appeared to be forthcoming.

Frederica shifted, reaching up to massage her neck, then looked over to her men, watching as George and Griffin's eyes met.

"Well, get on with it, then. *Tempus fugit*," she bit out.

She looked down, once again skimming Kelly's sleeping form. From the reports she'd read, *well before finding out it was Kelly they'd referred to*, his ribs had been cracked, his eyelashes plucked, his eyes blackened and bloody and the vessels within, burst; several toes broken, along with his fingers, and a few of his fingernails missing or smashed.

He'd been battered and beaten and quite thoroughly tortured, all of it within the cells of a Royal ship, the *HMS Nightingale*. All of it carried out in secret by the Society. She could only hazard a guess as to why, though Owain likely knew.

He *always* knew.

Then, Kelly was scheduled to be executed, but before the Society could carry out the deed, the *HMS Nightingale* had exploded. Kelly was thrown from the ship into the River Mersey, rescued by a fisherman, picked up once again by the Society, and eventually tossed here, in some bizarre tiny cottage that looked like a miniature barn near the small town of Runcorn. He'd been unconscious most of that time and was lucky to be alive, the bastard.

That was a fortnight ago, at least, and judging by the sight of him, Kelly had a long road to recovery. If he recovered at all.

Griffin laid Kelly's right arm upon the floor, and both men backed away, quietly, as if the man lying unconscious before them would suddenly awaken and pose an insurmountable threat.

And yet, all three of them stared at the man a moment in companionable silence before George, always one to point out the obvious, eventually said, "Things would go a whole lot easier, if he'd just wake up."

That was actually debatable.

And entirely irrelevant. They had to move him. Now.

"We'll need rope," said George.

"And Johnnie," Griffin added.

Frederica nodded her agreement. "Go see what you can find. We'll have to assume he's not waking up." Frederica's eye caught on one of Kelly's bent fingers.

Truly, unconsciousness would be a blessing at this point.

After the two men shuffled out of the room, Freddie leaned down impulsively and gripped Kelly's face in her hands, his skin burning hot to the touch with fever, the stubble of his beard rough against her palms, and whispered fiercely: "Wake up, damn you."

He didn't even flinch.

Chapter Eight

Kelly moaned. It felt like his bed was rocking. Had he passed out while fornicating? He'd never done that before, but there was always a first for everything.

But he didn't feel like he'd been fucking. For one thing, he felt woozy and disoriented with a sinking feeling about his head, and his skin was cold, but inside he was on fire...but not a good kind of fire, like when one was about to have an orgasm. Or when one spotted the love of their life across a crowded room...

More like someone had poured lava in his veins—had someone given him opium?

He sniffed the air for that tell-tale smell, and a faint scent tickled his nose, drawing forth a distant memory, but it wasn't of opium...

Freddie?

He flailed and tried to sit up, but it was as if his limbs wouldn't obey. He opened his eyes, frantically searching, but everything was hazy and bleary and indistinct. Then, suddenly, an angel appeared above him, concern marring her brow. She seemed familiar, too...

He smiled. "Well, aren't you a s-sight... Mm... You remind me of someone...silly of me, I know. 'Tis impossible, you see. She died."

The angel didn't respond, merely rested her hand on his head, then felt the side of his neck.

"Pardon me," he tried reaching for her hand, "but I'm not in the best state for love-making at the moment. I need...something. Not sure what."

The Angel spoke, "Kelly be quiet, someone's coming."

But he was damned if her words made sense with his head stuffed with cotton wool. Someone was coming? *Lucky bastard.*

He must be in that brothel in Blackpool. But it didn't look like the brothel. And it didn't smell like it, either. And he didn't like the disoriented feeling and the fire in his veins and the sharp pains in his sides— all things he didn't usually equate with brothels. Pleasure, yes. Orgasms, definitely. But right now, everything hurt but didn't. It was bizarre, and he didn't like the sensation at all.

He tried once more to sit up, but his arms refused to obey. "Do you have any l-laudanum? I'm quite keen to return to my love. I see her there in my dreams, you see. She has hair like yours, I think. And her laugh...I remember it quite well when I sleep. It's comforting."

His angel moved closer. "Shhh, Kelly. Be quiet and stay down."

Still, her words made no sense. "I beg your pardon, but—"

Suddenly, she tossed something over his head, and his world went dark. How very rude. Wait. Had she tossed a blanket over him? Ah, that made sense. Her husband must be on the way, and she attempted to hide him. Bless her. He should tell her he'd take care of everything.

He tried to speak through the ticking. "M mnn hndlm thhhs, lve."

She jabbed him in the ribs for his efforts, and the pain was unbearable for such a wee jab.

What followed was blackness; then nothing, a blessed relief.

Chapter Nine

Runcorn—Once Again

The job of moving Kelly had been a Herculean task of logistics and skill.

Throughout it all, Kelly remained unconscious or delirious—twelve stone of dead weight did not make for an easy race through the countryside, even with a wagon. Thank God for Johnnie.

Further, numerous men, all of them nefarious, continued putting up one hell of a chase. And not to be ignored, but certainly never admitted aloud, Frederica's resentment toward this assignment lingered. Even after a fortnight.

Oh, who was she kidding? Her antipathy was growing by leaps and bounds. Owain must want Kelly *badly* to send *her* on this mission.

How many times had she questioned the wisdom of all this? A dozen? More? Hell, she must have asked herself a thousand times in a fortnight why she didn't leave Kelly in a brothel somewhere and ride back to Wales to tell Owain where he could shove all his missions and plans.

But the *pièce de résistance*? They were back in Runcorn, or at least, she and Kelly were. And they were alone.

The reasoning? Who would ever expect them to go back to Runcorn? The society men were relentless, and Freddie and her team could not keep up the pace required to keep ahead of them, Kelly being dead weight and all.

This time, they were in a remote cottage owned by Viscount Sharpe, one of Owain's many aliases. George and Griffin were ordered to stay away, communications to be kept to a minimum and direct communication allowed only in an emergency. They were her scouts, her distant guard—running interference and leading the bad men away —for as long as possible.

Johnnie had put up quite the fight; he didn't want to leave her side while these men were still after them, Little Dick furiously bent on revenge. But eventually he'd capitulated; she'd really left him no choice.

So, it was up to her and her alone to keep Kelly alive.

Great.

Frederica glanced down to the source of all her troubles, once more lying unconscious, though on a bed and without the chains this time.

More of the bruising and scabbing on Kelly's face had healed over the last fortnight, revealing the hard jaw and formidable nose of his once treasured face, though his nose had acquired a new bump and a slight bend to the right due to a break courtesy of whatever horrors he'd endured over the past couple of months.

And despite recent evidence to the contrary, time had been good to Ciarán Kelly. He still had a thick head of hair, black as the night sky with only a small trace of silver at the temples. And beneath the remnants of bruising and scabbing still present, he had relatively smooth skin with only a few minor scars, indicative of a life lived to the edge, but blessed.

He had survived. He would survive.

Frederica sighed and collapsed into a battered chair by the wall of Kelly's room. She leaned one elbow on the arm and rubbed the area between her eyes, the beginnings of a headache making its presence known.

"Wake up, Ciarán," she mumbled.

"Mmmm..."

Frederica paused and glanced over, searching for signs he would finally awaken with his wits intact after all these weeks. His lips moved as he tried to speak, and she sat up and leaned in close.

"What was that?" she teased, "You want turtle soup and a paramour? Tsk, tsk. So very you, Kelly."

She snorted and reflexively drew in a deep breath while still close, *too close.*

The past two weeks had been an onslaught of *too close.* Tending an ailing man, *this* ailing man. Too close. And the emotions that had bubbled forth in that time. Too close. Once again, she smelled shaving soap and unintentionally savored his scent, which was earthy, fresh, and distinctly male.

Entirely too close!

Goddammit. His smell is still the same, and utterly un-fucking-forgettable, apparently.

Kelly turned his head toward her, his cheek brushing her own and searing her with a quick brand of heat.

She jerked back, away from the intimacy of the moment, but not before she heard him mumble, "Ah, Freddie...I've missed ye, love."

Frederica swallowed her surprise. He had said so many things in his delirium. Things she couldn't possibly trust. Things that made her *feel.*

But he couldn't possibly know it was her, and she couldn't possibly be allowed to feel.

"Can't honestly say the same," she forced out.

Yes, she might remember the way he smelled, but that fact changed nothing. Neither did any of the words he'd said, nor the many times he'd called her name in his sleep. Words meant nothing to Ciarán Kelly. Hadn't she learned that the hard way?

She would do well to remember that fact when his whispers tugged at her heartstrings.

He didn't respond to her reply, which was for the best. Sure, it had been an honest retort, but a hostile confrontation went fully against her mission.

Probably.

Lingering resentment coiled within, gathering up old memories she'd long since buried, teasing her that after all these years, she would finally have a reckoning. She was owed it—wanted it. Desperately. Despite her conflicting *need* to bury the past.

Kelly moved then, twisting subtly beneath the sheets, and she froze once again, waiting. Anticipating.

Before, they'd been on the run, and their race across the north of England kept her mind occupied and away from their shared past. But now, she had nothing much to do but wait and anticipate.

Any minute now, he would open his eyes. She primed herself for the instant he would see her. Recognize her. Before, he'd been delirious with fever and sick, spouting nonsense about lovemaking and angels and some woman who comforted him, but he couldn't remember her. Now, he was cool to the touch, his fever broken, and he just needed to awaken. She was ready, composed. *Finally!*

She rubbed her hands down her trouser-clad legs, her damp palms calling her out as a liar about being poised and in control.

A finger twitched. His leg shifted. And her anticipation exploded, she had to actively stop her leg from bouncing in a nervous tick as she waited. Oh, yes. Any moment now, Kelly's eyes would flash. He'd be thrilled, then devastating remorse would settle in, the guilt over-whelming and nigh on unbearable. And she'd relish every last drop, finally achieving closure.

After all these years.

Kelly shifted his head, *Now or never, you bastard,* then his eyes flut-tered once, twice, squeezed tight, then opened wide, unveiling the steely grey-blue she remembered so clearly, *too clearly,* and she stole a quick breath.

Good God, he is beautiful. Still.

It took a moment, his eyes blinking rapidly, before Kelly adjusted to the light, though dim, his gaze fixed on the ceiling.

Freddie choked back an unexpected sob of emotion wrapped around an odd surge of anger, it was all so very twisted and compli-cated, and forced herself to sit quietly by and watch, allowing him time to adjust to his surroundings. *She was a damn saint for her patience.*

She used that time to compose herself, trying to ignore the bewil-dering lump in her throat, *hating* that she was reacting at all. *After everything.*

Remember the mission.

Remember your secrets.

You know what's at stake.

He began to look around, and she watched him, once more anticipating the moment their eyes would meet with a bizarre combination of excitement and dread. She wanted to flee the house and pretend she'd never been here at all. She wanted to shout out his name and claim his attention right now, no longer content to wait. She wanted to curse him for everything. To scream out all the injustices she'd endured, which at this very moment, she felt justified in heaping on his loathsome, lying, still ridiculously beautiful head.

Of course, she was justified. He was to blame.

When she needed him most, he didn't come! He. Did. Not. Come.

And it had torn her apart! She'd ached for him to come to her rescue. For it all to be a grand misunderstanding. For him to hold to his promise. But most of all, for him to be by her side with what was coming—

She curled her fingers into fists over the top of her trouser-clad legs, fully angry now. She gave up on forcing a veneer of indifference; she definitely didn't feel indifferent, but anger? Yes, anger she could accept.

It was her right! Owain would get over it.

She pressed her lips together and bit her cheek. Waiting for the opportune moment to unleash her fury.

In contrast, he took his time, studying the far wall and the absurdly frilly curtains covering the room's lone window. The drapes were lacy and delicate and chartreuse, of all things.

His shoulders shook once as a chuckle burst from his lips.

Look at me! Face me! She screamed in her mind. Outwardly, she remained seated, her legs crossed, arms open and relaxed.

His gaze drifted over to the wall at the foot of the bed. A large painting of a naked woman sleeping on a fancy divan graced that wall, practically taking up the entire space. All twelve feet of it. Based on the furnishings in this simple cottage, limited though they were, the previous Viscount Sharpe had an obsessive love for the female body. Kelly would most certainly approve.

She must have made a sound for Kelly whipped his head in her direction, his eyes downcast, and spotted her clenched fists. When had that happened? She forced her fingers to relax once again.

A look of confusion flitted across his face, and Freddie nearly burst, an inappropriate laugh of pure nervous energy bubbling up and clawing its way up her throat.

She hadn't felt this out of sorts since Owain had caught her attempting to lift his wallet all those years ago. She'd still been so naive, so fresh back then.

Kelly followed the line of her arm, her shoulder. How did he remain so blissfully calm when both anxiety and fury were rolling off her shoulders in great, heaping waves of emotion? Couldn't he sense it?

She clamped her lips together and braced herself. Preparing for the first sign of recognition. Her heart sped up its pace, which was already racing at breakneck speed, and her mouth turned dry though she daren't show a single sign of her discomfiture.

This was it. He would see her and feel remorse. Or try to flirt. She would remain composed, then eviscerate him, and swallow every other unwanted emotion battling about inside her. Damn the mission.

His gaze wandered across her chest. She forced a smirk at his pause. Was that an appreciative glance at her bosom? Likely, for he smiled just then, the rogue.

He carried on, his gaze caressing her shoulders, her collarbone, then gliding up her neck. He stared at her mouth for an indecent amount of time. She had to actively refrain from wetting her lips, but the urge to do so was marked, and it pissed. Her. Off.

This was not going according to plan.

She snatched another sharp breath.

His eyes snapped to hers.

Her stomach dropped, and her heart surged, the traitorous organ.

He was so. damn. beautiful. And familiar. And her past all rolled up in one. And he looked like—

She gripped the arms of the chair and cut off that thought.

Kelly searched her face for a moment more, his eyes a curious question, then he smiled, a familiar lopsided lift of one corner of his

mouth, and with the ease of a practiced lothario, drew out, "Mmm...
Morning..."

It was too much.

He coughed to clear his throat, his voice scratchy and rough from
abuse, then disuse.

Frederica leapt to her feet, preparing to flay him alive with her
tongue, but before she could give voice to her dedicated fury, her eye
caught on an odd little cherub hanging in the corner by the ceiling,
capping off the crown molding and dragging her away from filthy, frilly,
sick rooms and traitorous ex-fiancées and depositing her back home.
To Wales. To the life, the people—the person—who awaited her there,
the reminder timely and *blessedly* necessary.

She slammed her mouth closed and resumed her seat; her lips
pressed together in a tight line.

Inside, was another matter entirely. Her emotions ricocheted off
the walls of her hardened soul. She could feel the very real urge to
twist her hands together but shook off the sensation. She had pluck,
dammit. She was independent. She was strong.

And he was her past. *Nothing*. More.

He lay there, his head cocked as if trying to solve a puzzle. As if
trying to piece her together.

Ha! He'd never managed it before.

His gaze swept over her, faster this time, and his smile grew. "Well,
aren't you a sight for sore eyes."

She remained silent; she was indifferent to his odious charm, and
her tongue still burned to eviscerate him. She guarded her animosity
and held on to her ire—anything to focus her mind on the mission and
keep her tongue planted firmly behind her teeth.

He closed his eyes, briefly, and drew in a long, deep breath. "I miss
yer smell, I tell ya, so familiar and comforting."

Frederica rolled her eyes, not for a moment thinking he meant her,
specifically. More likely, he meant women in general. He still appeared
somewhat disoriented, a glazed look covered his eyes, despite his
suggestive remarks. Perhaps, his fever had returned.

Frederica jumped to her feet, busying herself straightening his
sheets. It was either that or reach for his throat and throttle him, now

that he was awake for her to do so, decidedly not an action conducive to the reason she was here in the first place, nor the way she should behave toward a sick man. God, why couldn't she remember that fact?

Frederica turned her back and forced air in through her nose, slowly, calmly. She exhaled, letting the air pass her lips in a controlled manner. She repeated the process once again, securing her inner peace, refocusing on her goal, all the while sensing Kelly's gaze on her back.

Damn it. Once upon a time, she'd *loved* him. It had nearly broken her.

But now, she was a different person. Strong. Capable.

And here for a purpose. A job. Something greater than their past. Greater than everything.

Composed once again, Freddie resumed her seat.

Movement caught her attention. His hand trembled as he lifted his arm and reached over, his blunt-tipped fingers just grazing the tops of hers, which were now resting on the bed.

"Has it been so very long?" he asked, his voice soft.

She nodded her head, but kept her eyes fixed on his hand, lying there atop hers. *She* remembered. Seven years and three months to be precise. *Of course*, he didn't recall. She likely wouldn't either if she hadn't a very good reason to remember. *That* more than anything, placed another tether on her emotions, on her, at times, lethal tongue.

He squeezed her hand, lightly, his touch weak for he'd broken two of his fingers on this hand alone, and they no longer lay quite so straight.

When he didn't relax his grip straight away, she glanced up in time to see him frown and wondered at his sudden change in demeanor.

He stared at her a moment, studying her.

But then his frown turned to worry.

And worry to fear.

She watched these new emotions rapidly unfold, helpless to do a thing about it as terror raced across his face.

Her heart began to pound, unexpected fear bloomed, feeding off his.

This was all wrong. She *never* wanted to see that look again. On anyone.

He twisted in his sheets, now, a full-blown panic flaring to life in his eyes.

"No!" he screamed.

She awkwardly grasped his uncovered hand with both of hers and kept her voice steady as she tried to calm his unexpected agitation. "Shhh... Ciarán, you should rest a little more. You're— Why don't I go fetch—"

He squeezed her hands and pulled her forward with a sudden and surprising surge of inhuman strength. His other hand reached out from nowhere and grasped her behind the neck, pulling her close. He lifted his upper torso and met her part way. The sheets fell to his waist then, revealing his naked chest and the large swaths of bandages that encircled his recently broken ribs. His forehead touched hers, and his eyes, so serious now, locked with hers.

"Lady. What's. Your. Name?" He squeezed his eyes closed for a minute, then reopened them, his seriousness replaced with absolute horror. "Oh hell..."

He began to hyperventilate and shake all over.

This was normal. This was—

He gasped once, twice, then with bleak orbs of wounded steel, speared her with a look and asked, "Ah, God. What's mine?!"

Then, his eyes rolled back in his head, and just like that, he fainted.

Chapter Ten

Frederica threw open the cottage door and stumbled through the opening. She staggered to a stop on the small stoop and gripped the door frame with one hand while bending over at the waist, her other hand pressing down on her thigh, her breath sawing in and out.

Amnesia, Ciarán?

Frederica felt a stinging in her eyes, and she jerked upright, swiping at unwelcome tears. She rubbed her fingers together and glared at the moisture there. What the hell is this? *This* was ridiculous. They were strangers now, certainly no longer friends. And he would recover. He was young and strong. It was possible—probable even.

Ugh.

She rubbed a fist in one eye and stepped off the front stoop, then began pacing over a well-worn circle.

She'd dreamt of meeting him again, oh, numerous times, but in her dreams, their chance encounter had been nothing like this.

In her dreams, he was hale and whole.

In her dreams, he remembered her and ached with profound regret over abandoning her.

In her dreams, she didn't bloody care even as he begged and

pleaded and succumbed to his envy. She'd relished showing him every-thing he'd lost by leaving her to her fate.

She'd imagined him on his knees at her feet.

And covered with boils!

In truth, Frederica acknowledged these were hardly the dreams of a woman who was indifferent, but then she was only human and had been very much in love with a rogue.

A rogue with a silver tongue and a marvelous wit...

...and no bloody sense of loyalty whatsoever.

But she'd never imagined him like this.

Frederica stopped in her tracks, raised her face to the bright blue sky, and screamed. Out loud. For all the world to hear. For as long as she could. She startled the birds from their nests and sent numerous squirrels racing away; round and around the trunks of nearby trees they ran, desperate to escape the mad woman bellowing in their midst.

She drew on every ounce of energy spawned by the emotions swirling around in every inch of her body, from her toes to the roots of her hair, and threw it all into that scream. She didn't care. Besides, no one was near to hear.

With a grin on her face, her scream evolved into a laugh. A full-bodied, maniacal around the edges, laugh—the type that might find you in Bedlam kind of laugh. And it felt good.

No, great.

God, she'd needed the release. A way to expel her pent-up frustra-tion. An outlet for the emotional upheaval she'd just endured in that stupid sleeping loft at the hands of a former lover.

Very former. Seven years!

She raised her fist and between great bursts of laughter, shouted to the heavens. "But I wanted a reckoning before I spat in his face! Or revenge. Something. I just wanted him to feel remorse and shame and *suffer* for it, dammit. Suffer as I suffered!"

But she didn't expect to *feel*!

Her laughter trailed off into shorter, softer bursts until there was nothing left. Until she felt hungover. Aged. Tired.

Drained.

Freddie dropped to the ground in a field, then gradually rolled onto her back, cushioning her head on her hands, her fingers laced together. She watched the clouds sail by overhead as she slowed her breathing, inhaling the fresh scents of late fall while step by step, she pulled her thoughts out of the past and into the moment. She touched the locket she wore on a slim chain and breathed.

There were more important things in the world than Ciarán Kelly. It would serve her well to remember that going forward.

She had a job to do. She'd signed on for this. True, she never would have predicted Kelly being a part of her mission, but that fact was truly irrelevant. The Society had to fall. Hadn't Owain demonstrated why so effectively all those years ago? When he'd showed her a list of the murders, the torn apart families who suffered even now?

And she was stronger than all of this, dammit.

Could she set aside her ire and feign, at best, friendship, at worst, indifference? Long enough to achieve Owain's goals. Her goals?

Yes. Of course, she could.

For now.

With great strength, Frederica pushed aside her mental exhaustion and rolled up her sleeves, figuratively turning her mind to practical matters to consider what she knew. She'd come across a man once before, with a large tumor on his head, who'd had amnesia. Those who knew him said he'd retained many characteristics of his personality, though he remembered no one. He really had been a friendly old man and witty. Curious, she'd read a couple of books about amnesia not long after meeting him.

She knew there was nothing a doctor could do to heal Kelly. She refused to consider bloodletting, which she'd have to perform on her own anyway.

She also knew her best option was to find ways to jar his memory—sights, smells, sounds...familiar things that might touch a deeper memory.

She'd not known him in recent years. Could she force herself to revisit their past in such a way that it would jar his memory, a shared history that might have meaning, but one she desperately wanted to stay where it belonged—in the past?

Her first instinct was a resounding NO!

Once more, Frederica thought of Owain and their mission and knew what Owain would say: *Yes.* Of course.

Worse, despite Kelly's weakened state, she'd have to do so sooner rather than later, for she also knew that time was of the essence. The longer his brain withheld his past, the less likely he'd recover his memory at all. And she suspected that whatever his memory held, it was important to Owain, else why send her here at all?

But...

Wouldn't the more immediate concern be gaining his trust?

And if she told the literal truth, well, that would gain them nothing but more distrust, ergo... Perhaps something slightly resembling the truth but sure to gain his trust and help jog his memory was in order.

She knew he worked for the Duke of Stonebridge, so perhaps *they* worked for the Duke of Stonebridge...?

And when he did finally regain his memories and realized her stories were more lies than truth?

Well...as Plato said, "Our need will be the real creator." Surely, even Kelly would understand that. Hell, it was probably one of his mottos.

But perhaps, she would be lucky, and they'd be in Wales long before having to confront the truth.

All of it.

Resigned, Frederica stood and returned to the cottage, shuffling her feet in the loose gravel serving as a path to the stoop. She approached the wide-open door slowly, with all the excitement of a woman facing the hangman's noose, feeling old once more, and tired.

Freddie glanced up toward the open window with the frilly curtains ruffling in the breeze and plastered on a smile. "Swallow my lies, you silver-tongued bastard. I've got a job to do."

A sudden shout disturbed the quiet solitude of their hideaway cottage, and a voice screamed, "Freddie!"

"Dammit," she bit out.

Yet without hesitating, Frederica ran.

Chapter Eleven

T he dream started innocently enough, as dreams often do, but
the images came in snippets and flashes of impressions and
thought rather than a continuous stream of action.

Kelly saw a field of wildflowers bordering a well-kept garden, familiar he supposed, its bluebells dancing in the breeze.

He saw a beautiful, red-haired woman, young and lithe with a twinkle in her eye and a carefree laugh she freely shared as she skipped along a garden path in a flowing dress of blue.

He saw an older man standing with a younger version of himself. They were in a dark-paneled library or perhaps a study. The father was stern and cross and eyed Kelly with a mixture of distaste and distrust, a sour twist to his lips and eyes narrowed to slits. The son seemed less hostile, a touch of innocence marked his features, but still distant and wary.

He saw the older man once again; this time, they were outside in the dark. The man bristled with fury; another man held a pistol. He could sense more men behind him, but he daren't look away from the two before him. They shouted at him, but he couldn't hear or make out their words. Then, pain—blinding and intense. As he fell towards the ground and into sweet oblivion, he caught a glimpse of the woman once again. She was lying on the ground, curled into a fetal position, clutching her stomach and crying, and wearing a white dress soaked in blood.

Inside his head, he heard her scream clear as day, "Help me! K—" and then a booming male voice bellowed, "You've killed her with your bastard, you filthy Irish!"

Kelly jerked awake.

His first conscious thought was: Where is she? He blinked his eyes, attempting to shake away the darkness while he searched for the injured woman. But...he wasn't outside, and the room was bright. Daylight?

His second thought: Where the fuck am I?

A hint of pain fed his bewilderment. He glanced around, wildly taking in his surroundings. The absurd chartreuse curtains and the painting at the foot of the bed felt distantly familiar.

Reality returned in stages until he realized he'd been dreaming. Kelly shook off the remnants of the disturbing vision with a swipe of one hand down his face and immediately regretted the action as his ribs screamed in protest. He used his bedsheets to dab at the sweat gathered on his brow, feeling intensely relieved to be awake and free of the more alarming aspects of his nightmare.

He couldn't recall anybody's name from the dream. Nor the name of the locations he'd pictured. Hell, he could hardly tell what was real and what wasn't, for that matter. Were those people even real, a shared past, or an invention of his broken mind?

God, he had amnesia. *Amnesia.* Panic threatened, and he swallowed, forcing down the beginning rise of terror. He needed to focus. On what he knew; on what was real.

Kelly heard the rapid clamor of someone scurrying up a ladder, presumably he was in a lofted room, and he scrambled to compose himself, determined to appear stronger than he felt. He would heal. He would be fine, his current condition a setback and utterly surreal. And he needed to convey that fact in no uncertain terms. He must.

You have no bloody memory, fool.

It would come. It *would.* It. Must...

You don't know who to trust...

He glanced down, noting the obvious signs of abuse: the wrappings around his waist, the ache in his head. He held up a hand, his battered, broken hand. Panic once more began to intrude upon his reality. Who was he kidding? He was one step away from Bedlam.

A woman burst through the door, then, breathing hard, and he dropped his hand, letting escape a sigh of relief as his anxiety immediately subsided upon sight of her, even if only for a moment. Even if he didn't understand why.

"Kelly?" Her eyes roamed over him.

She was breathtaking, and for a moment, his thoughts scattered. Then, he recognized her as a slightly older version of the woman from his dream. Whoever she was, she clearly wasn't dead.

He shoved aside his tumultuous thoughts and forced himself to focus on the basics. On what he needed to know. On what she'd just said.

His mind whispered, *Survive,* and on instinct, he listened.

"Is that my name, then?" he asked. He strove for charming and added a deliberate wink; it felt right if a bit odd, considering.

Did she notice he slammed his lips shut after, swallowing back another flare of dread? Did she notice his smile, his wink, was forced?

I am going insane.

He fought back the encroaching darkness and searched his mind to see if the name, Kelly, fit, but unlike the way he felt when he saw this woman, he felt nothing either for or against the name, Kelly, only simple indifference. He shook his head.

She narrowed her eyes, confusion and, yes, distrust, marring her brow. "You still don't remember?"

He glanced away, taking in the frilly curtains, and swallowed, using the opportunity to cement what felt like his crumbling composure. When he turned back, he was all open charm. "No, love."

And was immediately drawn back to the curtains. *They* were safe.

Coward.

"Look, you called for me with an alarming degree of urgency—" Startled, he wrenched his head back around and winced, a breath of air escaped, "—screamed it, more like, and I just assumed your memory had returned." She narrowed her eyes. "People with amnesia don't normally call out for someone they've forgotten."

Kelly chuckled, ignoring the twinge of protest from his ribs, and maintained his forced grin, just. "Impossible."

The idea was absurd. Hell, this entire situation was absurd. Besides, how could he call her name when he bloody well didn't know it?

She drew her hands together, fingertips to fingertips and a study in patience, and dipped her head. "Nevertheless, you did."

Kelly considered her; she wasn't lying. Else, she was *very* good at hiding it. Either was a distinct possibility.

After a few moments, he admitted, "I dreamt about you. I don't know if it's real or not."

She smiled and settled into the chair beside his bed. "And?"

Why did the smile feel like a lie? It was in the way her knuckles whitened briefly and the corners of her mouth tightened just before she spoke, and it pricked his curiosity. She leaned on the arm of the chair and rubbed at her brow with one finger.

"Tell me," she prompted.

Kelly studied her, this puzzling woman with brilliant red hair and dark eyes, who wore a gentleman's clothes. "It was really just a series of impressions and images."

While he considered the best way to tell her, 'I dreamt you had died.', he asked, "Do we know each other? I mean apart from now, in this cottage." An evasion, sure. But he had to *know*.

And decide if it was truth.

She shrugged, but her eyes shifted away. "We've met before."

Ah. She also withheld something. *Perhaps, a lot of somethings.*

"Why do I feel like you understate things considerably?" he prodded.

She chuckled but didn't answer his question.

Funny. It seemed neither of them were openly forthcoming individuals... or they were both frauds. He knew his reasons for withholding his thoughts. What were hers?

Kelly cleared his throat, once again striving to appear unconcerned, charming even. "Why don't we start over? My name is..."

When she didn't respond right away, he prompted using his falsetto in imitation of her, his hand splayed across his chest. "Kellen Kevin Kelly the third. Royal Duke and Heir to the Throne of Kelland."

Humor had always been an effective way to disarm.

How the fuck do I know that?!

Her lips pursed. "Of course. Your name is Mr. Ciarán Kelly, and I am Frederica...Glyndŵr. Er, Mrs. Frederica Glyndŵr."

"Mrs.?"

She lifted her chin and said, "Yes."

He chuckled, though nothing was remotely funny. "Just checking. For a moment, you seemed, unsure."

She lifted one brow. "Am not."

"And I just yelled out, Mrs. Glyndŵr, to the heavens?"

She sighed and rubbed her palms down her trouser clad thighs. "Not precisely."

"Not precisely?" he nudged. Now, who was evasive? "I thought I—"

"Freddie." She blurted out and punched the arms of the chair. "You called me Freddie."

"Freddie." It felt strangely right to say it and yet foreign at the same time. "A nickname, I take it?"

She dipped her head in acknowledgement, and he filed that away for further consideration.

"How do we know each other, Mrs. Glyndŵr?"

Her smiled widened. "We both work for the same people, naturally."

He raised a brow, surely there was more to it than that.

She continued, "You're an agent, a spy, working for the Duke of Stonebridge."

Well that somewhat explained his instincts and fractured thinking.

"You as well?" he asked.

She dipped her head. "Yes."

Interesting, there was a slight hesitation just before she said the word. Possibly, she was lying.

"What about my family?"

She answered readily enough. "When I met you, it was just you and your father. Your mother had died when you were young. No siblings that I'm aware of."

Truth.

"And now? My father?"

She looked at him directly. "I'm sorry. I honestly don't know."

Again, truth. And if they were partners, why wouldn't she know? So many questions...

"Do you think anyone is looking for me?" Despite his attempt to appear unconcerned, and for a while there it had gotten easy, his heart thumped harder, faster, and he fought the urge to clench his own fists as he awaited her answer.

"I'm sure there are quite a few people looking for you right about now." She glanced meaningfully at the wrapping around his ribs.

He deliberately ignored her pointed remark despite the fact she was answering his own question. He wanted nothing more than to wet his lips, which felt dry as dust now, but he maintained a stranglehold on his composure. Just. God, for five minutes, he'd kept the horror of his situation at bay. Forcing his heart rate to slow, he fought harder. "So how did we meet...Freddie?"

Freddie straightened her spine and narrowed her eyes. "I thought we were going to discuss this dream of yours. Once again, you've changed the subject." She held up a finger. "and don't call me that."

He nodded in acquiescence to her request, but he was being dishonest. Honestly. He was definitely calling her Freddie from now on. Once again, he felt faint traces of amusement, despite the dire situation he was so obviously in. Oh, they definitely had a shared past. An intimate one. He just knew it. It would explain her hesitancy.

Either that or she was absolutely a liar.

Regarding her accusation that he'd changed the subject, he winked and said, "So I did."

Kelly rubbed his hands down the sheets covering his thighs, as much to gather his thoughts as to fight back the feelings of panic that still hovered around the edges of his mind, waiting for a crack in his control, the opportunity to overwhelm, like a darkness on the edge of his vision. He *craved* knowledge of his own self, of course, and of her... to understand who she was and how they knew each other, but with the obvious signs of abuse, his instincts also screamed to tread carefully...best to keep his thoughts close to his chest. For how could he possibly know who to trust?

If she were the enemy, it behooved him to appear as if he weren't a threat. As if he were innocent. As if he couldn't remember a thing...

Up until he did.

Yet it was so easy to relax his guard with her. His soul wanted badly to trust.

Survive...

He swallowed, covering up another burst of dread, and regarded Freddie once more. "I saw you. A much, much, m—" She raised one brow, and he forced a grin. "—younger version of you," he winked away his teasing, "walking on a path running between a formal garden of roses and a field of wildflowers."

She dipped her head and ignored his attempt to charm. "Sounds like my—" She cleared her throat. "Sounds like Cornwall."

What had she intended to say?

Saving that question for later, he continued. "A man and, presumably, his son were there, standing in a study or library of some sort with dark paneled walls. The father actively disliked me."

She toyed with a fingernail, seemingly unaffected. "My father and brother, Duncan. Probably."

Acting on instinct, he did not tell her about the scene in the dark. Instead, he waved his hand in the air, ignored the jolt of pain the action caused, and forced a flippant tone, "The rest is really rather boring." Interesting that she didn't contradict the idea that her father didn't like him.

She narrowed her eyes in accusation, but he flattened his lips, refusing to expound further, and she didn't press him for more.

So, she didn't believe him. Of course not, for apparently, he'd had a nightmare during which he screamed out her name. Her distrust was fine, warranted even.

Hell, neither one of them were being entirely truthful with one another, that much was obvious, which was saying something considering he had very little memory of things to hide.

"So, where did you find me? How did you find me? And how did you come to be my caretaker, not that I'm complaining, mind?"

"To be honest, Kelly, I found you chained up in a dungeon, beaten half to death. That was several weeks ago. But you needn't worry. For now, very few know where you are. And we'd like to keep it that way, until you've healed some more."

"We?"

She glanced away. "The duke. Your partners."

He changed the subject yet again, deliberately striving to be absurd, redirection at its finest, because she so clearly lied, and he had no way to force her to the tell the truth. Yet. "Do I have any clothes? I'm keen to be on my way now."

She cocked her head and chuckled, her sarcasm evident to anyone. "Oh? Plans to leave soon? Where are you headed? What? Are you just going to travel the countryside with several cracked ribs, weak fingers, and—"

"Are you calling me weak?" It felt natural to attempt to disarm her with charm, like a default setting in his brain.

Her smirk shouted 'Yes' in no uncertain terms, but she said, "Not in any way you imply, but Mr. Kelly, let's be realistic. That's a healthy dose of denial you have going on there."

Denial? He was miles away from anything resembling denial. *She* was in denial if she thought hanging around here waiting for the men who so clearly tortured him to arrive was a reasonable idea.

He searched her face. Then again, maybe they were already here?

Kelly forced a smile he didn't feel and said, "So, it is. May I assume you have a plan for where we go from here?'

"It just so happens, I do. We need you able to move so we can travel to Wales. We're to meet—"

A loud crash sounded from below, and faster than lightning, Freddie whipped out a knife from her boot. Clearly, she'd done the like once or twice before. She pressed a finger to her lips and stood, then slunk out the open door to his room.

He slammed his fist on the mattress. He might not know who he was, but he wasn't an invalid who would wait abed to be taken and tortured again.

Kelly tossed the covers aside, completely unashamed of his nudity, and slid his legs over the edge of the bed. Then, using the bed post for support, he pulled himself upright. Sweat broke out on his brow, and he swallowed back the urge to heave, his mouth watering in preparation to cast up his accounts. It was unpleasant, make no mistake, but he refused to give into weakness.

He drew in a slow breath. Forcing the air through in a controlled manner. In his nose, out his mouth. Repeat.

God damn, he was standing on his own two feet. Finally. "About *bloody* time," he muttered.

For a moment, he remained that way—upright beside the bed, breathing in and out—long enough to normalize his heart rate and command the pain and nausea to subside, at least a little. He focused on the wooden floor beneath his bare feet. Cool, smooth, and timeworn.

But knowing that any moment she might return or be in real trouble on the ground floor, he shuffled forward as soon as things were manageable (a stage above barely tolerable), one foot at a time, his teeth clenched against the desire to groan out loud with every step.

It seemed to take forever, but finally and with great care, he stood before the crack in the door and listened...

Another crash sounded, then Freddie called out, "Stop!"

Chapter Twelve

At the Same Time: Dawe House, London

Lord Dawe,

I have news of great import to share. It has come to my attention that a certain Irish asset has unexpectedly resurfaced in England following a brisk swim down the River Mersey, and then a fortnight later, promptly disappeared once again.

I suspect there will be more than a few raised brows when this information comes to light—loose ends are ever so vexatious.

I will, of course, pass on more information as I come by it. Until then, I remain,

Your most steadfast sponsor, &c.,

— VISCOUNT SHARPE

Lord Dawe laid the missive atop the stack of papers before him, smoothing the message until the foolscap lay flat once again, small creases and a waxy stain the only visible sign it had once been folded and sealed. He straightened the stack before him, mostly letters of inquiry regarding the destruction of the *HMS Nightingale*, the majority, and most persistent, of which were from that young upstart, Sir Robert Peel—an Irish lover if there ever was one.

The interest into the *HMS Nightingale* was a bigger pain in the ass than they'd anticipated, and a mess he must address—his associates were already breathing down his neck about it.

Now, this.

How many times must he kill Ciarán Kelly before the man finally took the hint and died already?

And now he must needs recruit a new man, someone cunning and mercenary, who could keep a sharp eye on their newest Society member, Viscount Sharpe.

Perhaps, it was finally time to allow his son, Duncan, to do more than just stand by his side.

At the Same Time: The Library, Stonebridge House, London

Lord Alaistair MacLeod watched as the Duke of Stonebridge handed a missive to Lord Clifford Ross, Marquess of Dansbury.

"I'll be damned," said Dansbury as he handed the missive over to MacLeod.

It read:

Duke,
   Kelly is alive.

— SPYDER

"*Shite*" was all he could manage.

His reaction caused both Dansbury and Lady Beatryce to laugh. MacLeod watched as Dansbury glanced over to his wife, who winked in return.

God, he wished Amelia were here...

Amelia was out and about with Stonebridge's wife, Grace, organizing the printing of pamphlets in support of immigration, or some such.

"Yes, well," replied the Duke of Stonebridge, a suppressed twitch of his lips the only sign of his good humor. MacLeod wondered at their good humor. He himself wasn't so sure the news *was* good.

The duke walked over to the side bar, pulled down four glasses, and pulled the stopper off a decanter of whisky.

MacLeod darted a look at the ornate ormolu clock resting on the mantle shelf of the nearby fireplace. 11:30. In the morning. Still, he supposed the occasion called for it.

Despite the fact that they all believed Kelly had betrayed his fellow agents for the Crown, they had been attempting to rescue him; he'd been badly beaten and tied up in the brig of the *HMS Nightingale* when the Nightingale exploded. They were lucky to be alive. Kelly, in particular, had been thrown into the frigid waters of the River Mersey and lost to them, despite their immense efforts.

Or so they thought.

The men and Lady Beatryce filed over to the duke and each accepted a glass. Each of them, likely, reliving that dark night. They'd all been there.

"You may want to take a seat," commanded the duke with a raised brow. Clearly, he wasn't making a request despite his polite words.

Of course, there was more. Hence, this morning's double shot of whisky.

Everyone but the duke took a seat on one of the two camel backed sofa's facing each other in the center of the room. The duke sipped his whisky, and the rest of the team followed suit. As the men waited for Stonebridge to speak, the tension became palpable.

MacLeod leaned forward, elbows on his knees, his glass of whisky dangling between his legs, his hand only loosely gripping the crystal over the rim while his gaze remained focused on the table before him, mainly so he wouldn't react to an unintentional crossways glance and crush the glass with his hand. He wasn't sure he wanted to hear what the duke was about to say. Regardless of whether or not Kelly was acting as a double agent under the duke's orders, Kelly had still kidnapped Amelia, MacLeod's fiancé, and *that* was something he could never forgive. Even if Amelia had escaped and was now fine. Even if Amelia herself willed MacLeod not to judge Kelly too harshly.

It was a tall order, even coming from the woman he loved. MacLeod had never been so frightened in his life, than during those weeks Amelia was missing.

MacLeod swallowed another shot of whisky, rage igniting once more at the memory.

MacLeod glanced up as Dansbury reclined and crossed one leg over the other, one arm resting across the back of the couch behind his wife; his fingers toyed lazily with some of the loose curls of Beatryce's hair. His other hand casually balanced his tumbler on his knee.

Amelia was Dansbury's sister. How could he remain so blasé about the situation?

Stonebridge downed the remaining contents of his glass and set it aside before leaning against his desk and casually crossing his legs. He braced himself on the desk a moment, his gaze on his feet or somewhere thereabouts, then he looked up and crossed his arms.

"Kelly has been working as a double agent on my orders."

The announcement was met with silence, the pronouncement not wholly unexpected at this point.

MacLeod swallowed the rest of his whisky and slammed his glass on the table. It may have cracked, but who the hell cared? Dansbury seemed to tighten his grip on his, but otherwise, remained steady. Lady Beatryce didn't even flinch.

The duke continued. "The incident six weeks ago on the *HMS Nightingale* makes it clear Kelly's cover was blown. Or at the very least, the Society decided they had no further use for him."

Still, no one else uttered a word. MacLeod suspected everyone one watched *him,* waiting for him to explode. But he maintained a tight leash on his anger—just. He felt a muscle tick in his jaw as he clenched his teeth, biting back his dark thoughts, which threatened to explode from his mouth at any moment.

The duke uncharacteristically broke form and ran a hand through his hair. "Why aren't you saying anything? I expected much yelling and arguing by now. Accusations at the very least. Your silence is disconcerting as hell."

Dansbury smiled and took another sip of his whisky. *What the fook did he have to smile aboot?*

MacLeod toyed with the idea of giving the duke what he wanted. MacLeod still bore the bruises from being caught in the explosion on the *Nightingale*. He was lucky to be alive, and though he was typically judicious with his words, Kelly. Had. Kidnapped. His. Fiancé. The fury he felt now was seconds away from erupting into a tirade the likes of which none of these men had ever before witnessed from him. *They really did no' want to see that happen.*

MacLeod's knuckles turned white where his hands rested, clenched into fists, on his kilted knees. He glanced furiously at the table before him, his jaw taut. Rage throbbed through his veins, but still, he said nothing.

Lady Beatryce stood, surprising everyone, it seemed, apart from the Duke who continued to watch *him*. MacLeod, his head still bent, followed Beatryce with his eyes.

She came to stop next to the duke, hands clasped before her, and leaned back against the desk, mirroring his stance.

She cleared her throat, delicately, and spoke up. "Even more surprising, I believe, is that this information came from our contact, Spyder. It hasn't escaped anyone's notice that the man always seems to be several steps ahead of our investigation and is always in possession of just the kind of information we need. I am pleased to report that we have a strong lead as to this man's identity, and I have a new person—a woman—prepared to infiltrate his household. Based on careful analysis of his contact with our agents, we believe the man is Welsh, from the nobility, well-educated, and has been contacting various agents under different aliases. I will have more to report in the next several months."

As Lady Beatryce returned to her seat on the couch, the duke murmured, "Thank you, Lady Beatryce."

My how far they'd come over the past year. It wasn't so long ago they counted Lady Beatryce their enemy; her father certainly had been. Now, the duke had her taking a lead role in this mission? *What next, sending Amelia undercover?*

The duke folded his arms. "We don't yet know whether Spyder—"

MacLeod leaped to his feet, unable to take any more of this, and the duke straightened.

MacLeod bit out, "Och, how can ye be sure? Kelly might have been playin' ye." He squared off with the duke, whose stance turned defensive. "The mon took my Amelia. She could have died, *daingead*. Those men—of the society—have no compunction aboot killin' on a whim. Was that part of yer plan, too, Duke? Was ma woman's life worth it to ye?"

The duke slashed a hand through the air, "Kelly never would have let anything happen to her."

MacLeod snorted in disbelief.

The duke fisted his hands on his hips. "I'd stake my life on it."

Silence.

Then, MacLeod said, "Ye're more than welcome to gamble your life. Or that of *your* wife's. But never Amelia's. So, tell me. Did you know?"

Everyone knew what he asked. Did the duke know about the plan to kidnap Amelia?

The duke sighed and pinched the bridge of his nose. "No. I didn't know."

MacLeod turned and threw himself back in his seat, his jaw clenched and fire throbbing in his veins. Point made.

Castle Ddu

Owain's rings clinked together as he unrolled the latest missive, courtesy of his personal pigeon post.

Dear Asshole, He has amnesia. And fuck you.

— F

Owain looked up and threw a quick glance out the window. His lips twitched before settling into a full-blown smile. Then, he pulled his leg from over the arm of his chair and stood. He jogged down the steps of his dais in search of paper and a quill.

Ah, Frederica. Is this the beginning of the end of our friendship?

Chapter Thirteen

S o, perhaps yelling "Stop!" wasn't the most logical thing to say, but it'd worked. It got his attention.

Frederica reached down and picked up said he, the largest, fluffiest, fattest cat she'd ever seen in her life, and immediately began stroking him beneath his fuzzy little chin. He was ridiculously soft. And hairy. And perfect. Though he had created a bit of a mess.

The cat lifted his grey head, to offer her better access, his purrs practically a roar of pleasure.

She sighed. "Aw, who's a good kitty kitty?" God, how she loved cats. Adorable little balls of fluff—with wicked blades hidden within their dainty little paws. And this one had serendipitous timing, despite creating such a ruckus. She hadn't felt like herself in weeks; he was *just* what she needed.

The cat added a little rumbling chirp to his hum, and Frederica let out a tiny squeal of delight.

Of course, she'd deny the entire thing should someone from her team suggest such a thing.

She lifted the cat to eye level and lowered her voice. "I think I'll call you...General Llwyd. Would you like that?"

The cat nuzzled her cheek in response.

"Oh my, I could just cuddle you all day, yes I could—"

"What the fuck?"

General Llwyd leapt out of her arms, and Freddie brushed away lingering fur from the end of her nose. It was Kelly, of course. Who else would it be?

She rolled her eyes, then scanned the room before her, her back to Kelly, but the cat was nowhere to be seen. He'd probably bolted through the gaping front door.

Frederica settled her hands on her hips and searched through the opening and said aloud, "Now you've done it. You've run him off." She lifted on to her toes. Maybe he hadn't gone far.

"The cat?"

Frederica spun around. "Of course...the...cat—"

The first thing she noticed was the sword he gripped with both hands. *Where had he gotten that?*

The second thing she noticed was his *sword*. His *other* sword.

Oh.

Oh, my.

She wet her lips. He was naked. 100% gloriously bare. But wholly different from the lying-on-his-death-bed bare. This was the standing-on-his—own-two-powerful-feet kind of bare. Very different things.

And he was utterly magnificent. Still. More so, damn him.

Freddie sucked in a deep breath, it was *Kelly*, then glanced up and narrowed her eyes. "Of course, the cat. Who else?" She swallowed and nodded to his weapon. Not *that* one. The other one. "Where did you get the sword? And Jesus, how did you get down? You should be abed—"

"Wasn't. Easy." He gritted out, gripping the sword—his weapon—the hard one— *Jesus*.

She wanted to fan herself.

She didn't. Thank God. "Were you coming to...protect me?"

He grimaced.

"Kelly?"

He said nothing, just flattened his lips, then he wove on his feet and promptly fell to the floor.

Oh.

73

Well—at least, he didn't land on his—either one, she supposed, but primarily the deadly one.

Which didn't entirely clarify things.

Of course, had he fallen on the *steel* sword, it would have saved her the trouble of having to drag him to the couch. But then, Owain would be wholly disappointed in the failed mission. *Sigh.*

Perhaps, she should just leave him there on the floor. He'd be guaranteed to wake with a crick in his neck. Would serve him right for scaring off the cat.

Frederica sighed, then gripped both of Kelly's hands and pulled.

He was now back to sick-bed-naked, so the cut of his hip no longer tangled her brain. Instead, she simply embraced the consistent feeling of animosity she held towards him; it was far preferable to the other, unwanted attraction thingy.

He might be a magnificent specimen of manhood, sure, but that didn't mean a thing. He was still, Kelly.

She tugged again.

He was just a job. Nothing more.

AN HOUR LATER, HE FINALLY WOKE. HIS MOUTH AUTOMATICALLY turned down in a tight frown.

Noting the rosy tinge to his cheeks, she reached for his forehead, but he battered her hand away, failing to hide his wince of pain.

"I'm fine," he said.

She snorted. "You look flushed. Are you sure your fever's not returned?"

"I assure you, you'll be the first to know."

"My, someone's cranky."

Now, he snorted.

And she was not afraid to call him on it. "An hour ago you were all winks and toothy grins. What happened?"

He flattened his lips. "My grins are not toothy."

She shrugged. Maybe not, but she'd never tell *him* that. Instead, she replied, "Depends on your perspective."

"Why don't I put it to you this way. We've established I may be flirting with...trouble. You hear an odd crash and race away, knife in hand. Then, nothing. You don't come back. Anything could have happened to you."

She patted his shoulder. "Aw, Kelly did you come to my rescue?"

"No, I came to mine."

Of course. Rakes only ever thought of themselves. Shouldn't she know that by now?

Chapter Fourteen

A week later, Kelly sat in bed, back in the loft, and stared out the window at a sea of patchwork green and dry-stone walls.

His head still ached, his mind stumbling through a persistent and uncomfortable dark fog. Worse, it was as if his entire collection of memories...his whole life...was only a hairsbreadth out of reach. If only he could stretch his mental fingers just a little bit further, everything would come tumbling back, flooding his mind all at once. Then, he'd be fine. A person complete.

Someone *familiar*.

Alas, he was a stranger even to himself.

Ciarán tensed when he heard Freddie enter the room. He still didn't remember her. And yet...

"Afternoon," she said, her tone practical and efficient.

He continued to stare out the room's lone window, the better to collect his muddled thoughts. At least the constant flair of panic and dread he'd felt three days ago had subsided. Somewhat. He mostly felt guarded, now, at times angry.

His new normal.

Oh, he made attempts to put her at ease, continuing to use humor and charm as a means of deflection...other than that brief argument after the cat incident.

But this afternoon, he simply wasn't feeling it. He was ready to *do* something.

He ground his teeth. "Hmmm..." was all he managed.

Still, she didn't complain—besides, it was better than a growl or a grunt. Like yesterday.

So maybe he wasn't always all smiles and charisma.

She came in daily. Forcing him to move his legs, his fingers, everything. His ill-fated trip down the ladder last week, entirely too soon for his physical state at the time, had been ill-conceived and proved a true setback for his recovery. So, at first, her exercises were pure torture. But he grew stronger every day. And now, he bore it all feigning more weakness than he truly felt while probing her for information. He pretended he was still too weak to seek her out on his own. Which meant he was forced to just sit here. With nothing to do.

But worse, nothing to remember.

He would lose his damn mind long before some faceless, nefarious people arrived at their door, something he suspected was a possibility based on Freddie's actions with the cat.

When she wasn't torturing him with physical stretches that went well beyond what was reasonably necessary, the sadist, she also talked about her home. Apparently, he'd been there before. And she said all the right words about her life there, her family, his presence. But there was an edge to her voice when she spoke of Cornwall, as if she withheld something important...as if the memories of her life there were painful to recall. Though whenever he tried to press her about it, she laughed at him like he was mad and changed the subject. Even her laugh was forced. All wrong and not a laugh at all.

And he still didn't think he could trust her.

She didn't say a lot about his role as a spy. Only that they'd worked a few cases together, but for the most part, did not.

"Fancy some supper?" Despite the question, her tone was commanding. Impersonal.

He continued to stare out the window. Rude, sure, but for some strange reason he feared looking at her. Like it would hurt...as if a locked box in his soul screamed her name whenever it sensed her, the sound muffled but the pain of its horrific wail still distantly present as an uncomfortable ache beneath the surface of his skin. All of it made worse by the suspicion that she lied.

He rubbed absentmindedly at his chest to soothe a phantom ache.

It was clear, especially during moments when her veneer of civility lifted the tiniest bit and her animosity revealed itself, that they were not lovers, at least not recently, though perhaps they had been? That would make sense and would explain her thinking that he might rediscover himself through her talking about her home in Cornwall.

Kelly smelled his supper a moment before he felt her weight against the bed, and he looked around to see Freddie placing a tray of food over his lap.

He sniffed to be sure and frowned. "I may not remember my past, madam, but I do know, with unquestionable certainty, that I despise turnips." He glanced at her. "Especially boiled ones."

She placed her hands on her hips, a scowl shaping her well-formed lips. "Ah. Grumpy, I see. Well, we don't have the luxury of a cook, now do we?" She nodded to the bowl on his lap. "You'll take what I can manage on my own."

And just like that, his temper eased. Kelly's lips twitched as he fought to withhold a smile. Strangely, her fiery spirit diffused his own irritability, which he knew was ludicrous. Perhaps, he was by nature, averse.

He regarded his dinner as he pushed the turnips around in his bowl with a fork. "Not the nurturing type, are you?" he quipped.

He heard her snort before asking, "Would you rather I dump the bowl of turnips on your head?"

Her tone was sweet...with an edge of steel.

Kelly felt the beginnings of a genuine smile. Aye, their banter may not be familiar, but it was enjoyable all the same.

Eventually, he quit pretending he was going to eat squishy plant roots and tossed down his fork, taking a breath to steel himself for her piercing gaze before looking up and regarding his culinary tormentor.

"What shall we do tomorrow?" he asked. "Shall we take a stroll down Rotten Row? Visit the menagerie or the Emporium?" Kelly folded his arms across this chest, anger and frustration exploding once again from out of nowhere. Had he been this mercurial before, or was it a function of the situation he founded himself in?

He ran his hand through his hair, ignoring the small jolt of pain from his damaged fingers. "And why the fuck do I remember those places exist, yet I do not recall my own name with any degree of certainty?"

Freddie pursed her lips and sat on the edge of his bed. She picked up his fork, and he followed her movements warily, his mouth clamped shut. Despite the mixed feelings he seemed to harbor toward her, he held on to a robust sense of distrust, warranted he'd bet.

She scooped up a forkful of turnip and held it up.

He caught her gaze and shook his head no, once.

She scowled at him, but then her look turned thoughtful, and she chewed on her delightfully plump lower lip just before she asked, "Why do you think you remember those places, specifically?"

Later, he'd blame what happened next on those delightfully captivating lips.

He opened his mouth to respond, his eyes locked, *involuntarily he might add*, on her well-formed mouth, and she shoved the fork between his lips, faster than an adder strike.

Dammit.

She was quick.

He nearly gagged, but *he didn't bloody dare.*

He chewed his mush and glared at her all the while; she crossed her arms with a self-satisfied smirk, a confident lift to her chin.

He refused to grimace at the foul taste, and absolutely forbade himself to vomit, though the mush tasted as vile as he'd expected. Yet with a defiant set to his jaw, he grabbed the fork and scooped up another heaping mass of the sordid shite.

He challenged her with a look as he put the whole damn thing in his mouth.

Then, another.

And another.

Still, she dared him right back, one brow raised in confident brilliance.

They didn't speak.

They didn't smirk.

And they never looked away.

Suddenly, he felt a sharp ache, and he dropped his fork, his hands flying to his head to shut out the onslaught of pain while a fragment of memory surfaced. He squeezed his eyes shut as if doing so would relieve the ache in his head.

"Kelly?" It was Freddie, but her voice was muffled as if he had cotton wool in his ears. He could feel her pulling at his arms, but that too felt detached and distant, numb.

He *had* eaten turnips before, a scene of him doing just that replayed itself in his mind, a small snapshot to be sure, but clear as if it'd happened only yesterday. He could smell the sea; hear the sounds of gulls cawing on the wind.

He saw bars.

Kelly shook his head in denial, uncomfortable with the implication of this particular recollection.

As the pain began to subside, he dropped his hands and looked up at Freddie, feeling a touch of bleakness as he grasped to hold onto this new piece of his past, no matter how small. No matter how...unpleasant.

Oh yes, he'd had boiled turnips before, but not in a comfortable, if primitive, cottage with a beautiful caretaker by his side.

Rather, he'd had them alone. In a dark, dank prison cell...

Later...

Frederica unraveled the latest missive she'd collected.

F,

   I know you are furious.

Furious doesn't even begin to describe it, asshole.

You must see this through.

Fuck you, Owain, already seeing to the task.

Do whatever it takes to restore his memory, and then bring him to me. To that end, I've enclosed a sketch of a woman who may or may not help in that vein. Show it to him. Her name is Mrs. Amelia Chase.
    Make haste. Others will be coming for him. Be careful. Trust no one.

No, shit.

-Your favorite asshole

Frederica chuckled over Owain's signature, though she was still reasonably displeased with him. The man did have a sense of humor at times. Then, she slowly pulled out the referenced portrait, hidden between the cover sheets of Owain's missive.

Frederica ran her finger over the portrait, swallowing a sudden lump the size of a boulder that had found its way into her throat. Mrs. Amelia Chase. The was no question about it; the woman was very beautiful. But who was she? Or more precisely, who was she to Kelly?

Is *she* the reason he'd abandoned her all those years ago?

An unexpected wave of sadness washed over Frederica, making her stomach drop and her heart ache. Her cheeks heated uncomfortably. She turned away from what felt like the woman's knowing gaze. God, what was wrong with her? She glanced back down at the woman's likeness in her hands and being honest with herself, recognized her feelings for what they were: envy. And oh, didn't she just hate *that*—the unexpected feeling of jealousy and animosity she felt towards an unknown woman. There was no logical reason for such feelings. Sure, the woman appeared beautiful and self-assured. Sensual even. But those things should not affect Freddie so—the woman hadn't done anything to deserve such bitterness. Further, Kelly was nothing to Frederica, now, and hadn't been for years, so this burst of envy over what may or may not be evidence of an affair with Kelly, a man Freddie no longer had any claim to, was ridiculous and unfair. Women were always at a disadvantage; such was the way of the world, and her place in it didn't offer many opportunities to develop the keen bonds of friendship with women, a fact she deeply regretted. She felt that women needed to support each other, always, even if it was just in the spirit of sisterhood. She'd rarely been at odds with a woman in her life.

Men on the other hand...

Ugh. Feelings sometimes made no sense whatsoever. Frederica set the sketch aside, vowing to confront, er—show, him the likeness. In time.

And tomorrow, they would step up their game. He needed to be walking yesterday.

She began to pen a new missive. Owain needed to come clean. Now was not the time to be keeping her in the dark.

Chapter Fifteen

Dawe House, London

Lord Dawe placed a bag of coins on the edge of his desk, then folded his hands in front of him. The ruffians fouling the air of his office shifted on their feet, each man eyeing the reward purse hungrily. Lord Dawe caught the eye of their leader, Harry Boyle.

"I want every man you can muster. Every boy. Every woman. Every child." His voice crept up, growing louder and louder with each word he spoke. "I don't—"

Spittle flew from Lord Dawe's lips, and he paused to remove his hand kerchief and dab at his mouth. All eyes were on him now and no one dared utter a word.

Lord Dawe tucked the kerchief back into his pocket and resumed with more aplomb. "I don't care how much it costs me. I want Ciarán Kelly found!"

He was yelling again, and he clamped his lips shut and looked down, reaching for the papers on his desk. They were ordered and precise. He straightened them again. "That is all," he said, without looking up. He heard the scrambling of many booted feet as the men fought to quit the room, and the jingle of coins as someone, most likely Boyle, pocketed the purse from his desk.

The room quieted, apart from the low shuffling of a softer set of footsteps.

"Son. Don't leave. Not yet."

Lord Dawe finished straightening one final stack of papers and sat, then glanced up at his son, Lord Duncan Dawe, who now stood before his desk.

"I have a different, but no less important task for you. Leave the men to Kelly. I want you to find out what you can about Viscount Sharpe."

His son cleared his throat. "The new man?"

Lord Dawe drummed his fingers on the desk. "Yes."

Duncan spread his arms. "He passed the tests, had all the requisite sponsors, made a sizeable donation, even completed the *initiation*—"

Lord Dawe raised a brow and stopped drumming his fingers.

His son bowed. "As you wish, father."

Early the Next Morning: Stonebridge House, London...

From the warmth of Stonebridge's library, MacLeod stared out the window and studied the quiet pavement and shadowy outline of nearby objects, dancing in the flickering light of gas lamps standing sentinel outside Stonebridge House, his arm propped against the window trim. He sought insight and inspiration, a way to diffuse the fury and resentment burning in his gut. Though several days had passed, thoughts surrounding the implication of the Duke and Kelly's machinations marched back and forth across his mind like a general inspecting his troops and finding them lacking, repugnant even.

The duke had other men gathering intel on Kelly's whereabouts, but everything was moving so damn slow, and MacLeod was itching to *do* something. But the duke was his boss, and if he said wait, they waited.

MacLeod clenched his raised hand and battered his head against his arm, wanting nothing more than to send his fist through the leaded glass window.

Kelly...

To say he hated deception would be hypocritical coming from a man whose occupation was that of a spy.

But it was one thing to deceive bad men and quite another to betray a friend.

MacLeod tilted his head back, relaxed his hand, and closed his eyes as Amelia slid her arms around his waist from behind, offering comfort and ease from his worries. Her cheek rested on his shoulder, infusing him with warmth, and his lips slid into a grateful smile. He settled his right hand over hers.

"Darling, you're up early..." she pressed from behind, the warmth of her breath on his shoulder sending soothing ripples skating down his arm.

He glanced at the clock standing guard atop the mantel, 4:30, and squeezed her clasped hands, then turned within her arms, swallowing her in his own embrace. "Och, love. Ma mind canna seem ta rest."

He pressed his lips to her forehead, and she burrowed further into the cavern of his hold.

"Kelly?" She asked, her voice soft.

"Aye." He hated discussing the man with her, despite her protestations that she held no animosity towards Kelly for his role in kidnapping her. For his part in hunting them down. For killing her horse.

She pressed for more. "And you're desperate to do something..."

"Ye know me so well, my love. The duke—" MacLeod swallowed his complaint.

"The duke knows you're not exactly objective at the moment."

"Aye, I know it." MacLeod squeezed her, then pulled back.

Together, they crossed the room and settled into one of the duke's couches, reclining into a corner that faced the fire, Amelia curled against his chest.

MacLeod stroked her loose hair, marveling at the play of firelight on the golden highlights woven amidst strands of cognac colored tresses. "Amelia?"

"Hmmm,"

He swirled the tips of his fingers down her back, knowing how much she enjoyed a light back rub. "Did Kelly...," He paused, unable to find the words to press her for more. Unwilling to be the man who couldn't trust.

Amelia sat up, her hands pressed against his chest, and looked at him in query. "What is it, darling?"

He tried to pull her back into the cradle of his arms, but she resisted, pulling away and settling beside him on the couch. She arranged her night gown, straightening the fabric as if she were dressed for tea in a fancy gown and not in her night clothes, then folded her hands in her lap and looked at him expectantly. "Ask me anything."

A small chuckle escaped, and he shook his head. God, he loved this woman. He opened his mouth to speak, but she forestalled him, her hand raised. "Pretend you are interrogating me as you would any other suspect."

"Mel..."

She tucked one leg under her and leaned forward, practically bouncing on the sofa as she warmed to the idea of her ludicrous suggestion. "I'm serious, Alaistair. Perhaps, something'll jog my memory."

"Mel, no. I couldn't possibly—you don't want to experience—"

She battered her eyelashes. "Wouldn't I?"

"Mel..."

Her grin turned sultry, sexy. She pulled at the ribbon of her night rail, loosening the laces and offering the barest glimpse of her chest. "The making up part sure would be fun."

He barked out a laugh and stood. She practically bounced in her seat once again, a knowing smile on her face and the hint of a blush on her cheek.

Aye, he couldn't resist her. He clasped his hands behind his back and paced the room as he considered where to begin. He maintained an even tone when he asked, "Did the man known to ye as Spyder or Kelly ever, in yer presence, mention the name Dawe..."

"No."

He spun around, facing her. "Did either of them suggest they knew anything aboot the men involved in the Secret Society for the Purification of England?"

"No."

"Did they speak of the Society at all?"

"Yes. Spyder did. Kelly was uncharacteristically mute."

They'd covered this ground before. More than once. He ran his fingers through his hair, then began pacing again.

He heard her sigh. "MacLeod, I don't think you're truly trying hard enough."

His shoulders stiffened. Was she *challenging* him?

He released a slow breath and relaxed his hands, his shoulders, his tight smile. Lazily, he turned around and stalked to where she was seated. She stopped bouncing and froze, though her face was —*expectant*.

He leaned over her, his fists planted into the cushions on either side of her. He was close enough now to hear her swallow, to note the sharp intake of breath. She wet her lips and an answering heat flared to life in his veins. He tucked into her neck, a hairsbreadth away from touching the soft skin with his lips. God, he loved this woman. "Mel —" She shivered; a hot breath of air escaped. "Are ye challengin' me, lass?"

She licked her lips and nodded.

He smiled and offered a nudge. "Are ye temptin' me?"

"Y-yes—"

"Verra guid—"

He planted a deliberate kiss in the crook of her neck, and another, up, closer to her ear. She moaned, and he continued *probing*, his brogue thickening with his desire. "Is there nothin' further ye want ta tell meh?"

She shook her head, strands of silky hair brushed his cheek, and he pulled back, the better to see the flush caressing her face. Och, she was beautiful. He leaned in for a kiss.

She stopped him with a hand to his chest. "Alaistair?"

"Aye, my love?"

"I think you should go after Kelly."

That gave him pause, a flash of anger threatened to ignite. He suppressed the instinct and considered her request. He sat beside her and gathered her hands in his. "Why?"

Her face, so earnest, so beloved, she said, "Because you're an honorable man."

He cocked his head, ready to deny her claim, but she continued, "He needs the opportunity to explain. Clearly, the society wants him dead." She was referring to the fact that they'd found Kelly in the brig of an old, retired Royal Navy ship, the *HMS Nightingale*. He'd been beaten to a bloody pulp, and they'd lost him when the ship exploded as they were attempting to disembark.

"Mel—"

She shook her head, her hand still pressed to his chest. A lone tear escaped and slid down her cheek. "He was your friend, Alaistair. Trust him."

Chapter Sixteen

The Next Morning

Frederica tossed a rather large jug of water right into Kelly's sleeping face. "Rise and shine you laze-a-bed. We have to *move*." She had to bite back a smile at how satisfying it was to toss all that water. She knew it had been totally unnecessary.

Or not, depending on one's point of view.

Kelly bolted upright, a surprising feat considering his injuries, and shook his head of water in that way men do, which always left her with a headache when she'd tried the same as a child, then raked his wet hair back and out of his face with both hands. He said nothing.

Slowly, he looked her way and offered her a beguiling smile.

Considering the sheets were down to his waist and his sleepshirt was now plastered to his skin, the effect was most unsettling to her insides, and she nearly squirmed. Which was absurd. Absurd!

They were both frauds, especially him. And even though she had to pretend she liked him; she really didn't. So, this attraction was particularly inconvenient.

And they had a *past*. One that was insurmountable. *He'd left—* Freddie slammed her mind closed on that thought.

Boils. Boils. Boils. Boils. It would be her new mantra.

Really, though, how had he managed to be awoken in such a way while maintaining such complete control of his temper? She'd have been sputtering in outrage and spitting mad, a curse or three on her tongue and looking like a water-logged cat.

It wasn't fair.

He swiped at his face again—so she might have used more water than was precisely necessary—and continued to take his time, so she prompted, "This is no time to be a slag. Let's get your arse moving and fix this. We've wasted enough time in bed."

Her cheeks threatened to set fire to the nearby frilly curtains at her unfortunate choice of words.

Kelly smiled—of course, he'd pick up on her unintentional innuendo—and opened his mouth to respond with something obscene, she was sure.

She shook her head no with a hard look of warning. "Don't." Despite her blushes, she was in no mood for his silver tongue.

He smiled and winked anyway, then looked down and pulled at his wet sleep shirt. "Did you just toss a jug of water on me?"

The obvious note of wonder in his voice was somewhat amusing. And the smallest bit charming.

No. No it wasn't.

She planted her hands on her hips. "Be thankful I didn't go with Plan A."

Kelly glanced up, one side of his mouth quirked, his eyes asking the obvious question.

She shook her head. "You don't want to know." Besides, she wanted to save that promising option as a resource in the event of future need. Clearly, a jug of water wasn't enough to ruffle this man's feathers.

Frederica smirked and tossed him a pair of trousers, a linen shirt, and a length of cotton for drying himself. "Can you manage without my help?" she taunted.

It was time for him to leave this bed.

He scowled and began pulling off his night shirt. It'd clearly ridden up in the night, and he managed to remove the garment with relative ease, a small groan or two the only sign of any discomfort.

Or had she been the one groaning? Out of habit, she reached for her locket and gave it a slide on its chain.

Kelly had been a much younger man when she'd seen him last. Now, at the age of twenty-seven, he had a smattering of hair across his chest, including a line of it that arrowed down beneath the covers. Her eyes traced its path.

Wait...had the covers just...jumped?

Frederica's eyes flew to his. "I see what you're about."

Kelly slanted his mouth into a shameless grin that made her stomach flip and her hands begin to tremble. Still, he said naught.

Then, his eyes dropped once more, and Freddie felt the scorch of his gaze like a brand.

She aimed for indifference, yet her voice shook as she said, "You're undressing me with your eyes, rogue."

Kelly lifted his eyes, silver steel flashed with blazing heat.

Freddie clenched her fists, willing away unwelcome desire. She swallowed the lump that'd settled in her throat while squeezing her legs together to keep from squirming. She tingled. *There.* For the naked chest on display for her now was all man. Virile, healthy man. Even the smattering of bruising, cuts, and scars did not detract from his... magnificence. Rather the opposite in fact. This man was a warrior beneath his lothario façade.

And, God, did he know it.

She scowled when she saw the look on his face that said he knew it. And that he knew *she'd* noticed, damn his eyes.

In truth, there was more to a man...a real man...than muscles and strength. Honor. Reliability. Honesty, to name but a few. Though, she was beginning to believe such an ideal creature was entirely mythological.

Still, she was a woman—alive—and appreciated male beauty.

Frederica turned and busied herself tidying up a room that didn't need it while he put on his shirt; studiously ignoring every moan and creek he uttered. "We need to get you ready. We need—"

She heard Kelly laugh. "I'm a lover not a fighter, but I can hold my own. Though at the moment, I need help with these trousers."

Her shoulders jerked up at his unexpected statement. Of course, he did. She knew it.

She counted to ten, firming her resolve. She could do this. He was only a man. Hell, she'd done it several times over the last fortnight, why would tonight be any different?

She tried to imagine him as sick-bed naked, not virile-healthy-man naked.

She spun around, forcing a bravado she definitely didn't feel. "Right then." She reached for his covers, but he stayed her hand.

She sighed. "What now?"

"Tell me, are you happy?"

"What? That's none of your business."

He tried again, "Tell me once more how you came to be my...well, my nurse, so to speak."

Frederica narrowed her eyes. He wanted to discuss that now? They'd been over this. She shook her head. "Once again, you're stalling."

He shrugged. "I need a moment."

Was that the hint of a blush staining his cheeks? Never.

She rolled her eyes and tsked. "Oh, please. It's nothing I haven't seen before."

Sick-bed naked, sick-bed naked, she chanted.

This time, his eyes shifted away. "Ahem, yes, well..."

Really? She didn't have time for his sudden bout of missishness... If she were to survive dressing this man who she was clearly unadvisedly and inconveniently attracted to—*still*—she needed this part over with. Now. While her resolve was firm.

Frederica smirked, and without warning, yanked off his covers, revealing what lay beneath...in all his manly glory.

And then quite literally quit breathing.

Oh.

Oh.

Oh.

He was...er...ready. For fornication.

And quite, quite large.

And very, very—*disastrously*—appealing.

So maybe she hadn't quite seen it all before.

For a moment or ten, who knew how long, she couldn't move—not even to unlock her eyes which seemed to have attached themselves to the sight of his formidable cock, jutting out from a thick nest of dark, black hair.

Distantly, she heard him chuckle and say, "That's not helping."

His comment was like the proverbial bucket of ice water, and she glanced away. She was shaken by the sight of him and all his *glory,* and worse, by her inconvenient yet compulsory attraction to him.

Or at least to his cock.

For the first time in years, she was unsettled. Words tripped over each other as they tumbled forth from her mouth. "Uh. You've got a... I see. Um..." She threw the covers back over his body and spun for the door. "I'll just...uh...I'll give you a moment, then, shall I?" It wasn't a real question.

Their enemies could have been in the room brandishing swords and pistols, and still, she wouldn't have cared. She didn't care, rather she bolted out the door like the weakling she apparently was. To hell with today's plans for dressing a rogue.

His laughter chased her down the hall, and she could have sworn she heard him add, "Coward," between chuckles.

She was. A coward. At least, at that moment.

She didn't really care.

She may have seen him before, but he was so much younger, then. A man, but not yet a *man.*

What a difference seven years makes.

God, even after all these years, their chemistry was explosive.

Even though she hated him.

Right?

Chapter Seventeen

The Next Day

Frederica bustled into the house, her arms laden with turnips and ran smack into a warm body, dropping her crop of root vegetables.

Kelly.

Instinctively, she grabbed hold of his arms to steady him.

Or was he steadying her? For he'd done the same to her.

The heat from his large hands, which wrapped around her upper arms, seared her...but not with pain. A jolt of heat bolted through her body, striking various places. *Intimate places.*

She licked her lips and stared at him. He returned the look, emotion swirling in his steely gaze. She became aware of the beat of her heart. Her next breath. His face. His lips. And nothing else.

She shook her head, self-preservation kicking in. Then, she dropped her hands and fought his pull, figuratively speaking.

Somehow, he'd dressed and climbed down from the loft on his own, a small bead of sweat near his hairline the only sign of difficulty.

As if on cue, together, they looked down at the mess.

"Here," he said from somewhere above, "Let me help you with these."

And he stomped on one with his boot. Then, another. A third, he kicked out of the still-open door of the cottage.

Or so she suspected. She tried to look. Honest she did, but her gaze was snagged by the obvious flex of thigh muscles encased in trousers that were far too small for him, despite the many weeks of being asleep in a coma and before that, torture.

She swallowed the lump in her throat and forced herself to look at the mess he'd created. She would not look to see if she could detect the outline of his formidable cock.

She would not.

The image of his proud manhood seemed to be permanently seared into her brain after yesterday's disastrous discovery of his virility and her susceptibility to it—to him, despite their disastrous past. Hence, the inappropriate and unwanted direction of her thoughts.

Once again, Frederica clenched her hands into fists. It was a good thing she kept her nails closely trimmed for she suspected she'd be forming her hands into fists quite often around him.

She looked him in the eye. "You are an idiot."

He smiled. "Holy Christ, I love it when you talk to me that way."

She shook her head. "Don't you ever take anything seriously?"

"God, I hope not."

Sometimes, the man was insufferable, and she marched off, her gaze firmly on her destination.

She returned with a broom in her hand and thrust it at him. "Since you're so fucking hale, clean it up." Then, she stormed out the front door in search of more turnips.

She'd boil them for him instead of roasting them with the rabbit she'd caught this morning.

She'd keep the rabbit for herself.

When she returned to the cottage an hour later, he was seated at a table near the cooking hearth, and he watched her, saying nothing, one corner of his mouth hitched up in a grin as if chuckling to himself.

She ignored him and strode past to the tall wooden table she used to prep food for cooking. She dropped the new batch of turnips, freshly washed in the nearby stream, on the table, then pulled down a meat cleaver. Over the top, perhaps. Intentional, definitely. She held it up, staring at it a moment with a smirk, then glanced his way, one brow lifted. Assessing.

He cleared his throat, and she looked back at the knife, not bothering to hide a small smile.

Then, she attacked the turnips. With relish. Her grin widened as she imagined his head on the table instead.

Thwack. Thwack. Thwack.

"May I ask you a question?" His yelled over the noise.

She paused and glared at him. Then, *Thwack.*

He laughed, but she ignored it.

"I'll take that as a yes." *Thwack.* "What else do you know about me, as a person? My character?"

She continued prepping *his* dinner and answered, "Well, let's see..." *Thwack.* "You're a well-known rake." *Thwack.* "Unreliable and a tad dishonest." *Thwack. Thwack.* "Perhaps, a little bit," *Thwack.* "disrespectful." *Thwack.* She set down the meat cleaver and glanced up. "From Ireland originally."

He rubbed thoughtfully at his chin. "Hmmm...I'm beginning to doubt the veracity of your answers. You seem to carry a healthy dose of animosity towards me."

"Oh?" she showed her teeth. "Is it showing?"

Without looking, she punctuated her sarcastic reply with another *thwack* at the turnips, for good measure.

Then, she scooped up her mangled mess and dumped them in a pot of water.

He chuckled. "Can't you find one positive thing about me?"

She shrugged her shoulders and salted the water. "You're a handsome man."

He snorted. "Besides that."

She hung the pot over a fire and turned to face him, her hands on her hips. "Well, I've never taken you for lacking in any self-esteem, nor for requiring a woman to stroke your ego. It is already *so* large." She rolled her eyes as she said the last.

"Freddie...", he growled.

She laughed. She couldn't help it. She crossed her arms and put a finger to her lips in thought. "All right. Um...I *can* say I've honestly never seen you angry. Serious? Yes, occasionally." She looked and noticed his toothy girn. "...*very occasionally*. But never angry or cross. Never mean."

He glanced out the nearby window, his eyes unfocused, but his questions seemed pointed. What was he searching for, precisely? "Why do you ask?"

He turned back and shrugged. "I remember next to nothing of myself, my past, the people I knew, or the things I have done. Why wouldn't I ask?"

She cocked her head. "Of course." But he seemed so focused on... her eyes widened...finding the good in himself?

And for a moment in a bright shaft of sunlight from the morning sun, she swore she saw anguish in his emotion-filled eyes. He looked away, abruptly.

Was he remembering more than what he was letting on?

She nearly felt sorry for the man. Nearly.

But then he looked at her once again, pulling on his lothario mask. One corner of his mouth lifted in a familiar grin, drawing her attention to his lips as accurately as a sign pointing the way home.

She looked away with no inconsiderable amount effort. Then, she reached for a large spoon and spun around to her pot.

Time to stir the turnips.

She could have sworn she heard him once again murmur, "Coward."

Freddie spun back around brandishing her spoon, but his attention had already returned outside, his gaze thoughtful, taking the steam out of her retort.

She faced the pot of turnips again and asked, "How are your fingers today?"

"Hm?"

She glanced over her shoulder to find Kelly's attention on her once more. "Your fingers? How are they?"

He looked down at his hands and flexed them both, tightening his hands into fists and then opening them flat again. "I can move them. A little pain, still weak."

"What do you suppose happened?" She nodded toward his hands. Her mind whispered, *torture*.

"A fight?" There was no mistaking the question in his tone.

Freddie knocked her spoon on the edge of the pot, then turned to face Kelly, laying the spoon on the table. "Hmm. Possibly, but combined with the burn marks?"

She stared at Kelly, trying to decipher what he didn't say. *Admit it, Kelly. You were beaten to within an inch of your life...*

He shrugged, while continuing to stare at his hands, twisting them this way and that. Considering his scars. Then, he glanced at her and steel eyes met hazel. "I couldn't say. Possibly some sort of accident, but a fight seems more likely."

Disappointed, she crossed her arms. "You lost then?"

He snorted. "I'm alive, aren't I?"

She smiled in response to his lopsided grin. "When we first found you, barely."

Her quip was met with silence. Kelly once again, looked out the nearby window.

But really, they were dancing around the idea that he'd been tortured. Why wouldn't he say it?

Why didn't she?

Possibly because saying the words made them real, and the entire idea was horrifying. She wouldn't wish what he'd clearly been through on anyone—even a man she mostly wished covered in boils!

And the fact he couldn't remember it at all? Freddie didn't know if that was a blessing or a curse for he still suffered the pain without any understanding or knowledge of why. Or from whom. And those men were still out there. Looking for him even now. Looking for them both.

She slammed her hands down on the table and leaned forward, bracing herself. Kelly's head whipped around in surprise. "Admit it Kelly. You were tortured."

He shrugged and threw her a smile and a chuckle. He glanced away; his gaze drawn back to the view of the distant horizon, and said, "I suppose spies who get caught tend to expect a beating. But really, why would anybody want to torture me?"

Why indeed. She could name quite a few reasons without having to think too hard about it.

It was time to try harder to jog his memory. Even though it would reveal her lies. And it was time they get moving.

Thank God, she'd sent for her team.

Chapter Eighteen

In the Meantime, Back in London

Alistair MacLeod followed the dark ruffian through the winding streets of St. Giles. MacLeod had gotten a reliable tip that this man might have information as to the whereabouts of Kelly, and the idiot would-be criminal wasn't doing a very good job of remaining unobtrusive. It was a wonder the man ever found a single job in this line of work, where invisibility was everything. Hell, it was surprising he was even alive.

In light of that, even a blind man wouldn't have missed the drop. The mark stopped and clumsily shoved the note he'd been handed into his pocket. Then, began walking, albeit faster now.

MacLeod couldn't believe his eyes when the missive fell right out of the man's pocket almost immediately and flopped to the pavement. MacLeod crossed the distance and bent to retrieve the missive while the nitwit continued on his merry way.

Inside, the note read:

Father,

Rumor has it there's been strange happenings around Runcorn; a group matching the people we're looking for have been seen in the area, including a woman with an unconscious man, clearly beaten. It's possible they never left. I also learned there's a property near Runcorn owned by Viscount Sharpe. Lots of odd ends don't add up. I'm tracking down another lead before heading to Runcon myself.

— *D*

MacLeod had no reason to delay, and his instinct told him he'd find Kelly there, in Runcorn. He'd gather his things from Stonebridge House and be there by tomorrow night.

Two Hours Later: Dawe House, London

Lord Dawe stood in the doorway to his study, arms akimbo. He took a deep breath and stretched. Everything was going according to plan, and it felt good.

The sound of booted feet charging up the stairs snapped him out of his reverie. Surprisingly, it was his son.

"Duncan? What are you doing here?"

Duncan slowed to a stop before him. "I had to grab a few things before I headed out."

Lord Dawe chuffed. "Headed out? Where?"

Duncan narrowed his eyes. "Didn't you get my message?"

Lord Dawe shook his head, alarmed. "I never received a message."

Duncan carded a hand through his hair. "Shit. We found evidence of activity in Runcorn. We think Kelly's there."

Lord Dawe spat and snapped his fingers. "Well, step to it...make haste, boy. Someone's intercepted the message and has a head start, you fool."

God save him from incompetence.

Meanwhile, in Wales...

Owain pulled off his wet shirt, his muscles sore from exertion. He dipped a square of linen in a basin of water and began to wash, starting with his neck, then down to his chest, the cold water soothing his overheated skin; his nipples puckered in response. He followed his own movements in the tall, looking glass before him, his gaze touching on every scar, every tattoo. Each mark a memory—some dark, some not so much—of his past.

He paused on one tattoo in particular, remembering the time he'd first discovered Freddie, who'd had the nerve to pick *his* pocket. A first.

He'd been captivated in an instant.

Owain smiled at the memory.

Then, his gaze dropped to the mark of the Society, and his smile fell. He clenched his hand into a fist causing excess water to sluice from his rag, trailing from his fist to the front of the basin and down to the floor. *Those bastards were a Goddamn menace.*

A sound pulled him from his dark thoughts, and he glanced up, certain he was being watched; he suspected it was his new housekeeper.

He smiled in the mirror, convinced he could see her azure eyes in the shadows, staring back.

What did she see with those all-knowing eyes?

He dipped his rag in the basin and called out, "You can come out, Mary Claire. I know you're there."

She didn't say a word.

He paused, his hand hovering over the basin. "Do you like what you see?" he prompted.

Still, nothing.

No matter. Let her watch. She was proving an interesting conundrum, this beautiful woman who pretended to be his housekeeper while forever watching his every move.

He squeezed excess water from his rag, and once again, dragged the linen across his chest, slowly, curiously finding his skin had grown even more heated, knowing she watched from the shadows.

Oh, yes. If the mouse wanted to play, the cat was ready.

And willing.

Chapter Nineteen

A Few Days Later

"Here." Freddie stood across from Kelly, who was seated at the kitchen table.

He glanced at her hand, one brow raised. "A deck of cards? We're to play whist? Poker?"

She rolled her eyes. "Humor me. Just shuffle them."

Kelly took the cards, and it was as if his hands had a mind of their own, for he began shuffling them expertly, without hesitation. The cards practically danced in his palms. He clearly knew the shape of them, how to maneuver them so they leapt to do his bidding, as if he were born with a deck in his hand.

Seeing him there, expertly controlling them, brought Freddie's mind to a distant time and place:

"No, no. Like this." Kelly jerked his hand and seemingly before her eyes, a single card was held in his grasp.

"How did you do that?"

"Magic."

She pushed against his chest. "Sirrah, I wasn't born yesterday. Tell me."
"It's easy really, just sleight of hand."

Kelly slapped the deck on the table, jarring her from her reluctant remembrances.

Who knew such innocent card tricks would ending up being the key to her very survival?

Kelly considered her, "You knew?"

Freddie bit her lip, not wanting to return to their past but knowing she had to. "Aye. It's how we first met."

He picked up the cards again and began shuffling them absently. "Go on."

Freddie let loose a long sigh, then began the tale, the story of their life. "There was a local fair, and you were seated at some tables," She nodded at his hands. "shuffling cards."

Kelly paused and glanced at her, one brow raised yet again and looking utterly unconvinced. "For money?"

She clasped her hands together. "Oh, no. If you must know, you were entertaining a group of ladies, impressing them with your *unique* skills." He winked at her then, and she abruptly stood and paced away, stopping at the far wall and leaning against it. "You were on one side of a long table, the women piled together on the other, practically climbing over each other to gain your attention, your favor. The table was situated in front of a large tent with a striped awning at the edge of a wood..."

She leaned her head back against the wall and closed her eyes, remembering. She didn't want to continue, to risk revealing any hint as to how it had all appeared from her perspective—how he'd made her insides quiver when he'd smiled her way—but she knew she must take the chance if only to help him remember. "You looked at me and winked. I was standing off to the side near the tree line, watching but not really part of the assembled crowd." She looked down and shuffled her feet at the memory. She'd been a somewhat shy girl then, and all too easily her feelings from that time came tumbling back. He'd been beautiful and charming with a playful twinkle, saying all the right things to make all the women sigh and bat their eyes, desperate to gain his notice. But there was a difference in his smile when she'd caught him looking her way. More real, somehow. She shook off that part of her memories, and said, "You disappointed your women then, by dismissing them with a promise that they'd seen all of your tricks."

Freddie lifted her head and looked at him, a smile on her face to make light of his teasing ways. The memory fond, despite everything. "And then you approached me and said—"

But Kelly wasn't even watching her, his was gaze unfocused, his mind clearly far away. But then, he abruptly started laughing. He slapped his hand on the table and guffawed, then swiped at his eyes. His laughter was contagious, and she found herself smiling in return. Then, chuckling along with him as he remembered, "Might I show you the secret of my—" he covered his mouth with his hand, but another snicker escaped despite his efforts. "—tits."

Together, they burst out laughing all over again. Freddie wiped at the tears in her eyes. "Y-you remember!"

"Oh, aye. God." He stood then and made his way over to her, leaning back against the wall and standing by her side. He crossed his legs and observed his booted feet. "I remember feeling so embarrassed." He shook his head and glanced to the ceiling. "No—embarrassed is too simple. I was. I was devastated. My tongue had never failed me. Until that moment. The most critical moment in my life."

He turned toward her, one shoulder against the wall, his face serious of a sudden. "I took one look at you and all thought fled my mind." As if to mimic the past, he searched her face once again.

Her breath caught, and she tried to swallow the sudden lump in her throat. She licked her lips, and his eyes dropped to her mouth. She heard his breath hitch and saw his eyes flare. He reached out, gently, and brushed a lock of hair away, his eyes following the path his hands took.

His hands *shook*.

He was so close, his breath caressed her cheek as he spoke, softly, gently. "I thought you the bonniest thing I'd ever seen in me life, and I just wanted the rest of the world to leave so I could talk to you. Even if only for a minute."

It would have been all too easy to kiss him then. They'd just shared a moment through laughter. But that way lay danger, and she refused to go there. There were too many hurdles in their past to overcome. Too many secrets.

He leaned closer.

She put her hand to his chest. "Too bad a minute was all we ever had—"

Kelly swooped in anyway and cut her off with his kiss. A wonderful, familiar, bone melting meeting of mouths that was both familiar yet entirely new. Darker. Hotter. Stronger. More powerful. She immediately withdrew whatever reservations she'd had.

God, yes. She'd wanted to kiss him for *days*, though she'd hated feeling that way.

He pulled her into his chest, and his arms encircled her completely, the inferno of his body sending hers up in flames. And she couldn't get enough. She grabbed hold of his head and held on tight, deepening the kiss, her tongue tangling with his and begging for more, for if this was a mistake, she would make it a big one. She'd finally have it all—what she'd been aching for for days—might as well make tomorrow's regret worth it.

It was *so* worth it.

Kelly moaned, and she answered in kind as the hard evidence of his arousal pressed into her stomach, ratcheting up the heat. She ground against him, relishing the feel of the solid line of his rather formidable cock, knowing where this could lead if she allowed it. The utter bliss to be found at the end of this road at the hands of a master like Kelly was utterly unforgettable.

He dragged one hand up her back, pressing firmly, but then he gentled the kiss, nipping at her lips, offering her a gentle caress of his lips as he seemed to simply savor the touch of skin on skin, his hand coming around to gently stroke the edge of her jaw.

And suddenly, it was all too much, too *intimate*. Lust she could handle. But not, this...

Frederica shoved him away, the tenderness of the moment far too devastating to allow.

Besides, he could be married for all either of them knew. How could she forget that? The sketch—

Startled, Freddie opened her eyes to see Kelly looking at her, his quicksilver eyes soft with affection, and God, how she remembered that look. She'd seen it before; believed in it before. More fool her.

She pushed him away, stepping out of his arms with a firm, "No," then stormed out of the kitchen area, headed for the small, front room. She heard him curse, then noted the clear sound of his pursuit.

"Freddie, wait..."

She ignored him, heading for her bags, tucked into the far corner. She knelt down, rummaging around, ignoring Kelly as he paced behind her. She shut out the image of him running his hand through his short black hair. Where was it?

Her fingers closed around the edges of paper. Found it.

"Freddie, I'm sor—"

Frederica stood and spun to face him, one hand held up. "Don't. Apologize." She strode forward and handed him the sketch Owain had sent her; then, retreated, stepping back once, twice, watching as Kelly first stared at her, a question in his eyes, then dropped his gaze.

It was difficult to simply watch, to step back and maintain her distance, with her lips still tingling from their kiss. She clenched her hands into a fist, lest she touch her fingers to her lips, her eyes never leaving his face as he stared at the portrait of another woman.

Eventually, she could stand it no more. "Who is she?"

Chapter Twenty

Kelly collapsed into a nearby chair, the sketch pulled taut between both hands. He knew this woman. Kelly ran his fingers over the sweep of her hair, brown and gold and vibrant, the full lips, the soft, rounded cheeks, the beginnings of a red dress. He distantly heard Freddie mumble something about going out to fetch—something—and then the door behind him slammed shut. He didn't mean to ignore her, but looking at this portrait, he felt sure that any moment now, everything would come rushing back. His memories, his life. The very core of his being. The good and the bad.

Kelly suspected some of it was very, very bad, indeed.

It didn't matter, though. He would take anything, even if it were all bad.

God, if he could just grasp on to the edge of all those memories floating about in his mind, a hairsbreadth out of reach—

Kelly concentrated on the woman in the portrait. He pictured her lips moving, whispering silent words. A smile. A wink. Could she be a former lover? God, his *wife?*

He didn't think so, but then his memory wasn't exactly reliable at the moment.

Shit, he'd kissed Freddie. Was he betraying this woman by involving himself with another? Once more, he traced the edges of the woman's lips with his fingers. No, he still didn't think so. He felt nothing, romantically speaking, at the sight of her image, but then a woman was so much more than the looks she presented to the world, and while this woman was beautiful in every way, he didn't *know* her. He could just...tell.

Not like he *knew* Frederica.

Out of nowhere, a snippet of conversation surfaced in his mind, a husky voice, the accent strange and not like his own or Freddie's. "Do you know I find that type of stitching to be incredibly tedious to do? And so hard on the hands? I cannot fathom why anyone would want to spend time learning that technique. I believe it was created as a clever form of punishment by some mean-hearted harpy with nothing better to do with her time."

Yes. She'd said that; he knew it. He remembered feeling equal parts amused and irritated at the time. He also knew she wasn't British. American?

And then, "Did you know that hunting pigs in Hedgesville, South Carolina is illegal? Why on earth pigs? And only pigs. Everything else is fair game." *Snort.* "Fair game. Ha Ha," she'd quipped.

Kelly closed his eyes. Yes, these bits of conversation were spoken by the woman in the picture as they travelled in a carriage, headed—

Damn, he couldn't place it.

Again, in that husky alto, "Have you ever watched paint dry?"

Kelly snorted and heard the door behind him open, then close, and he assumed it was Freddie returning to the cottage. He tuned her out, not to be rude, but silently begged her not to say anything. He almost had it, the elusive memory of this woman's presence in his life. She was important, though not his wife. He'd—

Kelly nearly dropped the page. *Shit.* He'd *kidnapped* her.

Fuck!

All of the sudden, Kelly was yanked out of the chair, the portrait ripped from his hands. It felt as if he literally sailed through the air as he was flung across the room, unable to halt his forward momentum until he crashed into the nearby wall and promptly slumped to the floor. Booted feet advanced on a heavy tread, and Kelly dimly registered bare knees and a blue and green kilt before he was physically lifted from the floor, he certainly hadn't helped, and slammed against the wall, his back and head meeting the hard stones and abrasive mortar with a dangerous explosion of agony.

Through half-slitted eyes, he noted brawny arms and red hair and a grin that in no way could be mistaken for anything positive or friendly.

Kelly smiled through the pain in his head, "Ah, MacLeod."

MacLeod glanced to the floor, then returned his gaze, fury rolling off him in waves. A thick Scottish brogue pierced through the waves of pain. "Oh, hell no, no' again, ye wee shite. What the fook are ye duin' with a portrait of ma woman?" bellowed MacLeod.

Deeper pain exploded in Kelly's head, and his mind unlatched all at once, unlocking *everything*. His memories, all of them, tumbled out and onto the surface of his consciousness all at once. Family, friends, his mission, MacLeod, Amelia Chase, fuck—the absolute agony of torture. Freddie—

Freddie! Freddie was alive!

He grabbed hold of two large wrists, as the massive hands of Alistair MacLeod wrapped around Kelly's neck and began squeezing the very life out of him.

"Stop," he choked out.

MacLeod shook his head, then pulled Kelly close, and bellowed. "I asked ye a fooking question, ye bastard."

MacLeod was so close, Kelly could feel the man's breath on his cheek. Kelly opened his mouth to reply, but he never got the chance. A loud *thump* sounded, and MacLeod's eyes rolled to the back of his head a second before the large man collapsed to the ground at Kelly's feet.

Kelly bent forward, bracing himself on his knees, and looked up. Frederica stood on the other side of the Scot, her chest heaving, both hands wrapped around a decent-sized cast iron skillet. She tossed it to the floor by MacLeod's head, and it landed with a loud *thunk*.

She knelt, putting her fingers to MacLeod's neck, then nodded and stood. "We have to go. Now. He won't be down for long, and that man, he's—well, I only got the best of him through the element of surprise, and you're in no condition to—Kelly what is it?"

His eyes roamed over her, taking in every detail, overlaying the woman he'd known for the past weeks with the one he'd known so long ago. Dammit. She was supposed to be dead. Dead! He'd seen her fucking grave, her parents' home swathed in black, a black band on the arm of her father and brother.

He had a thousand questions, to hell with running from MacLeod. Besides, the man was his friend.

Then, the door burst open and three men poured into the room. Two were normal sized, but the third...

Kelly knew precisely who he was the minute he laid eyes on the man. Johnnie. Lord Fulton's brother. Hired henchmen for the Society.

He turned to Frederica, and his soul shattered for he knew right away she knew these men. He stumbled and nearly fell to his knees in grief.

God damn, she was working with the enemy!

It all made sense now. The lies. The hesitations. Her presence here. Anger, true horrifyingly powerful fury, flooded him, gripped him. His grief disappeared in an inferno of rage. He clenched his fists and roared, "You bitch!"

She jerked as if struck.

His breath sawing in and out, he turned to the more immediate threat. But it was clear he stood no chance against three men, one of them monstrously-sized. Damn but he could use MacLeod's help right about now. He debated bolting. But leave his friend? *Argh.* He wanted to howl in frustration, all his options were unacceptable.

MacLeod groaned then, slowly resurfacing. Thank God.

Freddie lurched forward and took charge. "Johnnie, you take Kelly. George, Griffin secure MacLeod; he's stirring."

As Johnnie grabbed hold of his arms, Kelly bore a hole in Freddie's head with his glare. In the end, his revenge was going to be supremely satisfying.

She tilted her chin away and added. "Secure MacLeod well enough to keep him from following, but not so much he cannot get away. If MacLeod's here, others won't be far behind, and who knows whose side they'll support."

He watched her eyes, so like those of his enemy and burned to know just how much Frederica Glyndŵr *née Dawe* knew of her own father's activities.

Did she know her father was the very man who'd had him tortured? Twice.

Tying up MacLeod was the work of a minute and just in time, too, for no sooner had they finished, then Macleod became fully aware and roared his complaint in no uncertain terms. Both of Freddie's men paled a bit and darted out of reach. Kelly couldn't blame them; MacLeod was a big man.

There was an urgency to the actions of the enemy now, as they raced to get away before MacLeod freed himself. Kelly struggled against them long enough to say, "MacLeod, we ate lunch every Sunday, remember?" *Aw, fuck. What else?* "What did you have? You never left any evidence. Remember...er... remember where? You know, that little café in London?"

Johnnie lifted him bodily, but Kelly grabbed hold of the door frame, stalling for time, his knuckles white as he gripped the frame with every last bit of strength he had, and continued his nonsense. "When I get out of here, you'll have to pick where we go next. Definitely not the same place as last month."

He called the last at the very moment he lost his grasp, and they dragged him out into the night. Kelly hoped to God the Scotsman could work out his code.

And that the brilliant little liar up ahead couldn't.

Chapter Twenty-One

It had taken him twenty minutes, and his wrists were bloody, but MacLeod was finally free of his restraints. By their own admission, Kelly's captors had intended to allow MacLeod to escape. He stepped out of the cottage and into the cool, night air of early evening. Everything was quiet, Kelly and his captors long gone.

Oddly, his horse remained hobbled where he'd left him. If they'd left him an escape, then surely all wasn't as it seemed, though Kelly likely didn't think so at the moment, and MacLeod almost chuckled at the thought.

Almost.

MacLeod mounted his steed and rubbed at the lump on the back of his head. Someone would still have to pay for the bump, though.

MacLeod started off at a slow trot, headed South, testing the ache in his head. The pain was manageable, though that hardly mattered; he had no time to waste before *D*—whoever that was, definitely not a friend—showed up to investigate.

He clucked his tongue at his horse and picked up the pace, using his race through the countryside to recount what he'd learned.

Kelly was once again captured and very much alive.

He didn't know who the people who now held Kelly were, much

less how they related to the Society, but they weren't all bad or they'd have murdered him or left him for the next wave of villains.

And Kelly seemed to be trying to relay some sort of message but spoke utter nonsense.

They'd never eaten lunch on Sundays, certainly not with any regularity.

And the word 'Remember' was often used as a signal when speaking in code, that either everything after was coded differently than the way it was before the word. Or to ignore the sentence with the word 'remember' in it. With Kelly, who knew. He was clearly making shite up as he went along.

So, considering Kelly's first statement: 'MacLeod, we ate lunch every Sunday, remember?' If one ignored 'MacLeod' because that's his name and ignored 'remember' because that was a standard code word, that left: 'We ate lunch every Sunday.' Not the least bit true. So. One letter for each word, perhaps? MacLeod tried it. We Ate Lunch Every Sunday. W A L E S. Wales was definitely a word. It couldn't be a coincidence, otherwise, Kelly spoke true nonsense.

MacLeod thought back to what else Kelly had said, up until the next 'remember.' He'd said: 'What did you have? You never left any evidence.'

Hm... First letter had been used, so what about the first word of each sentence? That would be: 'What you.' *Meh*, that made no sense. All right, last word: 'Have evidence.' Now, *that* sounded promising. The next sentence, Kelly used Remember twice. He could have been struggling to think quickly, considering the circumstances. MacLeod decided to ignore "Remember where?" and consider the rest of what Kelly had said: "You know, that little café in London? When I get out of here, you'll have to pick where we go next. Definitely not the same place as last month. I hope Stonebridge isn't jealous."

MacLeod continued decoding by pulling out the last word of each statement: 'London next month.'

Putting it all together, MacLeod came up with: 'Wales. Have evidence. London next month.'

MacLeod pulled to a stop at a fork in the road. Right led to Wales, left to London.

If MacLeod were interpreting Kelly's nonsense correctly, his captors were taking Kelly to Wales, but he had evidence and would be in London next month with it.

MacLeod had to assume Kelly meant he'd see everyone at the duke's house in London. Further, Kelly must be confident in his ability to escape his captors in Wales. To the man's credit, the chances of his success was high. For the leader was a woman.

Either that or Kelly was a candidate for Bedlam. With Kelly, either option was a distinct possibility.

MacLeod's decision now was everything. The mission could be at risk. His sanity was definitely at risk. Trust Kelly? After everything? Or go after Kelly and bring him to justice, at the very least, force him to explain. MacLeod thought to Amelia, back home, safe, and her words of wisdom.

With a sigh, MacLeod directed his horse left, to London. He wanted nothing more than to track Kelly to Wales, but in light of everything else, he had to report to Stonebridge.

Besides, hadn't Amelia begged him to trust Kelly? And MacLeod trusted Amelia.

But he hoped to God *her* trust wasn't misplaced.

Chapter Twenty-Two

He'd loved her for years. Drunk himself into oblivion too many times to count in a state of quiet, desperate, helpless fury over believing she'd died giving birth to his child. He'd fucking mourned them. Mourned them both.

Kelly leaned back on his elbows and crossed his legs at his booted feet, his pose deceptively relaxed. He was in the back of a cart, caged in like an animal. But his new nemesis was perched on the bench before him, driving. Her back was ramrod straight; her chin lifted. And he had nothing but time.

"What were you planning to tell me the moment I regained my memory? About all the lies—what were you going to say?"

If possible, she straightened further still.

She could have ignored him, but she tossed back. "Does it really matter?"

Of course, it matters. Aloud, he said, "Humor me."

She shrugged. "To be honest, I hadn't planned it out."

He snorted. "So not the truth, obviously."

She handed the reins to Johnnie, who sat beside her on the bench, and turned to face Kelly fully. "The *truth* is, it really depended upon the circumstances surrounding the moment you regained them."

He barked out a laugh, and not the humorous kind. "I'll bet. In fact, I'm willing to bet you secretly didn't want me to get them back."

She nodded. "To be honest, the thought had crossed my mind."

He bit back a growl. The truth, when he heard it, was far worse than the lies.

She continued, "I had to judge—"

"Love, you'd already judged me and found me guilty from the moment you released me from that dungeon. But, why *did* you lie?"

She shrugged again. "I needed you to trust me, so claiming to be partners was the quickest, most efficient way."

Of course. "How very practical of you." And somehow, again, the truth was worse than anything else she could have said.

God, everything he ever knew about her was a lie. She was clearly planning to take him to the Society, so they could finish what they started. She was being tightlipped, of course. And it was painful to know.

She planted her hands on her hips. "Since we're opening up and sharing our *feelings*." She accompanied that with an eye roll. "Why did you leave?"

"Leave?"

She crossed her arms. "Of course, you've forgotten, I should have known. Yes, leave. Seven years ago. We were supposed to—supposed to meet. You never showed. You left me—"

He tightened his hands into fists. "Left you? Sure, and that's exactly what I did. Just set out in the world and left behind the spoiled, naive little princess I had foolishly loved." She flinched once again, as if shot through with an arrow, and turned her back to him, facing forward on the bench once more. Good. It would only be a fraction of the pain he'd felt when her father had had him tortured. Both times. Hell, maybe it was even her idea, maybe it—

That was it! She was just prying him for information, trying to learn what he could remember. How much he knew. The burnings, the beatings, the torture...she fucking *knew*.

"My God, you knew all along didn't you? You knew what your father had done to me?"

She tossed over her shoulder, "Of course, I did."

Now, it was his turn to flinch. No matter his own harsh words, *that* stung. Like reliving the past all over again.

He was going to *enjoy* arresting her when this was all over. He chuckled.

She spun back around. "What are you laughing about?"

"Nothing much. I was just recalling how they broke my fingers. Oh, and then there was the day they busted my ribs; that sure was something. And you know what else...well, of course you do, you were there...but I most *fondly* remember the time they were holding my head under urine-laced and feces-infested water until I choked on it, breathing in shit and filth and piss, then vomiting it all up and swallowing it all, all over again. Over and over, they pulled me out and pushed me back in until I shit myself and I very nearly begged to be shot. *Nearly.* Oh, how you must have laughed. I'll think about your laughter the next time I revisit that moment in my nightmares. And then, do you remember—"

She slapped her hand on Johnnie's shoulder and yelled, "Stop the cart."

They hadn't even come to a complete stop before she bolted from the bench. Kelly leaned up on his side and watched as she darted off into the woods. He rolled onto his back and rested his hands on his head, an awful smile bunched his cheeks, and he closed his eyes as if he would fall asleep without a care in the world. "Good," he murmured to himself. "Maybe, she's feeling a bit guilty."

Chapter Twenty-Three

Freddie ran recklessly through the woods without a care as to where she was going. Or how far. Eventually, she slammed against a medium-sized tree, figured it was as good a time as any to stop, then she bent at the waist and cast up her accounts. Violently.

When she finished and was merely dry heaving air, she stepped back, and suddenly, George was there, handing her a cloth and a flask of water. He stood back, giving her space, as she rinsed her mouth and wiped her face.

Father had had Kelly tortured?

She knew her father was a bad man, hell hadn't he abandoned her in St. Giles with nothing but the clothes on her back and proclaimed her dead to the world? All for the unforgivable crime of being in love with an Irishman? That was pure evil in and of itself. He'd even had a grave made in her honor, the perfect touch when pretending to be the grieving father.

But this...torturing an innocent man in such a vile way?

Was her own Father *working* for the Society? Did Owain know?

Freddie shook her head at her own idiocy. Of course, he knew. That man knew everything. They were all just puppets in his games of power play. Which begged the question—what else did Owain know? And just whose side was he on, besides his own?

Freddie felt a moment of guilt for doubting Owain; who'd been there in her darkest hour. When he kept secrets, he always had reasons.

She glanced to George. "Did you know who we were going to rescue from the beginning?"

George relaxed against a tree and crossed his arms. He dipped his head. "I did."

Freddie lifted her chin. "And while he was being so talksy, did Owain tell you about my past with Kelly?"

George smiled. "Only in so much as that once you found out who we were rescuing, it was probably best we avoid provoking you for a few days, even in jest."

She thought back to George and Griffin's behavior the day they rescued Kelly and narrowed her eyes. "You lie."

George shrugged. "Does it really matter what I know? I judge a person by their actions, those I witness firsthand. I have enough worries of my own to deal with to care about someone else's past, mistakes or no."

Something in his expression made Freddie stop. He was right. George was a black man in a world that saw him as other. He had bigger concerns to care about than her checkered past.

She rested a hand on his arm. "I'm sorry. For questioning you, George."

"It's alright. Given the circumstances, I understand. And you have every right to know the truth."

Freddie held up the flask and square of cloth. "Thanks for these. If you don't mind, I just need a few minutes more."

George stood away from the tree. "Of course." And left.

Frederica found a log to perch on and sat, feeling emotionally raw, her throat tight, and wasn't that something? A fortnight ago, she was wishing boils upon Kelly's head, and now...

And now tears threatened, and she felt a sob building. It wasn't just the thought of torture and her father's duplicity in scarring the man she had loved, though that was a large part of her grief. But she also realized in a matter of a moment that despite believing he'd abandoned her to her fate all those years ago, she'd harbored a very small nugget of hope that there was some reason behind his abandonment. That perhaps, he'd tried to come and couldn't for reasons unknown.

But no. He had just left.

She'd have never admitted to that aloud, but now that that hope was utterly extinguished? She felt the missing spark like a tangible thing...like wearing slippers a size too small or a coat with the buttons misaligned.

Like once again losing another piece of one's soul.

Had she truly been a spoiled little princess? She didn't like to think so, but it was possible.

And entirely irrelevant. Her stint in St. Giles had removed all vestiges of that flaw. How long before she'd become a thief to survive? Two days. How long before she'd become an expert at it? Maybe, a week?

She was a fast learner.

Perhaps, she'd started to thaw towards Kelly recently, that witty tongue and charming smile of his was ever potent. Today was a reminder that that way lay nothing but heartache. She needed to continue to keep the truth close to her chest and remember that Kelly was a master of charm and persuasion.

And could be just as ruthless with his words.

Her best option was to avoid him altogether and hope that when they got to Wales, things were still the way she'd left them.

With Owain, one never knew.

Freddie pulled herself together and sucked in a deep breath, swallowing grief that was far too late and far too futile. She was not responsible for her father's actions. And her past with Kelly was over. Had been for seven years.

And hadn't she'd gotten something beautiful out of the relationship? Without question, so she couldn't regret the experience at all.

Out of habit, Freddie reached for her locket only to find it missing. "Shit."

She searched the ground around her tree, but she knew her efforts were for naught. She'd taken it off while bathing and had inadvertently left it behind in her haste to leave amidst everything else going on.

But she had to retrieve it.

Freddie raced back to the road and their wagon.

"George, I need your horse."

George handed over the reins. "What is it?"

Out of the corner of her eye, Freddie caught sight of Kelly sitting up in the back of the wagon and did her best to ignore him. "I left something behind."

She raised her leg into the stirrup.

George rested his arm on hers and whispered furiously. "You can't go back there."

She paused. "I *have* to."

George held her gaze for a moment, then nodded his head once.

Freddie swung up into the saddle. "You all carry on ahead. You know where to meet. I'll catch up with you tomorrow."

Griffin and Johnnie shared a look. Johnnie began to stand, and Freddie said, "No, Johnnie. I'll be fine. We need you here." And she nodded in Kelly's general direction.

She took off at a gallop, intent on her mission and did her best to ignore the bellow from Kelly, who leapt to his feet and rattled the bars of his makeshift gaol. "Where is she going? Freddie, you get back here! Do you hear me? Come back! How can you let her just ride off like that? What if something happens—Freddie!"

His pleas mattered not. Her men wouldn't stop her, and besides, she had no choice. No one could know what was inside that locket.

Chapter Twenty-Four

Frederica dismounted deep in the woods surrounding Viscount Sharpe's cottage in Runcorn. She hobbled her horse and crept silently back to the house, then ducked behind a stack of firewood, frustrated to know her caution was warranted. Men, presumably from the Society, surrounded the place.

Dammit.

She prayed they wouldn't find her locket.

After ten minutes, Little Dick, of last month's *Wee Cock* debacle, strolled out onto the front stoop. Well, there was someone she had hoped to never see again, unless it was to watch him hang. Freddie rolled her eyes, then started when something brushed against her leg. She looked down to find the grey tabby rubbing against her. He let out a too-loud *meow*.

She raised a finger to her lips and jerked her head towards Little Dick. "Shhhh...we don't want them to know we're here."

The cat sat and blinked his eyes, then *meowed* again.

She darted a look to the cottage and side-whispered. "I'm sorry. I shouldn't have left you behind, either."

She glanced down at the cat, who had lifted his leg for a lick, clearly nonplussed by her excuses.

Frederica huffed, quietly. "Of course, I didn't forget you."

The cat carried on with his bath, disbelief evident in his actions.

Federica shook her head. "Fine. But you'll have to ride in my bag."

The cat paused, then stretched, a long drawn-out reach, complete with exposed claws and a dipped back, then leapt onto her lap, which was awkward considering she was squatting and the cat was no feather-weight. Frederica steadied herself with one hand on the stack of wood, then gave General Llwyd a good stroke before looking back to the cottage in time to witness her brother step out of the entrance.

Startled, she slapped a hand over her mouth and choked back a sob, as she fell to her rear. The cat harried off into the bushes, and Frederica squeezed her eyes closed as someone called out, "What was that?"

Please don't investigate.

Her brother replied, "Probably just some animal in the woods." She willed away more tears, his voice excruciatingly familiar.

After a few moments of silence, Frederica let out the breath she held and crawled back into a squat, daring another glimpse.

Her heart shattered at the sight of him. To see him standing there, a man now, in his prime and so handsome and fit, but a perfect stranger. It was almost too much. Frederica rubbed at the ache in her chest. What did he know? Everything? She found it so difficult to believe that the man who called her "Monkey," would have had any part of her abandonment.

But if he was here, it meant he was involved in the society!

She felt ill all over again. *Oh God, is my entire family a part of this!* Did Owain know it all? Had he kept the truth from her all these years?

Frederica nearly gasped out loud as Duncan lifted his hand, for from his fingers dangled her locket, the gold metal winking in the light.

She stifled her gasp with her hand. He would know immediately whose locket that was—

Duncan looked up as if he'd heard her, anguish in his eyes, and he squeezed his hand into a fist.

Dare she hope? Did he miss her as dearly as she'd missed him? Was he an innocent in her Father's machinations as she had been? He would know that locket, for he'd given it to her, and it was inscribed.

But most importantly, did he understand the significance of the miniatures held within? For that was the entire reason she'd risked her life to come back here and retrieve it.

Little Dick stepped back out of the house and approached her brother. "What've you got?"

Her brother tucked the locket in his coat. "Nothing." Duncan cleared his throat. "Kelly was definitely here; we found part of a message in the ashes of the fire confirming it." Her brother turned to Little Dick. "The woman who took Kelly. Tell me about her. What did she look like? Did she say her name?"

Little Dick spat in the dirt at his feet. "No. She was just some bitch who thought herself better than a man."

Frederica stifled the urge to snort. She had shown him just how much better she was than he, a man, that was for sure.

Her brother unexpectedly lunged forward and grabbed Little Dick by his cravat.

"Lord, what is wrong with you." Little Dick pushed back.

Her brother abruptly let go and carded one hand through his hair.

Little Dick spat again. "Red hair, similar to yours for that matter, taller than average. Spoke like a lady apart from the cursing. Wore trousers."

"Is that all?"

"Yes."

"Have you found anything else of significance here?"

"We found evidence of homing pigeons out back."

"Good. Round up the men; we've got what we came for," said her brother.

"Should we track them?"

"No."

Little Dick seemed prepared to argue, but Duncan cut him off. "We're to London with our report."

Little Dick did not seem pleased by that pronouncement; his animosity practically rolled off him in giant waves of anger. With eyes never leaving her brother, he called out, "You heard the man; everybody out."

Frederica willed her brother to watch his back but dared not reveal herself. Too many lives were at stake for her to take that chance. Besides, Little Dick's presence here was not a point in her brother's favor.

More than ever, she needed to make haste and get to Wales, for the situation had just grown exponentially more complicated.

And Owain's place was a week away, at least. Thank God, they would cross the border tonight.

Chapter Twenty-Five

The Next Afternoon: Wrexham, Wales

With a sigh of relief, Frederica dismounted at Owain's cottage located just outside the city of Wrexham. A small, three-room, stone cottage, it was a place he or his men only ever used as an overnight place to rest when traveling. They were still a week out from Castle Ddu in Dinas Powys.

Frederica was certainly relieved to be here, across the border and into Wales. Owain had a long reach on this side of the border, which meant they would be relatively safe, for people here generally wouldn't ask too many uncomfortable questions should they notice Kelly's confined state.

George leapt to his feet as she crossed the threshold. "How did it go?"

Frederica slammed her bags on the floor to the side of the door and winced as General Llwyd hissed and leapt out of her bag. "I was too late."

"What was that?" asked George, his eyes following the blur of fur as it raced across the room.

The cat slowed and began what was clearly a strut as he stalked over to Kelly, tail straight in the air and saying, 'smell me, I'm safe.' God, it seemed one couldn't trust the males of *any* species to remain loyal.

Kelly was sitting on the floor, leaning casually back against the wall with his knees raised, under Johnnie's vigilant surveillance. The cat rubbed his sides against Kelly's legs.

Kelly gave the feline a long stroke and promptly sneezed.

Frederica snorted. "A traitor is who that is." Then, she turned to George. "Did you take care of that important task we discussed before you left Wales?"

George rested a hand on her shoulder. "Don't worry. He's safe. No one can breech those walls. And no one goes in or out without alerting the guards. No one."

Frederica spun around and glared at Kelly, who was tickling the cat behind his ears, but watching her intently. She could hear the traitor's purrs from across the room. Freddie said to Kelly, "Don't pretend you're not listening to every word we say."

Kelly smiled. "Wasn't going to."

George pressed, "Is there a problem, Fred?"

She didn't hesitate. "Yes." And she and George shared a look. "Maybe you should go—"

George shook his head. "Frederica, he's safe. No one knows."

She folded her arms. "Even Owain?"

George responded honestly, "You and I both know there isn't a hole deep enough for *that*. But you need to trust Owain."

Frederica pinched the bridge of her nose, rubbing at the ache building between her eyes, and mumbled beneath her breath, "That's what I'm afraid of..."

George nodded. "So, what about the mouser?"

She followed George's gaze to the cat, who was now sprawled on his back across Kelly's lap. Frederica had been surprised to return to George's horse at Runcorn and find the cat curled up beneath the beast.

She glanced to Kelly. "I couldn't leave him."

Kelly smiled as he returned his gaze to the ball of fluff on his lap. "Yeah, she left you," he said, using infant talk. "Had I been free, I would have seen to your needs." The cat chirped, and Kelly said, "Right? Women." Then, he stage-whispered, "You should piss in her corset while she's sleeping. If she even has one..." Then, he sneezed once more.

Kelly looked her way once again, his eyes laughably red. "Who is this Owain?"

She answered honestly. "Sometimes, he's my husband."

Kelly froze. It was almost imperceptible, but she noticed. Then, he resumed his tickling and asked, "Sometimes?"

She waved away his question and grabbed a nearby wooden chair, spinning it around so she could sit and face him.

Once seated, she got straight to the point. "Why does Owain want you?"

Kelly snorted. "I should be asking you the same question. As far as I can tell, you are part of the Society and just taking me back so you can finish what you started."

Freddie crossed her arms. "Owain is working to bring down the society."

His reply was instant. "Ha! Sure doesn't look like it from where I'm sitting."

There was no point in refuting that statement, and since any answers along this line of questioning were purely conjecture, she switched tactics. "So, you spent time with the society as a spy, a double agent?"

His smile wasn't so genuine now. "Are you asking me a question? Or making an accusation."

"What is my father's involvement?"

He laughed. "Why would I reply, when you already know the answer?"

"Humor me."

He winked. "I'm not in the humoring mood but thank you anyway."

Argh. She wanted to pull out her hair. "When was the last time you saw my brother, Duncan?"

He kept his eyes locked with hers but remained mute.

"Is my brother involved in the Society?" she pressed.

Kelly barked out a single laugh. "As much as you are, I suspect. Daddy does a damn fine job of protecting his children, doesn't he? Covers your tracks quite well."

Well, that was deeply unsatisfying, because she was not involved in the society. So, the implication could mean anything...except she suspected her father was guilty as hell and even more so than she already assumed. Was Father behind *everything*?

She huffed out a breath of exasperation. "Who else is involved? Do you have names?"

Kelly shook his head in disbelief. "Why would I tell you any of this? And don't say humor me... How about this, you answer some of my questions, and I'll think about answering some of yours."

They stared at each other for a handful of minutes, each challenging the other. Eventually, Freddie looked to George. "Leave us."

George stood away from the wall he'd been holding up. "No."

Frederica rubbed at the bridge of her nose again. "He's not going to hurt me."

Johnnie cracked his knuckles and spoke up. "I can make him talk—"

"NO!" she exclaimed. Kelly had been through enough at this point.

George, ever the voice of reason, said, "How can you be sure?"

"I know him, alright? He won't hurt a woman." At least not in the way they were implying. She gestured at the lone exit from the house. "Besides, it's not like he's going anywhere, and I can handle myself."

Each of her team glared at Kelly as they begrudgingly left the room. She loved them for their concern but was frustrated by it all the same.

Once the door closed behind the men, she turned to face Kelly once again. "You tell me one truth I'll believe, and I'll reward you with the same. Maybe, we can both get something out of this."

He spread his hands. "I'm not promising anything, love."

Well, there was nothing for it but to try. "I know you work for the Duke of Stonebridge, along with the Marquess of Dansbury and Lord Alaistair MacLeod. I know you were sent undercover to infiltrate the Society and that somewhere along the lines they captured you and began the t-torture. We don't know how or why."

Kelly shook his head. "I don't need for you to recite my past to me. I have my memories back, remember? How about answer me this, are you married and why are you taking me to Wales?"

Fair enough. "First, no , I'm not married. Second, Owain wants to meet you; I told you. Believe it or not, he wants to see the Society fall; your goals are aligned. He either wants you to join us or at least participate in the sharing of information."

Kelly snorted. "And you believe him? Does he know you work for the society?"

"I don't."

"So, you say, but you must admit, your actions are decidedly suspicious. Besides, you told me—"

"I spoke in anger." She assumed he was referring to her admission that she'd known he'd been tortured.

Kelly laughed, but it was far from humorous. "And now I'm just supposed to believe you?"

She shrugged. "It's the truth, whether you believe it or not is on you."

"No, whether I believe it or not depends on how much I tell you."

"You're making me wish I'd accepted Johnnie's offer to help jog your memory. So, did you come across my brother or not?"

"No."

"What about my father?"

"As I said before, you father is the entire reason I was tortured. Your father is *very* involved, and you damn well know it."

She supposed she did; she just didn't want to face it, despite everything. And why was that?

A tear fell, and she swiped it away. Why the hell was she crying? Father was a monster. She'd known that. Obviously. Why did some piece of the child in her feel pain over new proof her father was a bad man? Was it some deep-down inherent belief that daughters were supposed to love and trust their fathers, forever? That fathers were supposed to adore their children in return? That they were all *good?* Reliable? Respectable? Was it the final death knell of some kernel of love left over from the little girl she'd once been that had her wiping away tears after every evidence to the contrary?

Kelly's voice broke through the silence. "I'm sorry, Freddie. You didn't know, did you?"

She stood up and turned her back, wiping away more tears as they continued to fall.

No, she didn't. But she didn't say it.

Kelly sighed. "Look. The truth is I am as interested in knowing what your Owain wants from me as you are. So, if you let me ride freely, we can make far better time."

She laughed as she wiped her hands on her trousers. "How do I know you won't try to escape?"

"You don't, love, but I can promise you this...I won't try before I meet this Owain you're so fond of."

He sat there, tickling the cat, a lopsided grin on his face, his shirt open to reveal the dark hairs of his chest, for he had no clothing suitable to the gentleman he usually portrayed himself to be. His demeanor displayed trust me, with a heaping of...well, something undeniably appealing. Perhaps, she just had an inherent character flaw that made her trust men she shouldn't. Her record in that area left much to be desired.

Frederica swallowed and forced her eyes back up to his face. Then, she held out her hand and said, "Deal."

It might have been the biggest mistake of her life. Or the best.

Time would tell.

Chapter Twenty-Six

Two Days Later

They rode alongside the newly completed Monmouthshire and Brecknock canal for about an hour before stopping on the opposite side of the River Clydach, and down a-ways, to make camp. The scenery was quite breathtaking and beckoned for a closer look, though they did their best to avoid the higher peaks of the Brecon Beacons as they traveled, otherwise their passage through would have been treacherous. Still, Kelly was relieved to part with his saddle for the night, even though it was far preferable to his gaol cart from before.

He'd mostly healed from his ordeal, but certain parts of his anatomy began to twinge and ache a bit faster than he was previously accustomed.

Despite Freddie's confidence they'd see no trouble in the towns due to this *Owain's* reach, she didn't appear to be taking many chances to test that assertion.

In terms of comradery, their travel since his partial freedom had been, well, certainly not friendly, but definitely a few steps up from cordial. And was getting more comfortable by the day. They'd even shared a laugh now and then.

He preferred talking with George overall, though he would be a liar if he didn't admit to taking a particular pleasure in baiting Frederica's ire. He truly was a degenerate.

He relished taunting her with the defection of her cat, even though he found he was allergic to said animal, which meant his eyes were continuously watering, never mind the brisk air, and his stomach muscles were tender from all the sneezing.

It was worth every ache.

Most of the time.

After two days of travel, he'd made peace with the idea that Frederica had no association with the Society. Despite her fierce attitude and quick temper, she didn't have the personality to be a part of something so horrendous. He saw it in the way she treated her teammates, including the newly recruited Johnnie. It was in the way she respected the maids and bartenders at the few taverns and inns they'd frequented.

And when his ledger had tallied undeniably in that direction, he had confirmed it with a few well-placed questions to Johnnie who confirmed she had no involvement he was aware of.

And if that wasn't enough to convince him, it was telling in the deference her teammates paid her, something one didn't see in an organization filled with men who had no moral compass. In every one of those cases, the men held onto power through fear and coercion.

Frederica's men would follow her anywhere.

Hell, wasn't he right there with them, following her to some unknown location in Wales?

He could have escaped at any moment, yet he didn't. *Why?* Wanting to meet this Owain for himself was only part of the reason, surely.

Her relationship with Owain was another matter entirely, and it bothered him to no end, this not knowing, even though he had no claim on her. Not anymore. So, her and Owain weren't married, but that didn't mean they didn't have a relationship of some sort, more than just friends or employer/employee. Was that, perhaps, the true reason he followed her to Wales? To know? Was he a glutton for punishment?

Perhaps, it was at least, part of the reason, at any rate.

Now, two hours before sunset, Kelly stood in a knee-deep section of the River Clydach and used his shirt to wash the grime from his body, allowing the cold water to sluice down his chest, a balm to his aching muscles. He'd washed his trousers and smalls first, which were now sprawled on a nearby rock, drying.

He wiped across his chest and around his waist with the linen, wincing a little when he brushed certain areas. He lifted the shirt in one hand while he slid his other hand across his stomach and to his side to probe his ribs. He glanced down. Everything looked as if it was healing nicely, only the faintest trace of bruising remained.

He slid his hand lower.

And lower still, his fingers touching fine hair. He'd been semi-aroused for the better part of the day watching Freddie command her men, watching them respect her in return. Her authority was...moving.

"Meow," came the nearby voice of General Llwyd and Kelly smiled.

He glanced over his shoulder, searching for the cat, and froze, as Frederica stepped out of the tree line.

She tossed her arms in the air. "He seemed to want me to... fol...low—*Oh*."

Her gaze followed the water trailing down his back...then landed on his arse.

He stifled a chuckle and squeezed his...*cheeks*. And added a little shake for good measure.

She jolted and briefly met his eyes, then looked away, but not before his body took notice of the swipe of her tongue across her lips and the flare of lust in her gaze. His cock perked up with unabashed interest. He closed his eyes and reached down to squeeze the misbehaving beast in an attempt to ward off a full-blown erection.

His actions had the opposite effect. Particularly, when he heard her sharp intake of breath.

He envisioned her tongue darting out to moisten her lips again. And her nipples peaked, begging for his tongue, for his caress. He could imagine her soft whimpers and the lust in her eyes—Kelly moaned and dragged his free hand down his face, while his other hand *tugged*, a subtle, inadvisable stroke. Just one...

Oh, God.

It felt as if streaks of lightning shot through his veins, all-together explosive and fucking amazing. But...imagine if it was *she* who touched—

Jesus. He cut off his highly detailed imagination and growled over his shoulder, "You might want to leave," then dove away from the shore, into deeper, icier water.

Just before he submerged, he could have sworn he heard her mumble, 'But what if I don't want to...,' and the thought nearly drove him out of his ever-loving mind.

Like a giddy school-boy, he kicked off from the bottom and arrowed to the surface, his heart racing wildly, but after frantically wiping the water from his eyes and searching the shore to no avail, he realized she was gone. Disappointment weighted him like a lead in his legs, and he pulled himself from the river like a man decades older than his own twenty-seven years.

Once on the bank, he shoved his legs into wet trousers, frustration making his movements jerky. He was confident she'd not really wanted to leave. Hell, she'd been undeniably mesmerized by his bare arse.

He left his shirt off, using it to towel his soaked hair, and strode back to a nearby clearing in search of a soft place to dry in the cool, clear air.

He paused, a smile firmly in place, when he caught sight of Freddie, alone and wearing a circular path in the grass.

She froze upon sight of him, bit her lip, then said, "I am sorry for intruding."

He tossed her a wink. "I'm not." And continued 'drying off.'

Her eyes watched his every movement.

Once again, his body took notice.

She jerked her gaze to his face, then darted a glance over his shoulder. Without warning, she shouted, "Kelly, look out!" and dove for him, knocking him to the ground as a gunshot exploded from behind.

He heard footsteps rapidly retreating through the woods, but he only had eyes for Freddie. She looked at him wildly for a moment, searching his face, then her eyes flared, and she slammed her lips to his, her tongue swooping in. The kiss was explosive but explosively short, and then she was off, accidentally catching his balls with her knee as she scrambled to her feet to chase down a would-be assassin.

"Freddie, wait!" It took him a minute to shake off the pain and the healthy dose of lust, then he was after her, racing as swiftly as he could. "Freddie!"

Fear drove him harder, faster. She was going to get herself killed, and the thought terrified him far more than it should have.

When he caught up with her, she had the assassin face down on the ground, her knee in his back.

Kelly was equal parts relieved and livid. "What do you think you're doing?" He raked his hands through his hair and paced the ground, but kept an eye on the downed man, ready to jump on him should he even think to get up.

She didn't answer him for a moment, simply stood and swept the dirt from one knee as the rest of her team arrived, guns trained on the would-be murderer on the ground.

Freddie brushed the dirt from her hands. "If you haven't noticed by now, I don't need protection. I'm perfectly capable of taking care of myself."

She turned back to the cutthroat and nudged him over and on to his back with her foot.

It was Lord Fulton. Johnnie let out a soft whimper. If he recalled correctly, Lord Fulton was Johnnie's brother.

Frederica crossed her arms and said, "Ah. Little Dick, we meet again." She shook her head. "You should have returned to London with your men."

Little Dick shot daggers at Freddie but remained mute. Kelly was ready to end the man's life in that moment.

Frederica looked to George. "Restrain him. I'm sure Owain will be happy to have a new guest in his dungeons, especially this one." She glanced at Lord Fulton. "Even better, Owain has an oubliette." She squatted beside the downed man. "Do you know what that is? An oubliette? It's an arsehole of a dungeon." She snorted. "An arsehole for an arsehole of a dungeon. Perfect."

She stood and walked away, stopping beside Johnnie and resting a gentle hand on the giant's arm. "Are you all right?"

She was so much like she'd been in the past, concern for her team foremost and evident. Kindness to everyone. He glanced to Lord Fulton, well, to those that were deserving.

She was remarkable. Still. And he was finding it harder and harder as the miles passed by to remember why they were at odds.

Johnnie's eyes trailed Lord Fulton as the prisoner walked away with George, then nodded.

After all the men had left, Frederica stopped before Kelly and asked, "Now, where were we?"

Before either of them had taken their next breath, they were in each other's arms, lips colliding in a heated battle for victory. For life. For the past. And possibly, for the future. For relief at finding each other again. For surviving everything thrown their way.

She was bolder now, stronger, and he felt it all in the way she kissed. She knew what she wanted, and she took it...and God damn, did he crave it. His heart raced and soared, and he found himself pulling back, staring at her in disbelief, then diving in again, nibbling at her lips, cupping her beloved face.

Oh, God, he was home. Finally.

This woman, whom he'd thought dead. Whom he'd *loved*. Then, mourned. God, how he'd mourned. Just the thought of his grief threatened to bring him to his knees. Right now.

But no! She was here. In the flesh. Kissing him like her life depended on it, and suddenly hope bloomed in his chest. Possibilities came alive he never, ever imagined could become reality.

And he was kissing her in return putting every ounce of his grief, his past love, his relief at finding her again, and his hope for the future —all of it—into that kiss.

A kiss for the ages.

For the love of youth.

For the love of two who'd been through hell and come out on the other side, harder and stronger and the better for it. Then, found each other again against every odd. Together again.

His thumbs swiped across her cheeks, his kiss turning tender. He wanted desperately to savor every single inch of this moment, inscribe it in his soul, for he'd never in a thousand years imagined he'd find himself in her arms once again, and he didn't want to take this gift for granted. To miss a thing about it. To be unable to recall it at will. Whenever he needed its comfort.

If this was a dream, he never wanted to wake.

Could they just forget the society, and remain here, in this wood, forever? The two of them alone. Weren't they owed this moment? This time?

"Oh God, Freddie. *Leannán* ."

He slid his hands down her arms, mapping out her familiar curves. Committing everything to memory. Refamiliarizing himself with what he'd lost and found once again.

Seven years without her, and he'd never gotten over her. Never.

He nearly shouted to the heavens when, out of nowhere, she gripped his backside and squeezed. It was all the permission he needed to carry on.

He slid one hand down the front of her trousers, one broad finger arrowing to her core, capturing the dew pooling there.

"Ah, Saint Fionnán weep." He begged, wanting nothing more than a long, lingering taste of her womanly essence.

"Kelly, Kelly, Kelly... Stop!" Seemingly out of nowhere, Freddie shoved him away, jerking him out of blissful heaven, while shaking her head, adding, "It's too soon. Too soon."

He squeezed his eyes closed, desperately trying to clear away the lust, while respecting her command. But he wondered at her abrupt change in her demeanor. Of course.

Her gaze skipped away when he finally opened his eyes, and she didn't even look his way as she said, "We should head back and finish setting up camp."

"All right." His voice cracked from the strain. "I'll be there. In a minute."

What the hell had just happened?

Whatever it was, he was determined to understand, but first, he'd give her the space she required.

THE NEXT FEW DAYS WERE FILLED WITH WEARY TRAVEL. KELLY decided not to confront Freddie about her abrupt halt of their romantic interlude for he could admit that considering everything, they'd moved at quite a fast pace toward a reconciliation of sorts. He couldn't entirely blame her for her hesitation.

At first, she'd kept her distance, her conversation stilted and focused on their travel plans. But as the days passed, he could sense her softening. A shared look here, a touch there. A soft glance.

They were united by a past—a connection—not easily severed. Despite everything.

And then on day four, her laughter returned. God, *her laugh*.

General Llwyd, proud of his hunting prowess, had gifted Kelly with a disemboweled field mouse. And Kelly had responded with, "Praise Saint Patrick, just what I've always wanted, you marvelous mouser, you."

And that was enough to set off Freddie's mirth.

Oh, how that sexy rumble still managed to fill him with a lethal combination of joy, contentment, and...hope.

It was the last thing on his mind as he rested his head for sleep, exhausted, but imagining all the possibilities of a brighter future. Their future.

Chapter Twenty-Seven

One Week Later: Castell Ddu, Dinas Powys, Wales

Castle Ddu was as dark as the name implied, the stones making up the buildings appearing black in the fading light, its towers shooting up through the mist like skeletal fingers stretching for the sky. They'd passed no people on their trek through the village leading up to the castle, though one could hardly blame them for it with this cool, murky weather.

By contrast, the vegetation was lushly green and very much alive, which was an extreme juxtaposition against such a gloomy, crenellated centerpiece.

They dismounted in the baily and a group of men led the horses and Lord Fulton across the cobbles to the stables. No one else was there to greet them, and George, Griffin, and Johnnie scattered in various directions, so Kelly blindly followed Freddie into the keep itself.

Kelly crossed into the great hall, a cavernous mostly empty space, and approached the man seated across a black throne on a dais situated at the opposite end of the enormous room; their booted footsteps echoed loudly despite the rushes. Kelly rather thought the man at the far end met them here in an attempt to intimidate; surely, the mysterious Owain had a space somewhere in this massive tomb with more modern conveniences.

Kelly stopped before the black throne and its equally dismal dais and instantly became aware of three things.

Owain was arrogant.

Owain was dangerous.

And Owain was someone Kelly already knew.

Kelly narrowed his eyes. "*You.*"

The man inclined his head. "And you're not in chains, so I suspect things are going better than I'd hoped." Owain glanced to Freddie. "I fully expected her to walk in here and attempt to punch me in the face with you following behind on a leash."

Surely, hope, wasn't the word he was looking for?

Freddie crossed her arms and replied, "There's still time."

Kelly shook his head. "Puppet Master? Spyder? Viscount Sharpe are all one and the same?"

Owain dipped his head again. "Yes."

Of course. "Any other aliases I should know about?"

"Those are the few that matter. To you at any rate."

"And I suppose I'm not to know your real name." Kelly didn't tell the man he already knew it. Best to keep what knowledge he could, close to his chest. For a man who peddled in knowledge, information was key.

The man folded his hands. "Depends on whether or not you earn that right."

Kelly couldn't help but laugh. "You wanted me here." Kelly spread his arms as if to say, 'and here I am.'

Owain chuckled and shook his head, "So, I did. But let's continue on with the introductions, shall we? At the moment, I'm more interested in what you two have discussed since your reunion a month ago. I'm guessing you two have had much to say to each other. Any truths or all lies? Based on my assessments of your individual personalities, I'd say you have both been rather stubborn."

Freddie blurted out. "I don't appreciate your keeping me in the dark about this. You deprived me of my right to make my own informed decisions."

Owain simply chuckled. "Oh, darling, you have no idea." He gestured to Kelly. "Did he tell you the reason he abandoned you all those years ago?"

Kelly narrowed his eyes. Spyder couldn't possibly *know,* could he? And who knew what sort of lies he'd tell Freddie, whatever would suit his purposes was his first guess. The last thing Kelly needed was this arsehole making everything worse. Out loud, Kelly said, "Fuck you." Because surely, he couldn't *know*.

Owain ignored him. "Your father and his men had him beaten and impressed into a prison hulk. He was on a ship bound for Australia. By the time I tracked him down and set up the scenario for his escape, he was already there. Once he was finally free, he raced directly back to you only to have your father tell him you'd died in early childbirth with his Irish bastard."

Kelly didn't miss her sharp intake of breath, but he refused to look her way, hiding the fact that he was stunned Spyder knew so much. Hiding the fact that being faced with the reminder of the way he'd felt the day he learned Freddie was dead was pure fucking anguish. *Still.* As if it had happened yesterday. He'd been in hell for months, mourning her. Mourning them both.

Hell, he'd never fully recovered. Like a permanent scar on his soul.

Owain continued. "I can see you're both equally surprised. Don't worry, Kelly. She's been keeping quite a few secrets herself." And the look he threw Freddie was nothing less than a warning.

Kelly slammed his mind shut against his own memories of the past, funny and not funny after all those days of yearning to remember anything at all. He was prepared to—hell, what was he prepared to do? Defend her? He glanced to Freddie, who was shaking her head, tears streaming down her cheeks. It killed him to see her cry. But she didn't look his way. And as she kept reminding him, she didn't need his help. Hell, Kelly didn't even know how *to* help.

She sobbed out. "No, don't, Owain. Oh God, please don't."

Whatever it was, Freddie was deadly serious. And desparate. Kelly stepped forward to intervene anyway. Fuck this man.

Owain shook his head and said, "I'm sorry, love. You can't keep this from him forever. He deserves to know. All of it."

Kelly froze and clenched his fists. Whatever *it* was, it was going to be bad; he knew it in his gut. And it involved him, which made him curious. Freddie was practically ready to collapse in anguish, and Kelly was torn between wanting to console her, wanting to punch Owain in the face, and wanting to know more than ever what *it* was.

Owain stepped down from the dais and headed for a gothic door in the rear of the room. He reached for the handle, but before opening it, said, "I'll leave you two alone for this..."

Then, he opened the door, ruffled the dark hair of a small child, and said, "Go on, son... Your mother's home."

FREDDIE FRANTICALLY SHOOK HER HEAD. SHE WASN'T READY. IT WAS too soon.

She closed her eyes just as a young voice, yelled, "Momma!" Then, she collapsed to her knees a moment before her young son threw his arms around her neck. His small voice proclaimed, "I've missed you, so much."

She squeezed him harder and said, "Oh, I've missed you, too." The last, she choked out on a sob.

After a few moments of trying in vain to shut out the reality of everything about to transpire, she chanced to open her eyes and look at Kelly, whose face had turned ashen as he stared at the young boy in her arms. Seven years old with eyes a unique, quicksilver eyes and ebony hair? There was no questioning his parentage.

Her son must have noticed her disquiet for he pulled back and asked, "Who is that momma?"

She allowed her son to turn fully around to face Ciarán, then, took a deep breath and said, "This is Ciarán Kelly."

Ciarán's eyes appeared to burn now, with an explosive intensity, as silver orbs stared into identical silver orbs. Kelly ran a hand down his face, then fell to his knees, his hand covering his own mouth, which shook with emotion, and his eyes filled with the sheen of tears. And anguish. And perhaps, a hint of joy?

She'd never seen a grown man cry. Until now.

And she knew right then, he didn't doubt the child was his.

She gave Finn a little nudge. "Go on, son. He's your father."

Fionnán took one hesitant step forward, then paused. "You look like me."

Kelly nodded and cleared his throat, but his voice cracked all the same. "So, I do." And once again, she could see the tremble in his lips.

Finn dragged his foot through the rushes and quietly said, "My name is Fionnán."

Kelly's voice was rough, tortured, when he replied. "Nice to meet you. I'm Ciarán."

Finn smiled and gestured with one hand. "May I?"

Kelly nodded, bit his lip, and held out his arms, "Come here, son."

Finn ran to Kelly, throwing his arms around his father's neck the same way he'd done with her only moments earlier. Freddie bit back another sob at the sight.

In a way, she was unsurprised at the instant connection. Her son loved to be touched and held and had been asking about his father for months, desperate to know who he was. She'd run out of excuses to offer his inquisitive mind and grown weary of having to lie.

Kelly rocked with Fionnán wrapped tightly in his arms. "Oh, son, I am so, so sorry. I didn't know. I didn't know."

Watching Kelly's shoulders shake as he, a grown man, a strong, capable man, sobbed with grief and joy upon meeting his son for the first time...

It *devastated* her.

And in that moment, she realized the truth she'd ignored for so many years. She had never let Kelly go, not fully. She should have known when she so strongly desired a confrontation, even after seven long years. Hadn't she thought it—the idea that her thoughts and actions were hardly that of woman who was indifferent?

And now, after seeing him filled with unequivocal love, after realizing that their entire life had been one giant misbegotten tragedy of immense proportions, and that this man was as honorable as she'd once believed him to be... She could admit her love for him was still true. She loved him! And she was tormented to realize all he had endured at the hands of her own family.

The entire fucking thing was tragic.

But how could they ever get past the truths she withheld? She'd actively hid his child from him for seven years. Who could forgive something like that? How could they ever move past it?

The answer was obvious and no less devastating: they couldn't.

True love can survive many things, but it cannot survive *every* betrayal...right?

Chapter Twenty-Eight

With great care, Freddie removed herself from the room to allow Kelly time alone with his son. She leaned against the outer wall and released a long, drawn-out breath. Her guilt now weighed heavily on her. She had done what she thought was best at the time, with the information she had in that moment, but now—now, she had many regrets. Keeping Kelly from his son for seven long years was one of them. And the biggest. The worst.

Freddie slowly pulled herself together and pushed away from the wall; her feet taking her toward the family wing of the castle—Owain's domain, for he had no family, unless you counted her and Finn, who were the closest to family he had. She picked up her pace as she advanced in that direction, funneling her remorse, turning regret into ire, for it seemed there was one person who had an entire catalogue of information he should have shared...information that could have made every difference in the world.

With a heavy tread, she sought out Owain. She found him in the northwest tower, in the private sitting room adjoining his bedroom.

She burst through the door and wasted no time with her accusations. "How in the hell could you keep all this from me?" she roared.

Owain, who was reclining on a black velvet settee before the fire, laughed once to himself and took a sip of whisky. Then, he rested the arm holding his glass on one upright knee. He stared at the fire as he said, "Would you believe I feared losing our...friendship?"

She snorted and tossed her hands in the air. "That's not friendship."

He took another sip but said nothing, his gaze lost to the fire.

She marched around the matching settee until she blocked his view. "Maybe, I could forgive you for keeping the secrets, though it burns every time I think of how I cursed Kelly's name in front of you and you said nothing. But here and now—it was definitely not your decision to decide it was time to reveal my child to him."

"*Your* child." Owain tossed back the contents of his drink and stood. "Don't you mean your's and Kelly's." He shrugged. "Besides, what's done is done."

Argh—how could he be so calm, so blasé about it all. Didn't he care about anything or anyone? Besides himself? She stamped her foot. "Yes, *my* child."

He said nothing.

Why wouldn't he fight and argue. She was spoiling for a good fight.

"Why did you do all this? I don't understand. Kelly has given you nothing. Did you bring him here just to witness us tear each other apart? Did you—"

Suddenly, the door sprang open and slammed against the wall. Kelly marched in on a wave of anger. He ignored Owain and glared at her, his eyes red with emotion. "How could you keep this from me?"

Owain mumbled, "Well *that's* a familiar refrain."

Freddie ignored both remarks and looked around Kelly. "Where's Finn?"

"With his nurse. Why the hell didn't you tell me?"

Freddie's eyes snapped to Kelly. There was a hint of raw emotion in the question that made her heart clinch. "My father told me you'd abandoned me because you wanted no part of our child's life."

Kelly's jaw ticked. "And you believed him?" He grabbed hold of both her arms and bent to look her in the eye, his were swirling with grief and anger, betrayal. "Freddie...after everything? After—," he checked himself, releasing her and stepping back. "I couldn't have possibly known you were carrying my child at the time of my disappearance."

Of course, he couldn't. "And I didn't understand that then—I was too young and naïve and foolish."

"And I had loved you above all else," he voice was a faint whisper.

Hearing those words, uttered so despondently and in the past tense, robbed her of her next breath.

Owain chose that moment to interject with a chuckle, and she flinched, unable to bare yet another shake of her emotions. Despite her inner turmoil, which must be obvious to both men, he said, "I suppose this means she hasn't told you what her father did to *her*..."

Freddie closed her eyes and shook her head, but clearly Owain was determined for every secret they ever had to be dragged out in the open today. God only knew for what purpose.

She lifted her chin and spoke before Owain could continue. "I ran away because my father was going to make me give up the baby."

Freddie looked to Owain for confirmation he would at least keep *this* secret until she was ready. He owed her.

But she should have known better. Owain only ever thought of himself.

Owain shook his head and said, "He abandoned her in St. Giles with a babe in her belly and nothing but the clothes on her back." He glanced to Kelly. "Forbade her to reach out to any family, or it would mean the death of her child. Told everyone she'd died. And then, she survived that hell hole. Alone."

The silence after that proclamation stretched on for what felt like hours, the only sound the crackling of the fire in the hearth.

"Jesus." Kelly broke the silence with a hand through his hair and a curse.

He turned his back and pressed both hands against the wall, then leaned in and hung his head. He was angry before, but now he seemed to be residing somewhere between rage and anguish. His fists were clinched until his knuckles turned white. She feared he was ready to punch the wall to the devastating effect of his hands.

It seemed their entire relationship, for lack of a better word, was shrouded by betrayal, secrets, and lies. A death knell for hope.

Chapter Twenty-Nine

Kelly entered Owain's office early the next morning after a fitful night's sleep. His entire reality had altered, forever changed, so it wasn't surprising he'd not slept.

In fact, it had been somewhat of a relief to receive what could only be described as a summons from Owain. Perhaps, they could get down to business. Whatever knowledge he and Owain shared would give Kelly something to chew on besides secrets and betrayals surrounding the woman he'd loved with every fiber of his being.

Kelly didn't care for Owain's attitude, but he was interested in getting this interview over with so he could return to his mission.

Owain stood at a side bar. "Whisky?"

Kelly stopped mid-room and crossed his arms. "No. I'd quite rather you get to the point. Why am I here?"

Owain took a sip of his own drink, then settled himself behind his desk. "I thought we could exchange information. Surely, you managed to gather some evidence during your time as an undercover spy. And as you can see, I'm on your side."

Kelly laughed. "I highly doubt that. You're on your own side."

Owain steepled his fingers. "I'm glad you've a clever mind."

Kelly shook his head. "Flattery?" He strode forward and braced himself on Owain's desk. "Did you think to see Freddie and I rip each other apart? Did it get you off?"

Owain laughed. "No, it takes a little more than that for a man of my years and experience."

Kelly stood back. "You're no more than two, perhaps three years older than I am."

Owain's eyes turned dark. "Try seven. And compared to *your* easy life, I've lived decades longer."

Kelly couldn't believe his ears. "Easy? You call my life easy?"

Owain smirked. "I suppose it is all rather relative."

That was an insult, without a doubt. Kelly folded his arms. "Do you have anything of substance to ask or share? Because this conversation is going nowhere."

Owain dipped his head. "As you say."

The man stood and removed a key from around his neck, a glimpse of a familiar tattoo flashed.

Kelly smirked and nodded pointedly. "Lovely tattoo you have there. I wonder how a man in your position comes by one of those?"

Owain pulled back his lacy, black sleeve. "This? It is the tattoo of the Society for the Purification of England. Like you, I felt the need to work undercover in order to gather evidence." He shook out the lace and inserted his key into a strongbox upon the desk and opened it. "It took me years to get to this point."

Owain pulled out a notebook and held it aloft. "I have the names here of every man who bears this tattoo that I have met, including location and placement of the tattoo—they're not all in the same place." He slammed the notebook down on the table. "What do you have?"

Kelly scratched at the beard growing wild upon his chin. "I have some pages from their account books. A list of people who have given the society money."

Owain raised his brows, the look suggesting he was both surprised yet pleased by this knowledge. "Do you have it with you?"

Kelly laughed. "No."

"Ah yes, of course, not. And it's—"

"It's safe."

"So, it would seem the three of us may have just enough evidence to bring the Society down."

"The three of us?"

Owain smiled. "I would never even think to leave Frederica out of this; it's far too personal for her."

Kelly took exception to that. "These men are extremely dangerous." Didn't the man care?

Owain laughed. "Son, haven't you figured it out by now? Frederica Dawe can take care of herself. She doesn't need us."

And then it hit him. The reason behind Owain's actions. "Oh, my God. You love her..."

Owain did not respond, not right away, but the proof was there in the tick of muscle in the man's cheek. It all made sense now. Owain had hoped that revealing their secrets *would* destroy any chance of reconciliation. Yet he revealed everything, even those secrets that worked against him, like admitting that Kelly hadn't abandoned Frederica all those years ago. What was that all about? Some strange, honorable, way to make the battle for Frederica all above board.

Owain raised his glass and said, "May the best man win."

Kelly turned and walked out, but not before saying, "The best man already has."

But was it the truth? And did he want to win?

KELLY SPENT A LARGE PORTION OF THE MORNING LEARNING HIS son's preferences—salmon was in, turnips were out, smart kid; black was the best, chartreuse made him want to vomit—and the bulk of the day filching what he would need to leave.

He hated to leave so soon after finding his son, but knowing Finn made Kelly's mission to bring down the Society more urgent than ever.

His son was clearly of Irish decent.

What would the man behind the Society for the Purification of England do if he knew his own grandson was half-Irish?

Kelly didn't want to find out—he wouldn't allow it.

Already, he would give his life for that little wonder of curiosity and joy, Fionnán Kelly. It might even come to that in the end.

LATE THAT EVENING, KELLY LET CREPT INTO FINN'S ROOM, surprised to learn it was far closer to his own room than Owain's.

"Father!"

"Shh... We don't want to wake your mother, lad." His son slapped his hand over his own mouth and stifled a giggle, his shoulders shaking wildly with his mirth. Kelly pretended his own mirth as he drew to a stop beside Finn's bed and sat on the edge. "I have something for you —two things for you, actually."

Fionnán laughter died, and he frowned. "You're leaving already, aren't you?"

Smart lad. Kelly brushed Finn's hair from his face, desperately wishing the answer was no. "Only just this once."

Fionnán crossed his arms. "I've heard that one before."

Kelly was at odds with what to say to that. 'Trust me,' seemed far too trite. He pulled his first gift from his pocket and handed it to his son. "I carved this for you last night." The boy's eyes lit with wonder; his sadness temporarily forgotten. "It's a Celtic knot on wood, and it means 'forever.' I give this to you as a symbol of my vow. You will be my son forever, and I *will* return to you."

Finn slipped the necklace over his head, and Kelly adjusted the leather band. He had never been more relieved to have the skills necessary to filch the leather and knife to make this gift for his son, for at the moment, he had nothing else to give but his love.

Fionnán smiled now, a shy smile, but a far sight better than his frown. "And the second gift?"

"And the second." Kelly laughed. "Is here." He picked up his bag and set it on the bed, then opened the flap and out tumbled the grey cat. "This here is General Llwyd. He can't go with me, either; though he really wants to. I need you to watch over him while I'm gone. Can you do that?"

Fionnán's eyes were wide now. "You really mean it?!"

Kelly once again ruffled his son's hair as the General curled into Fionnán's lap like he'd done the like a thousand times. "More than anything, son. More than anything."

"Can I ask something of you, Father?"

"Ask away—"

"Will you tell me a story?"

Kelly smiled, then pretended to think over the request. "Hmm... On one condition."

"Anything!"

"Oh, ho! Anything? Be careful promising too much before you have an idea of what you're agreeing to. But in this instance, condition is this—will you allow me to settle in beside you in the bed?"

Finn gladly made room, and Kelly settled in, his back against the headboard, and started sharing with his son his favorite tale as a youth, a character from which his son drew his own name—the story of the incredible Irish warrior, Finn McCool.

KELLY PULLED FIONNÁN'S DOOR CLOSED AS QUIETLY AS POSSIBLE SO as not to wake him. He hated leaving the boy so soon, but he needed to end this, now, if he ever hoped to be a part of the boy's life.

He turned and nearly jumped out of his skin to discover Freddie leaning against the opposite wall, which was embarrassing to say the least.

"We need to talk," she said.

He *really* didn't want to, but if they were going to both be a part of Fionnán's life, he needed to compromise, though he was well aware any court of law would rule in his favor. However, Kelly had no desire to part Finn from his mother. Somehow, they would have to come to some sort of arrangement so they could both be involved.

No matter what happened between them.

Kelly rubbed at the back of his neck, then shuttered away his emotions and held out a hand. "By all means, lead the way."

They entered her room, which was a relief for he didn't want her to see the evidence of his thieving and predict his plans.

She paced before the bed, then said, "We've got a situation."

That wasn't what he was expecting. He didn't know what he was expecting, but that wasn't' it.

"My brother was at the cottage in Runcorn. He found my locket. Inside are miniatures of my mother...and Fionnán."

Jesus Fucking Christ. Out loud, he said, "So, there's a good bet the society, and therefore your father, knows."

She nodded. "It's a possibility we must consider. Is it possible my brother is not as involved as we think?"

Kelly leaned against the door and crossed his arms and legs. "So, it's we now, is it?"

Freddie let out a long-suffering sigh. "Please don't argue semantics with me now. I'm not convinced my brother is fully involved. He's been doing questionable things for my father, sure. But...when I saw him... he seemed surprised to find out I'm alive."

Kelly frowned. "Could you be mistaken? Maybe, he thought you'd never make it out of St. Giles alive?"

Freddie nodded. "Perhaps, but—"

"We better hope to God that is the case." He dragged his hand down his face.

"Was my brother present when my father took you?"

Kelly froze. "No." He bit out. "It was just your father and some hired ruffians. They were large, filthy, and cared less about who I was or how I got there, only where they needed to take me and when they would be paid."

She strode forward. "Oh, God Kelly—I didn't know."

She looked as if to kiss him or cup his cheek, he didn't know which, but he thought she was probably acting on instinct. Regardless, he turned his cheek, making it clear her advances weren't wanted. Not yet. It was too soon. He was too *raw*.

Too conflicted, despite his bravado with Owain earlier.

Though his traitorous body vehemently denied any hint at confusion. His cock knew precisely who it wanted—Freddie.

Sure, he realized she could never be in league with the Society, but she also wasn't the person he once knew. And perhaps, Owain had a reason to believe she might choose him.

He rubbed at the ache in his chest brought on by that thought. Not that he could blame her—seven years was a long time, and Owain was a handsome, powerful man.

Besides, Kelly wasn't sure they could move past the secrecy, the lies. Wouldn't there always be a kernel of distrust between them?

And with Freddie, he refused to allow kisses and romantic touches when his inner feelings were in turmoil. Not after all the lies.

At least, that's what he told himself. *What a time for his honor to rear its head.*

But dammit, he *could* withstand her advances, at least once. Twice, might be pushing it, regardless of where they stood; their mutual attraction was as potent as it ever was—still.

He stood away from the door and raked a hand through his hair. "I must go."

Now, more than ever, the society must fall, and it was urgent. His *son* was in danger. He understood, now, why she'd raced away that first night on the road, despite the danger it placed her in. And with her actions, he was proud to acknowledge her bravery.

She loved their boy; he had no doubt of that.

But the society was a monster, twisted, and everywhere, with many heads...a Lernaean Hydra, deadly to those anywhere near it.

He glanced at her and swallowed any outward signs of his fear for Finn's safety. For her safety. She was worried enough already. He pulled out a false smile and strove to distract her with his charm. He winked.

She wasn't fooled; she narrowed her eyes. "Where are you going?"

He cocked his head. "Why, love, to bed, of course." He waggled his brows. "Want to join me?" which was a humorous thing to say after he'd just rebuffed her advances, and it was probably the reason she was suspicious of him now. Clever woman.

She crossed her arms. "Aren't you tired of trying to fill that void?"

He forced a laugh and glanced around. "What void? I'm perfectly content. Besides, to your earlier point, where else would I be going with no money, no food, and living within the walls of a veritable fortress."

He hoped to God she deemed him as incapable as he led her to believe. Because now more than ever, he needed to leave. Tonight!

Chapter Thirty

At the Same Time

Lord Dawe paced his office, wondering when his wretched son would finally return. He'd left for Runcorn two weeks ago and should be back by now.

A commotion out in the hall had the old man wildly racing to the door. He walked out slowly and glared down the stairs just as his son stepped into view. "Well, it's about time," he huffed out.

His son handed his hat, greatcoat, and gloves to the butler with a "Thank you, Matthew," then turned and began climbing the stairs taking his time. And since when did he call the servants by name?

Lord Dawe returned to his office and awaited his son there. He was straightening the stack of papers in front of him when Duncan walked through the door.

Lord Dawe rested his elbows on his desk and steepled his fingers. "Well."

His son didn't respond immediately, which was a first. In fact, he appeared to be...thinking.

Lord Dawe slammed his fists on the desktop and was about to prompt him to get on with in, when his son finally sat and said," Kelly was definitely there, but they were already gone when we arrived. I believe one of my messages to you was intercepted. Probably, one of Stonebridge's men."

Lord Dawe had the urge to toss the papers on his desk at his son. "You incompetent fool."

His son mumbled something.

"What did you say?"

"Nothing, father. Never fear, we now know Viscount Sharpe is involved, and I have a plan to set his trap."

Maybe, his son wasn't such an imbecile. "Traitors are intolerable! Do go on." He was salivating over the torture that awaited Viscount Sharpe. He wanted *that* man as much as he wanted Kelly!

"I'm envisioning a masquerade..."

ALISTAIR MACLEOD MARCHED INTO STONEBRIDGE'S OFFICE AND headed straight for the whisky decanter. Dansbury and Stonebridge both drew silent as he paraded past the pair of them, lounging on the matching camelback sofas. After swallowing back two fingers full of excellent Scots whisky, he refilled his glass and turned to face his friends.

"I saw Kelly."

Both men leapt to their feet. Stonebridge looked around as if expecting Kelly to hop out from behind a chair any minute now, and asked, "Is he here?"

"No."

"*Where* is he?" asked Dansbury.

"Wales."

"Wales?" Both men repeated.

"Aye. Do ye bloody well want to keep pepperin' me with questions, or shall I just tell ye what I ken?"

Stonebridge and Dansbury both laughed, and Stonebridge said, "Go on."

"Kelly plans to return in a month with evidence, make that three weeks nou. He's in Wales at the moment. He's in custody, but somehow, I think that won't last. The woman holding him has some sort of hold on him; I don't know what. But then, she's a woman, and it's Kelly we're talking aboot."

Stonebridge and Dansbury burst out laughing.

MacLeod shook his head. "I know, she's a woman, but...I think this one is different somehow."

Stonebridge swiped at the tears in his eyes. "Does she have red hair, rather tall?"

"Aye."

Stonebridge nodded, his chuckles subsiding. "They do have a past. Kelly will be here in three weeks, then."

"Aye. Let's hope his information is good."

"In the meantime, here."

Stonebridge handed MacLeod a stack of papers. "What the fook is this?"

Stonebridge leveled MacLeod with a serious gaze. "My wife, Grace, has made pamphlets in support of immigration. Since, you have some unexpected time on your hands, you can help us spread them about town."

MacLeod should have known better than to ask.

Chapter Thirty-One

Two Days Later

Kelly dismounted from his stolen horse a fair distance from the main road and set about making camp. He still hadn't crossed the border back into England, despite making all haste to get to Blackpool. It felt like time was slipping through his fingers, and with worry his constant companion, he was unsettled enough that sleeping was difficult. If it weren't for sheer exhaustion, he doubted he would sleep at all.

He had just finished setting his snares and had settled in beside the fire, when he chuckled out loud and said, "You might as well show yourself."

He laughed again as he heard the 'dammit' from the woods behind him, followed by soft footsteps.

He poked at the fire with a big stick as Frederica situated herself beside him.

"How did you know I was there?" she asked.

"I heard you snoring last night."

She swatted his arm. "I don't snore."

Kelly shrugged. "You're free to believe what you will."

She huffed and began rummaging in her bag.

He set his fire stick beside him and looked at her. "Why didn't you stop me from leaving?"

Freddie broke up a nearby by twig and began tossing bits into the fire. "I knew you were going because you wanted to keep our son safe."

Kelly did not know what to say to that. It was the truth. But did this mean they were working together now? No more lies? Or was she working for Owain? And planning to make off with whatever evidence he retrieved?

He felt a moment of guilt for even thinking it, but he was only human. Over the two days, he'd had more time than he'd cared to mull things over, and he was on the verge of making a choice. Still, he asked, "What does Owain think?"

"He doesn't know—yet."

Kelly jolted. "What about Fionnán?"

"He's safe."

Kelly seriously doubted that. "Even from the man who seems to know everything?"

"Owain...has his ways, sure. But he'd never hurt Fionnán. I know that now."

"Tell me this. Do you understand Owain's motives? In all of this. In you. With *us*. Because I'm not certain I understand what he gets out of everything he's doing—and everyone has a motive. Whether they like to admit it or not." He'd be damned if he was going to be so honorable as to tell Freddie the man was in love with her, despite his own conflicted thoughts.

"I don't know nearly enough about Owain's motives, I grant you that. But I know enough to leave my son with a trusted friend and follow after *you*..."

"Who is this trusted soul who holds such esteem in your eyes?"

"George."

Kelly nodded. Fair enough. He liked George, too.

But his sense of urgency did not relent, and now that he gave in and accepted she was going to follow him to Blackpool, regardless of his own wishes, he decided to make the most of the distraction.

He glanced to Freddie. "Tell me about St. Giles."

FREDDIE CHUCKLED WITH SELF-DEPRECATION. SHE HARDLY KNEW where to begin. She sighed and focused on the fire as she spoke. "My father, once he found out about the babe, tossed me in the family carriage and drove to Seven Dials. He laid out his options in no uncertain terms: 'Either get out here, and we never see you again. Or I take you to Bedlam. And believe you me, that bastard you carry will never see the light of day!'

"I got out, of course. And it didn't take long to shed the vestiges of my upbringing. One can't survive the streets of St. Giles and maintain propriety. Much of what I was taught growing up was useless in my new surroundings." She tossed another stick in the fire. "But hunger and fear for your unborn child is a strong motivator."

"I can imagine," he whispered, softly. She daren't look at him, lest she dissolve into tears at the memory. She swallowed an overwhelming feeling of emotion and continued her tale. "I was a beggar the second day, and a thief by the third." She nudged him in the arm with her shoulder. "Incidentally, your sleight of hand lessons from long ago turned out to be a life-saver."

He snorted, and she shrugged, then continued, "By the first week, I was really good. And surviving...and I must admit, my animosity toward you grew in those days. Anger for you not being there. For abandoning me—*us*."

He touched her shoulder. "But—"

On reflex, she squeezed his hand. "I know, now. Though the worst part of it all, were the rats."

She trailed off, lost to distant memory.

Eventually, Kelly prompted, "But..."

She shook herself. "But then, I picked the wrong pocket—Owain's. Well, I suppose it was the right pocket, in hindsight, but at the time, I didn't know that. I only knew that for the first time—I had been on my own for months by then, you see—but for the first time, I had been caught. Worse, the baby was showing by then, and I knew I was going to be in real trouble soon. His catching me threatened to be a setback I couldn't afford. But Owain was surprised and impressed with my skill and not entirely on the right side of the law at times. No one had ever been quite so successful at stealing from him; despite the fact he'd caught me, he was...intrigued. So, he made me an offer I couldn't refuse."

Kelly uttered a noise that could be called nothing but a growl, and she shook her head. "Not *that* kind of offer. He taught me skills I could never have imagined. Useful skills. Hell, the *most* useful skill. He taught me independence. And provided a safe haven for my son. *Our* son. Along with a chance to earn my own income so I never had to rely on anyone again. Kelly, I owe him everything."

"You do yourself a disservice. He couldn't have taught you things you had no aptitude for to begin with. You were always more than you seemed."

Freddie looked to Kelly and was surprised to find him arrested, staring at her as if...well, his look was inscrutable, but certainly not disgusted or inhospitable.

In fact, the longer their gazes lingered, the more convinced she was that he was captivated. Mesmerized. In a way he never had been before.

Perhaps, she was reading into his look her own desire, which was simmering now just beneath the surface of her skin, and had been building since she'd witnessed the immediate love he had for their son, and until he told her no, she was going to embrace her assumption. The attraction had always been there, but now that she could freely admit to herself she was in love with him, she wanted it all, even if only until the mission was over and the Society fell.

He could only refuse, and there was nothing more to her story to relate but mundane events.

She reached up and cupped his familiar cheek, and even though she refused to say the words, I love you, she closed her eyes and embraced the familiarity and willed her love into him. That he would know it, deep down, even if she couldn't say it. Even if he never would.

When his breath caught and he leaned into her hand, she took that as acceptance and slid onto his lap, resting her forehead against his, her arms on his broad shoulders. His own arms slipped around her waist, and he pulled her in close. She inhaled his scent, so familiar, and it brought back the feeling of youthful love. That first kiss. That first glimpse of forever.

But he was no young buck any longer. They were both grown. More experienced. More knowledgeable about what they wanted.

And she wanted Ciarán Kelly. As a man.

She kissed him then, with all the passion in her soul. For all the time they lost through the machinations of others. Through their own stubborn pride. He came to life beneath her, and she gloried in his acceptance of her kiss. She pulled back and began unlacing his shirt.

"Are you sure, *a chroí?*" he asked, softly.

She paused and looked him in the eye, altogether serious. "I've never been more certain."

He leaned back with a charming smile. "Then, you may proceed."

With that she yanked off his shirt and immediately drove her fingers into the fine hairs on his chest. The hard muscles and warmth of the skin beneath her hands had her squirming in no time, ratcheting up her desire in record time.

With a snap, their passion exploded. He attacked the buttons of her waistcoat, making quick work of the inconvenient garment, then reached for her falls. "Freddie, it's been..."

He groaned as she reached for the buttons of his own trousers, each preventing the other from achieving outright success. She slapped his hands away, and he raised them in submission with a laugh, but she had a second thought. "Never mind...you take care of you, and I'll..."

She didn't finish that thought; she didn't need to. She stood and fumbled with her own trousers as he addressed his. Or undressed as it were.

By the time she'd doffed hers and glanced up, his cock was standing tall and proud between his bare legs, his limbs spread wide, rewarding her with a perfectly clear view. "Come closer, *mo ghrá...*"

And, oh, what a magnificent view.

The man should be fucking proud.

He took his manhood in hand then, and she wasted no time straddling him once again. To say she experienced heaven when she slid down on his cock would not do the experience the justice it deserved. There simply were no words in the human language.

"Freddie," he growled; it ended on a groan.

She felt every glide of his flared head inside her, and it accelerated her excitement, making her squirm and moan, and she rode the feeling for all she was worth.

"Jesus, Freddie. My God, so fucking good...," his words trailed off on a sigh as his eye rolled back in his head. He gripped her with his powerful hands and squeezed, a gentle passionate, formidable hold.

It was glorious.

It was wonderful.

It was empowering.

She arched her back, and his hands left her hips, where he helped her stay on rhythm, settling them on her breasts, cupping them, weighing them. "Oh God, *mo shíorghra*, let me taste your rosy peaks. I've never seen such exquisite beauty in all my life."

She leaned forward, and he latched on, suckling her fiercely. She slowed her pace, enjoying the tug on her nipples and relishing the echoing pulse in her core. She was so close to ecstasy, it was difficult not to push him back and ride her way to completion. Now. For it had been so long. Seven years too long.

She squeezed her insides, and he let go, throwing his head back with a moan. "Freddie, fuck. Yes, just like that. You are killing me." His dirty talk pleased her, and she squeezed again in reward. She felt him harden within her and knew he was close.

So, she let go. And rode him.

Faster.

Harder.

Slamming herself on him, chasing the little death. The sound of skin meeting skin ratcheting up her desire, which was already so very explosive.

"I can't hold on much longer, *mo ghrá*. Now!"

He reached between them, touching his thumb to her distended nub, and she came on contact with a scream.

He lifted his hips and held onto her hers, riding her orgasm, increasing her pleasure, for as long as he could. The slap of their thighs echoed in the night and just as the tingling began to subside, he hardened one final time and exploded within her, yelling her name out loud, "Freddie!"

Chapter Thirty-Two

Three Days Later: Near Blackpool

Kelly and Frederica rode side by side on horseback, following the road on their final stretch to Blackpool. They'd passed Liverpool that morning, and it was now early afternoon.

Frederica laughed. "Did you have to say that to the Publican? Did you have to make fun of the name of his pub?"

Kelly shrugged and glanced over to Freddie, warmed by the now frequent sound and ease of her laughter. "Well, with a name like *The Olde Cock*... Can you blame me? Really?"

Freddie laughed again. "I suppose not."

They'd been traveling for three days, and every bit of it had been enjoyable. Exhausting but enjoyable all the same.

Kelly looked ahead again, then slowed their pace and stood in his stirrups. He shielded his eyes with one hand, a relief from squinting against the glare of the sun. Up ahead was a horse who roamed free, grazing on the grass by the side of the road. Kelly looked about but could see no one else nearby.

He nodded toward the beast. "There's a horse up ahead."

Freddie shaded her own eyes and looked, standing tall in her own stirrups. "Huh. Do you see anyone else?"

He shook his head. "No."

They rode slowly toward the horse, who didn't seem to be bothered by their approach. Once beside the great beast, Kelly tossed his reins to Freddie and slid from the saddle.

The horse looked up then, and Kelly soothed him with a soft voice. "Aren't you a beauty," he crooned.

He ran his hand up the horse's muzzle to his forehead, slowly petting the large beast. Then, he walked around, noting the detailed bridling, the tell-tale bells and saddle blanket, the unique stitching on the saddle itself. The colorful ribbons decorating the horse's mane.

But...there was evidence of blood on the blanket.

Kelly briefly closed his eyes and prayed to be wrong, then lifted the blanket and searched the horse's withers for the brand he knew he'd find.

When he found it, he dropped his head. "Shit."

"Kelly, what is it?"

He collected the horse's reins and turned to Freddie. They shared a look, her concern mirroring his own. He silently handed her the reins, then dug around in his saddle bag until he pulled out a pistol.

"Kelly..."

Kelly nodded. "Stay here."

Then, he turned on his heel and walked into the woods behind him. He knew she wouldn't really listen, but he'd tried anyway.

He crept cautiously, occasionally pausing to listen and smell the air. It wasn't long before he caught the scent of trouble—blood and the unforgettable stench of death.

He walked cautiously but steadily, and eventually stepped into a clearing where a cluster of colorful wagons stood proud in a large circle.

But there were no horses, no pets, no people. No children. No sounds. Nothing but the breeze gently rushing through the leaves of nearby trees and the occasional rustling of a nearby forest animal, likely a squirrel or a bird, foraging for food.

He'd stood there for so long, he was quite startled when Freddie rested a hand upon his shoulder and squeezed.

He covered her hand with his own and returned her squeeze and said, "You probably don't want to see this." Then, he patted her hand once more and stepped around the nearest wagon...into vulgar devastation.

Death.

Destruction.

Evil had visited these peoples.

Their bodies were piled unceremoniously in the middle of the circle created by their wagons. The men. The women.

The children.

Every one of them.

Their eyes appeared frozen in terror; their bodies mutilated by some madman—or madmen.

Freddie stopped beside him and grabbed hold of his hand, and they stood there, together, in mourning for these unknown people. Offering respect through a moment of silence and prayer.

Eventually, they turned toward each other, and Freddie asked, "Romani?"

He shook his head. "No." He took a deep breath. "Wandering Irish."

His people.

"Who would do such a thing?"

He looked away a moment, taking another chance to compose himself. It was impossible to imagine anyone could be capable of such a heinous crime, but Evil was a very real thing. He knew that all too well. Eventually, he straightened, looked at Freddie, so beautiful, her eyes heavy with sorrow and concern, and said, "I don't know. But we must see to them."

Freddie nodded her agreement, and together, they searched carefully through the wagons until they found the tools they needed for the task.

It took them two days to carefully see to the remains. Two days of mostly silence, while they toiled and did their best to honor the deceased.

The afternoon of the second day, as they turned to care for the last person, they found the evidence they both silently sought. The evidence that proved precisely who might be behind such an unthinkable massacre.

A familiar symbol was carved into the chest of the remaining man, who had probably been the group's leader and the first to die. The carving was crudely drawn, sure, but there was no doubt in either of their minds what the symbol represented: the Society for the Purification of England had been here. They were responsible.

And they would pay.

Chapter Thirty-Three

They packed up and left the morning of the third day, and for hours, Freddie and Kelly traveled in silence, each lost to their own thoughts. Both of them moved by the events of the last several days. Both saddened and needing more time. Time to process what they'd seen. And to contemplate—everything.

They hadn't known any of the people in that camp, but they could empathize with the horror of it all. Only a cold, unfeeling person could experience what they'd seen and remain unmoved, or not be saddened by the unnecessary and tragic loss of life. Of absolute murder on display. Of innocent victims left unburied for the vultures to pick apart.

The sun was shining and the air was crisp and refreshing, which hardly seemed appropriate when one was in no state to enjoy it. When so many innocents were no longer alive to experience it. And Freddie wanted to shout to God to stop it. To stop it all. To hide the sun, which felt like a smile. She wanted wind and rain and thunder. Weather more appropriate to her mood, even if it would make her miserable. *More* miserable.

For she was already feeling wretched, and the sun simply felt like a terrible joke at someone else's expense. Perhaps, at hers.

A few miles south of Blackpool, Kelly slowed. He cleared his throat, then said, "I think we should camp here for a few days before we head into town."

It was the first thing either of them had said all day.

Freddie nodded her agreement. She wasn't ready to face anyone, either.

They made camp in continued silence, working companionably as a team. As they'd managed to do with relative ease since they'd left Wales so many days ago. As if they'd worked together for years, partners who could read each other's intentions and adjust as necessary.

And that night, they made love beneath the stars once again.

For Freddie, it was a desperate need to celebrate the gift of life, though she couldn't help but feel a twinge of guilt for it. Guilt for the touch of relief that overcame her as she pulled Kelly into her embrace. For being relieved to have found him again, to have him here with her. For feeling alive while at the same time, she mourned.

Her emotions about it all were so very difficult to understand and manage but no less real, though she supposed it was natural to want to celebrate life when faced with death.

Kelly was peculiarly silent through their love-making, but no less focused on her, on them, on the newfound power of their connection.

They found their release together, each succumbing on a long exhale; their faces tilted toward the stars. Both of them floating away in ecstasy and filled with honest joy; together experiencing the full potency of their bond.

The next morning, they felt a little bit more like themselves. Freddie understood that the best thing she could do for those people now was to pull herself together and move on. To see justice served, the men who did this hanged.

Kelly had a few more items to see to before they traveled into town, so they agreed to stay put for at least another day.

And even though she could see signs of Kelly's jaw once more beginning to soften, his lips once more twitching as if to gift her with his coveted smile, she knew that both of them were driven—more determined than ever to see the Society fall.

Chapter Thirty-Four

Several Days Later: The Golden Goddess, Blackpool

"A brothel, Kelly? Really?"

Ciarán turned and raised a brow. He was dressed in the full complement of clothing any gentleman about Town would don, having *acquired* them while she slept the night before.

He stepped into her space and dipped down to meet her eyes. "Afraid, Freddie?" he said.

She snorted and waved him away. "Of course, not. They are just women and men earning a living. I suppose I'm really not surprised, that's all. Only *you* would keep important papers in a bawdyhouse of all places."

Ciarán shrugged and stepped aside with a bow.

Freddie entered first, head high, Ciarán following in her wake.

Inside, the main room off the hall was a complete surprise. For all her worldly experience, she'd never been in a brothel like this; the whores she knew in Cheapside mostly plied their wares in the street or in rooms that barely qualified as such.

Dark and draped in silks and rich velvets of black and cream, the room was excessively opulent. Women and men crowded the main parlor, the equivalent of a large sitting room in a wealthier home. Some patrons settled close on low, velvet settees, and some nestled together in alcoves, and for the most part, no one paid the newcomers any mind.

The majority were far too...*preoccupied.*

From behind her, Ciarán said, "Regina here?" He touched a hand to her elbow, and Freddie straightened her spine, lest she unconsciously lean into him in front of everyone like a wide-eyed, green girl.

A red-headed woman, dressed in a gorgeous gown of dark green velvet, her arms draped over a young man's shoulders, jerked her head to the ceiling. "She's in her room."

"With a client?" Ciarán asked.

The woman chuckled. "Not today, but since when has that ever stopped you, Kelly?"

The last word ended on a moan as another man had come up behind the woman and skimmed his hands up her sides, then cupped her breasts before pinching her nipples through the rich fabric of her gown.

Freddie swallowed. *Well...*

Ciarán stroked the side of her arm and settled his palm at her waist. Frederica jumped.

"Fair enough," he admitted, and the innocent words raised the bumps on her arms.

Frederica reversed out of the room, and Ciarán watched her, a bemused look about his face, his hand gliding across her back as she passed. She halted at the bottom of the stairs, then stepped aside, gesturing up the flight with a wide sweep of her hand. "After you, Sir Fucks-A-Lot—"

Ciarán laughed as he passed and proceeded up the stairs, Frederica close on his heels. She'd only taken two steps before she glanced back to the woman in green being *devoured* by two men. The woman's mouth was open on a silent moan; her head tossed back in wild abandon. A man's head appeared from beneath the woman's skirts, and Frederica gasped. Make that *three* men. Holy *hell.* The woman lifted her head and met Frederica's eyes from across the room. A slow smile spread across her lips, and she leaned forward, licking the side of one man's neck, her eyes locked on Freddie.

Frederica jolted, then raced up the stairs, having frozen midstride.

When she reached the landing, Ciarán turned to her and cocked his head. "All right?"

Her face felt like it was on fire, but Freddie nodded and said, "Y-Yes," her own voice husky and a touch breathless. *It was the race up the stairs, truly.*

He ran his eyes down her body, and she felt it everywhere, like a caress.

His eyes flashed, and he said, "Good," his own voice a tad gruffer than was usual.

He turned and stalked up the hall, stopping before the second door on the left. He rapped twice and a very feminine voice called out, "Enter."

Ciarán disappeared into the room amidst squeals of delight and exclamations of "Kelly!"

Frederica turned the corner just as the woman, a young beautiful blonde wearing nothing but a sheer peignoir, pulled back from Ciarán. *Had they been kissing?* The woman tilted her head in Freddie's direction, looking Freddie up and down; then walking her fingers up Kelly's chest, she said, "Mmm...nice. Dare I hope she is here to join us?" The woman threw Freddie a sultry smile, her eyes flashing with definite interest.

Ciarán grabbed hold of the woman's hands and brought them together, placing a kiss on her knuckles. "Not today, Regina. I'm just here for my things."

Regina pouted, her carmine lips full and deliciously red. "Boo."

But she held out her hand, palm up, and Kelly fished out the key they'd procured out of some tree in the forest outside Blackpool—*long story*—and dropped it in her outstretched hand.

Regina danced away with a twirl and bent over an open trunk, taking the opportunity to wiggle her arse in the air, teasing them all with a sensual show while she rummaged about inside. She produced a second key with a delightful, "Aha!"

Meanwhile, Freddie stepped up beside Ciarán, though she was absolutely not marking her territory.

At least, not fiercely.

Regina unlocked the doors of a large bureau, then pulled a lever hidden beneath a hat box, which revealed a false floor. Using the key Ciarán had handed her, she hefted a box from inside, lifted the lid, and pulled out a stack of papers, a miniature—Freddie stood on her toes and strained to get a better look—a book—

And a gun, complete with all the sundries for producing ammunition and cleaning the silver-handled pistol. Regina handed everything, one at a time, to Ciarán, who put all but the gun in a sack. Just as he tucked the gun away in his pocket, the door opened, and the woman in green walked in.

"There are men here, looking for the pair of you; you need to hide. Come with me. They've been in town for weeks, so they're determined." The woman looked Freddie and Ciarán, both, up and down with unveiled interest. "You may have to stay overnight."

Freddie's body was onboard with the idea—there was so much to explore here. But her heart was not in it. She found she might like the idea of watching, but she abhorred the idea of *sharing*.

They travelled down the hall and into an unoccupied room, then passed through a secret door within another wardrobe. This place was full of secrets, but she supposed it was prudent to have them when one ran a bawdyhouse.

After a few twists and turns and more stairs, down this time, they entered into a room tucked away in some hidden corner of the house. For that matter, they might not even be in the same house anymore, for they were on foot for a good ten minutes before arriving here, and not traveling at a leisurely pace.

Once they were alone, Freddie collapsed into a red velvet chair in the corner. "Who is the woman in green?"

Ciarán, who was watching discretely out the room's lone window, said, "Rowena. She's the bawd; she owns this entire place." He gestured vaguely with his hand, while maintaining his outward vigil.

Eventually, he pulled back and leaned against the wall. "The women are here because they want to be. They embrace a woman's right to choose her partners with full acknowledgement that women are sensual creatures who seek pleasure without fear of recrimination, without feeling shamed for desiring sex with others. It's quite unique and very special."

He smiled. "No judgement on relationship arrangements either—men and men, men and women, women and women, and every combination therein is allowed, so long as all the members are not participating under duress."

Freddie was pleased with his attitude. A man with respect for women's autonomy was a rare and wonderful thing. She gestured to Ciarán's sack. "What's in there."

He stared at the sack for a moment, then turned back to Freddie. She read hesitation in his eyes.

Freddie crossed her arms and lifted her chin. Though he had every right to distrust her, she expected some concession for risking her neck to come after him.

For giving him her body.

Perhaps, she wasn't owed any concessions, considering, but that didn't stop her for wanting them anyway. She was in love with the man, after all.

Eventually, he said, "The important bit is the papers. I stole a section of pages out of one of their accounting books. It's a list of people who have donated to the organization this year, but it's in code."

"Is that the reason they tortured you?"

A muscle ticked in his jaw. "That was but a thin excuse for they only found about that *after*. In truth, it was because your father found out about me and ordered my execution. He knew I'd never truly betray the Crown."

Of course. "Did you know he was the man behind it all?"

Ciarán shook his head. "No. Not until the torture started."

She didn't want to think about him being tortured, so she quickly changed the subject. "Can I see the pages? I have a way with codes."

Once again, Ciarán turned wary. "This is important evidence, Freddie. I've taken an oath, a vow. I shouldn't."

Shouldn't wasn't couldn't. But she understood. Somewhat. She was convinced it was mainly because he felt he couldn't trust her. And she genuinely couldn't blame him for that, but the idea still stung.

And it didn't mean she couldn't see them. Later.

But she'd *prefer* to have his agreement on the matter.

Chapter Thirty-Five

Kelly needed to get her mind off the papers in his possession. She balled her hands into fists. "Kelly. I can help."

He dragged a hand down his face. He wanted to trust her. God, he did. But he'd be a fool to do so. And while he genuinely believed she wasn't involved in the Society; she clearly had a fierce loyalty to Owain, despite the man's machinations. For all he knew, she could be here on *his* orders. For all he knew, she could be planning to take his evidence back to Owain at the first opportunity.

Though none of that fit with the night of ecstasy they shared on the way here and the woman he was beginning to know once again.

Inside, his gut told him his excuses were thin.

Still, Kelly shook his head. "I'm sure you can, love. You're devilishly clever."

"Argh," she cried out in frustration. "Why won't you trust me?"

He raised a brow and regretted it, for the look on her face told him he'd hurt her. But he would never lie to her.

She threw her hands up. "It's not like me holding the papers while you stand there watching would do me any good."

Kelly laughed. "Ha! I've seen you take down a man much larger than you. Remember MacLeod? I'd be a fool to underestimate you."

Freddie's face turned red. "I'm not sure whether you're offering me a compliment or an insult."

Kelly held up his hands in supplication. "A compliment, for sure. Besides, haven't you made it clear you don't need protection?"

Freddie waved away his remark and stood to pace. "Look, if you can't crack the code, you should at least let me try."

That stung. He wasn't an idiot. "No."

She froze. "No?"

"No."

Now, he wasn't backing down. Besides, Stonebridge would have his balls if he let her have them, code or no code. Friend or no friend. Trustworthy or not.

But he had to admit; he liked her ire. And he had to work at keeping the grin off his face.

She opened her mouth to speak, and he swooped in to kiss her. As with every other time, their passion exploded on impact. He could not get enough of her, of her sweet mouth, of her fierce temper.

He backed her toward the bed, but before settling her upon it, he pulled back. They hadn't talked about their intimacy thus far. And passion on the road wasn't like the possibilities here. Now.

Now, they were in a comfortable room. With a bed.

She sat on said bed.

Kelly stood at the bed's side and asked. "Freddie, is this all right?"

She stood once more, while nodding her head. Straight away, she dug her fingers into the knot of his cravat, practically climbing his body and a surge of urgency flooded him, but he had to know. He put his hands on her arms and dipped his head, a question in his eyes.

She laughed. "I'm the one stripping you, you fool. Now, shut up and kiss me."

Kissing had its drawbacks. He was pretty sure she was making the knot in his cravat tighter. He lifted her, and she wrapped her legs around his waist, thereby removing the tension in the knot of his cravat. Whatever...he wasn't really complaining because it placed the hard ridge of his cock right where he wanted it.

After she slid the cravat from his neck, he tossed her on the bed.

She bounced once, then he reached for her, managing to divest her of her trousers within a matter of seconds.

After that, he gave her one look, a warning, but he needn't have bothered, for she spread her legs in invitation.

He hesitated a moment and advised, "Don't forget, we're being hunted—Don't. Scream," then, he dove right in, his tongue latching onto her already distended clitoris.

Her taste hit his tongue, and he moaned, "Ah, sweet ambrosia."

He savored her a moment, then made use of his thumb and added a finger, crooking it just so, making her practically leap off the bed in ecstasy. It was satisfying to know she was trying desperately not to shout.

He pulled away and blew on her mound. "Uh-uh. No screaming, love." Then, returned to his ministrations.

He slid his free hand up her side, gently pinched a nipple along the way, and cupped her, lightly, over her mouth. She chuckled softly and bit the side of his hand, using him to battle her urge to cry out.

His cock hardened painfully in his own too-tight trousers as she bit down. It was a marvelous kind of pain, and he groaned against her woman's mound, absolute pleasure flooding him. He wanted her, now, but he wanted her to come, first, knowing it would heighten her pleasure when he finally entered her.

He increased the pressure of his fingers and used bold strokes that matched the rhythm of his tongue against her clitoris, and before long she was flying, coating his fingers and tongue with her sweet dew, possibly drawing blood from his hand, but he cared not.

She was worth it.

He lapped until her whimpers subsided, and only when she was boneless and satisfied, did he shun his own trousers and join her on the bed. He gripped his cock in one hand and looked her way. She smiled, slowly, lazily, and nodded her head.

"Hold on, *mo ghrá*," he said, and she wrapped her legs around his waist as he buried himself to the hilt.

The feeling was greater than anything he'd ever known, and he was hesitant to move for he wanted it to last. But he was eager for her, for them, for riding toward his pleasure in the only woman he'd ever loved, which made every difference in the fucking world.

But he couldn't lie there forever, and he couldn't wait. So, he drew back his hips and thrust home once more, quickly establishing a rhythm, pistoning his hips with very little finesse but an overabundance of desire.

Then, she began to squeeze around his cock, and his eyes literally rolled back in his head. He whispered fiercely, "Jesus, Freddie—ah, love do that again. God, that's it. Christ, you're amazing."

Aye, he was a babbler, but he spoke the God's honest truth.

Before long, he was groaning uncontrollably, and when he came, "Oh, shit, I'm coming," it was with a force that took his breath away. For once, all he could do was moan as he rode out his orgasm, the potent pleasure having robbed him of his tongue and his wits.

Chapter Thirty-Six

Kelly woke to the best post-sex bliss he'd ever experienced in his life. It was the truth; she was going to kill him after all, but damn, he would die a very happy man every step of the way.

He was about to make known his contentment with an audible sigh, but his instincts kicked in and alerted him to the unnatural quiet of the room.

He held still and opened his eyes. What he saw, tore at his scarred heart.

Freddie was by the fire, reading the papers he had forbade her to see.

He rolled onto his side and propped up his head with one hand. "I see you've been searching through my things."

She jumped and placed a hand to her heart. "Jesus, Ciarán, you scared me."

He laughed, but he was not amused. "Ever the sign of a guilty conscience. I'm quite sure I made it perfectly clear yesterday—"

"Look!" she interrupted and shook the papers. "This code uses a special cipher. You need the key to unlock it."

He shrugged his free shoulder. "Aye, that's generally how these things work."

She shook her head. "I've seen these symbols before, especially this combination." She pointed to the paper, which he clearly couldn't see from across the room. "This one represents my father. Fifty thousand pounds! But even better. I know where to find the key."

Kelly sat up then and began pulling on his smalls in haste. He forgot his ire, his mind awash with possibilities. "Where?"

"My father's house in the country. It's on the way to London." She stood, then, and began repacking his sack.

He paused. "Who said anything about going to London?"

Freddie turned to him and gave him a speaking look.

All right, so even an imbecile could figure that one out. But still. She was being unreasonable with her presumptions. "Besides, I thought your father's estate was in Cornwall?"

He waved away his remark with one hand as she reached for more of his things. "Oh, my father has estates all over England. And the cipher isn't in Cornwall. It's near Luton."

Definitely on the way to London.

She glanced at the papers in her hand. "These are all statements of money coming into the organization. Do you have any with expenses? Your evidence would be stronger with both."

He shook his head, while he buttoned his trousers. "No."

She stood, already dressed, and settled her hands on her hips. "Well, we have no time to lose. We can search for bills and expenses in the abbey as well. If my father knows you stole from the society, he'd have moved everything under his own protection because he doesn't trust anyone."

Kelly paused in the buttoning of his waistcoat. "We?" He shook his head. "No. It's too dangerous."

She tossed him a frosty glare. "I could have left in the night. With the papers. While you snored away your post-coital bliss. And I could have gone to my father's house all on my own, and you never would have known."

He snorted. "I don't snore."

She lifted her chin and said, "And I didn't leave. I stayed."

Perhaps, she had a point. "Freddie—"

"Kelly. I can do this. I am capable."

Dammit, that wasn't the point. Not really.

She was capable.

He was the one who was afraid. Afraid *for* her.

"And you know what else?" she added as he knotted his cravat blindly in the early morning dark. "You absolutely do snore."

Maybe, he did.

But even more curious, was the fact she didn't mention the miniature in his sack. She must have seen it.

How did she feel when she saw her own likeness staring back at her?

Chapter Thirty-Seven

Four days later: Dawe Park, Luton, North of London

Dawe Park was a former abbey just outside of Luton, about thirty miles north west of London.

They'd arrived around 2:00 a.m.

They'd made it through a side entrance, around the cloister, picked a lock, and had gain entrance to her father's study fifteen minutes later. Easy.

Perhaps, too easy.

Frederica shook off the disconcerting thought and glanced about the room. The moon was full, and the drapes had been mistakenly left open, which allowed in enough light to make out the general layout of the room. It had been eight years since she'd last stood within these walls and nothing had changed. The same old dark walnut desk stood sentry in the center; the same old Persian rug covered the stones beneath her feet. The same stale smell, old cheroots and musty leather, hung heavy on the air.

And the same old tapestry hung on the far wall, framed on either side by two windows.

Only this time, she wasn't a naïve little princess in a make-believe world, and for once, as she eyed the shadows making up the familiar furnishings and well-remembered wall-hanging, she could honestly say, "Thank God for tradition."

While Ciarán quietly tried to coax enough flame from the banked coals in the fireplace to light a candle, Frederica marched her way across the room, stopping before the ancient tapestry.

The threads were dyed in jeweled tones of blue, red, green, and gold, and were expertly woven together to form a large English oak, *of course*. Throughout its branches random, everyday items—an apple, a knife, an orange, a feather, and many, many more—were embroidered with care. As a child, she'd spent hours hunting for new objects to find amidst the branches and leaves.

And woven into the design of each object were symbols, like runes, one for each.

Clearly, those symbols could be used as a cipher.

The tapestry was large enough to make a statement in the room, creative enough to capture the imagination of a young girl, and most importantly, small enough to transport if necessary.

It was absolutely necessary.

She pulled the tapestry down and folded it neatly, then stuffed it in her sack with absolutely zero ceremony.

She turned to find Ciarán standing over her father's desk, a lit taper in his hand.

He ripped a handful of pages from a book and held them up. "Expenses." He stuffed them in his sack with equal ceremony—none—closed the book, and turned to leave, but suddenly, he froze and picked up a piece of parchment from the desktop.

"What is it?" she asked.

"Your father is hosting a masquerade. To be held in Cornwall. In four days." As she crossed the room to join him, he picked up another sheet. He held it up. "Look. This is a guest list. It's a Society event; they've used parchment inscribed with the Society's seal, here. The English oak with the S and P intertwined."

She scanned the list of coded names and recognized two, one other besides her father, and she swallowed. "S-Should we make a copy of the list?"

Seemingly lost in thought, Kelly didn't answer.

She knew instantly what he wasn't saying, and prompted him with, "They'll all be there. Under one roof."

He picked up the thought, smiling at her. "We could end this. All of it. All at once."

A door slammed from somewhere further down the hall, and she jumped. Together, they glanced at each other and said, "We should go." Definitely no time for copying a list.

Ciarán extinguished his flame, and they fled to the door. He cracked it, just, and paused to listen.

A female said, "Lady Dawe would like some heated milk."

Another replied, "Yes, ma'am."

Servants. And...her mother was here?

Ciarán jerked her from her thoughts, whispering, "Everything is clear. Let's go."

Freddie stepped out into the hall and hesitated.

She hadn't seen her mother in seven years. *Mama...*

Ciarán suddenly appeared before her, concern marring his brow. "Freddie, what is it?"

She looked at him; he appeared somewhat blurry from the tears threatening. "My mother, she's *here*. She's—"

Ciarán shook his head. "We cannot."

But Freddie resisted. "But I haven't seen her—"

Ciarán cupped her face in his hands; his eyes filled with compassion. "I know, *a chuisle mo chroí*. But it's too dangerous."

"But—"

Ciarán whispered fiercely, "You shall see her again, love. I vow it. But we have to go. *Now*."

And on that promise, she reluctantly allowed him to drag her away.

Freddie looked over her shoulder as she hurried out the door, *Soon, mama, soon.*

LORD DAWE STEPPED OUT OF THE SHADOWS OF THE EAST-SIDE cloister and rubbed his hands with glee, watching the traitorous pair leave while he waited for his son, who approached from behind, having hidden himself in the priest hole behind Dawe's desk, while Dawe's traitorous daughter plotted against them all, the bitch!

"Did they take the bait?" Dawe spat out.

Duncan replied, "They did." Though far too calmly for Dawe's liking.

He spun around and faced his son. "And the tapestry?"

Duncan dipped his head. "They have that, too."

He reached for Duncan's jacket. "The list? What about the list?"

Duncan brushed his hand away. "They looked it over it but left it behind."

Lord Dawe rubbed at his oiled beard. "Hmm. Anything else?"

Duncan looked him straight in the eye. "No."

Lord Dawe smiled then. "Good. They're as good as dead." His only regret was that he wouldn't be there to witness their executions first-hand. As an afterthought, he added, "Make sure you have Lord Faulkes draw up a Writ of Execution for the pair of them. I want to frame both documents and hang them in my study. Over the mantle will do."

Duncan said nothing, simply bowed and marched away.

No matter. The wretched whelp wouldn't dare double-cross his own father.

Chapter Thirty-Eight

The Yellow Goose, Just Outside London

They'd been racing at breakneck speed for weeks now, with only the stops in Blackpool and Luton offering any sort of respite. So, rather than carry on to London in the wee hours of the morning and unnecessarily waking everyone up, they chose to find accommodation just outside of London and ride into the city at a more reasonable hour later that morning.

Kelly stood in the stables, seeing to their horses, finding the familiar motions of seeing to his horse soothing for his unsettled mind.

He thought of Freddie and smiled. Possibly, they needn't leave until later in the afternoon. Mayhap, even early evening? The masquerade wasn't for four more days. A few hours in bed couldn't hurt...

Kelly shook off that train of thought lest he find himself grooming the horse while sporting a cock stand, a decidedly uncomfortable prospect.

The horse whinnied as if in agreement and telling him to get on with the grooming, and Kelly laughed.

Yet despite the promise of the untold delights that awaited him upstairs, a small churning in his gut left Kelly feeling distinctly unsettled.

Everything just seemed to be coming together far too easily. He shouldn't complain; they finally had the break they needed after years of investigations.

But had it been too effortless? The end promising to be conveniently wrapped up in one main event?

What if it was all a trap? He'd be a fool not to consider that possibility.

An hour later, with nothing more concrete than his suspicious mind, Kelly entered their shared chamber to find Freddie furiously scribbling away at the room's lone table, translating the accounting pages using the cipher on the odd tapestry she'd swiped from her father's office. The warning in his gut tightened further. Wouldn't her father notice the missing piece? And how soon?

Kelly began removing his jacket. "How are the translations going?"

"Mmm," was her indistinct reply.

He chuckled and took her response as a positive.

After hanging his coat on a peg in the wall, he approached Freddie and glanced over her shoulder. The names she had written weren't all that surprising. Middlebury, twenty thousand. Fulton, five thousand. And so on, and so on. So far, she'd written about ten names. Mostly men of the aristocracy whose political leanings were notoriously anti-immigration.

He watched as she hesitated a minute, then scrawled out 'Viscount Sharpe.' She paused with her quill in mid-air, halfway to the ink pot. She did not face him as she said, "Viscount Sharpe was on the guest list for the masquerade; his response was *yes*." Then, she plunged the quill in ink and carried on with her translations.

Viscount Sharpe. Spyder. Puppet Master. Owain. All one in the same. And a complicated situation for Freddie.

For them both.

He rested his hands on her shoulders and squeezed, then returned to the bed and began removing his boots.

The road from here on out would be fraught with danger. Worse, her loyalty was sure to be tested. Was she ready?

Was he?

And did it really matter? Because the truth was, he knew precisely what he needed to do.

Twenty minutes later, Freddie crawled into bed with him, finished with her work. She settled into his arms without hesitation and with what sounded like a long sigh of relief. He echoed the sentiment.

Though after a few moments of gliding her fingers gently through the hairs on his chest, she spoke softly, "I'll be all right, Ciarán. I'm not afraid. I can take care of myself."

He kissed her on the forehead and said, "I know, *mo ghrá*. But you must know; I'll always do what I have to do to protect you." He didn't want her anywhere near these people.

She glanced up and replied, "I don't need your protection. I need your support."

This time, when they made love, it was slow and thorough, though with no less passion. And no less intensity.

After, they embraced for long moments. They just laid there, together, joined—she fit so perfectly in his arms.

"Will you forgive me for not getting back to you in time? For not—for not finding you in St. Giles. For not *knowing*…"

Frederica sat up. "You ridiculous man. There's nothing to forgive, you *didn't* know…"

He squeezed her harder and kissed the side of her head, "Ah, Freddie, we've lost so much time."

She swallowed and pulled back, looking at him earnestly. A touch of uncertainty could be heard in her voice as she said, "Will you forgive me for hiding Finn?"

He pulled her close and touched his forehead to hers. "Aye, love, I already have. I wouldn't be here, otherwise."

God, he loved her. He did. He loved her and Finn more than anything in this world. He wanted them safe. Both of them. And for them to all be together, as a family.

And while his thirst for her was as high as it ever was, he knew that in all likelihood, this was good-bye, and he was already filled with regret.

For he knew what he had to do, and just precisely how much she would hate it.

But he'd rather her live and hate him, than die beside him.

He wouldn't survive mourning her again.

To suppress such maudlin thoughts, he directed their conversation to better things. "Tell me about my son. Not the kind of things I can ask him, for surely, I will. Tell me what I've missed..."

Chapter Thirty-Nine

When Frederica woke, she stretched the length of the bed, wiggled her toes for good measure, and immediately recognized two things before she'd even fully opened her eyes.

One. It was far later in the day than it should be based on the feel of the sun caressing her cheek.

And two. Ciarán Kelly was gone.

She fought back the instant lump in her throat that stretched the muscles in her neck as she lifted her head and glanced about the room, confirming her suspicions. She looked to the table. Her translations were gone. As was the tapestry.

She checked the peg by the door and swallowed hard.

All of his things had vanished.

She threw her head back and punched the pillow next to her, hating that near overwhelming feeling of sorrow. She'd vowed a dozen times she'd never allow herself to feel that level of grief again.

But she'd never imagined falling in love with Kelly once more, damn his silver eyes.

She reached for his pillow, intending to toss it across the room in added relief, forcing herself to pull on her anger and suppress her sorrow. But rather than feel soft linen beneath her fist, her hand landed on something else. She rolled over and discovered a flower and a note.

She rolled her eyes and mumbled, "What level of masculine shite is he going to explain to me now?"

As she began unfolding the missive, she mimicked in her best Irish accent, deepened for affect, "It's for your own protection, *mo ghrá*. I will always do what I have to protect you."

Snort.

She jerked the note the rest of the way open, calling out, "What about what I want, Kelly? What if I want you to do what *I* think is best for *me*, Kelly? Ever think about that?" then, read:

A chuisle mo chroi,

Probably means, 'love of my heart who must obey,' in Irish. Old masculine proverb. *Snort.*

I know you're angry. I can imagine how you must be cursing my name.

No shite. Give the man a cheroot.

I am sorry.

Not sorry enough and not as sorry as you will be.

I wish there was another way.

There are five thousand other ways. All would be better than this, you imbecile.

Please, return to our son.

Our son is safer than you will be in a few hours. And don't tell me what to do. As if I'm going to just sit back and wait while the love of my life faces pure evil.

I will join you in Wales when this is over, and our family is safe.

Ha!

Love,

— KELLY

Frederica crumbled his letter and tossed it at the fireplace. She missed, but hardly cared. Were all men this idiotic? Did he truly believe she was just going to run back to Wales and wait for him there? Should she start some useless embroidery project? A sampler of swords and idiotic men with their balls chopped off?

Did he even understand her at all?

Well. He was about to learn a thing or two. About women. About her. About what it meant that she would choose him over Owain.

She climbed out of bed, searching for her clothes, and as she shoved her legs into her trousers, grumbled, "Kelly better hope he is a fast learner, all evidence to the contrary, because here I come."

Frederica grabbed her sack, threw open the door, and came face to face with her brother, Duncan, his hand poised to knock.

She stepped back once, twice; her hand flew to her neck. "Duncan."

He caught her before she backed into the bed.

And pulled her into a warm embrace. Then, almost immediately stepped back and met her eyes. "God, let me look at you, Monkey. Jesus, it's so good to see you." He had tears in his eyes, and he looked careworn, the first she'd ever seen him that way. "I had no idea. No idea father was capable of such cruelty. I've learned a lot since I found your locket."

He let go with one hand and reached into his pocket. "Here."

Once more ,she swallowed a lump the size of a boulder as he handed her the treasured keepsake. She found herself uncharacteristically mute.

"Freddie, we must talk."

She blurted, "How did you find me?"

"I was watching for you. Father doesn't know you're here. He thinks I'm just following Kelly."

"Kelly's not here," she grumbled.

"I know. It's you I want to speak with." He tossed her a wry grin. "I didn't trust Kelly not to shoot first and ask questions later."

She snorted. "He's more of a lover," *or leaver*, "than a fighter." *Maybe.*

Her brother shook his head. "I wasn't willing to take that chance. Not where you're involved." He dragged a hand through his hair. "You look wonderful by the way. Mother is going to be overjoyed. It's been deuced difficult not to tell her. She still mourns you. Sometimes, I wonder, though, if she knows in her heart you're alive, but I daren't suggest it."

"God, I miss her. I almost went to her at the abbey..."

"Good thing you didn't. Father was there, hiding."

"What do you mean? Tell me."

"You must know...the masquerade is a trap. Well, the masquerade is real, but the location isn't. The party is in Luton, at the abbey. You were meant to find the information, and while we were all here, toasting to the Society's murderous, blind success, you lot would be on your way to Cornwall, walking into a trap. Accident and demise on the way. Brigands. Dumped in the sea. Never to be seen or heard from again."

"Jesus, Duncan. What about O—Viscount Sharpe?"

Her brother laughed. "We have special plans for him; I wasn't quite sure how to work that one out. Yet." He looked back at her. "Sorry, monkey. I had to be convincing. Father is always so damn suspicious. He doesn't trust anyone, not even me 100%. And his mind is, fracturing. He's mad with power and abuse. He kept me in the dark for so long, and I felt like such a Goddamn fool when I learned the truth. By the by, what happened to Lord Fulton?"

"Who is Lord Fulton?"

"A nasty piece of work and one of Father's best henchman who likes to pretend he's a gentleman, but he's only one by title. Has a brother named Johnnie we long suspected was abused but could never prove. Johnnie's been missing."

"Ah, Little Dick."

They shared a laugh.

"Little Dick?" he asked.

"Oh, we had a run in in Runcorn. I put him in his place; it's what I call him. He caught up to us in Wales, unfortunately for him. He's sitting away in Viscount Sharpe's oubliette at the moment, contemplating his small dick, probably. And Johnnie now works for me."

The relief on Duncan's face was evident. "Were you there, at Viscount Sharpe's place, watching us in Runcorn?"

She nodded. "I was. I'm sorry—I couldn't be sure you weren't involved—"

Once again, he pulled her into a warm embrace. "I knew it. Somehow, I knew. And I understand why you couldn't. In fact, it was right you remained hidden—what a mess that would have been. As it was, I couldn't mask my feelings fast enough, and Little Dick was suspicious ever since. But I knew he didn't stand a chance with Kelly there. That man would do anything for you."

She pulled away. "Let's get one thing quite clear. Little Dick didn't stand a chance because *I* was there."

"My apologies." He smiled, and he lifted her chin with his knuckle. "You really are quite remarkable, Monkey girl. I look forward to hearing everything." He gave her one more hug, then added, "I wish I could stay, but if I don't report to father soon, he'll become suspicious. Well, more suspicious. I hope to God this is over soon."

She settled a hand on his arm; her throat clogged with emotion. "Good luck. And thank you."

He rested a hand over hers and gave it a squeeze. "Godspeed. I love you, Monkey."

"I love you, too, Beanpole." It's what she used to call him when he was a teenager.

And it was true. She did love him.

The only real question was...could she trust him?

Chapter Forty

Stonebridge House, London

Kelly strode across the threshold into Stonebridge's study, assertively faking his confidence with every step he took, but from within, he was nervous at best and prepared for the worst. He expected mixed reactions at the very least.

He forced a smile and slammed shut the guilt that prodded his brain for leaving Freddie behind as he did. Then, he cleared his throat and proclaimed, "Well, gentlemen, I am proud to announce; I'm a father."

Well, he didn't have to fake *that*; he was damn proud to be a father.

The men burst out laughing, which was...good?

Maybe not. For they continued laughing. And laughing.

Kelly frowned. "I'm serious."

"Of course, you are," said Dansbury. MacLeod, as usual, said nothing.

Kelly growled. "I'll have you know; I have no bastards. I've invested heavily in condom manufacturing and research into making condoms safer and more effective. *And* more readily available to the less fortunate. Always play it safe, is my motto."

Kelly winced inside, *though, perhaps, not with Freddie.*

Stonebridge stood up from his desk and met him half-way.

Without warning, the man gave him a hug. "Well, done. Good to see you safe and well. Where is the little mini-Ciarán?"

Kelly cleared his throat, though finding the lengthy embrace oddly satisfying, "He's in Wales. You'll meet him eventually."

Kelly pulled back and looked his friend over. "It seems married life is treating you well."

He meant it. Before Grace, Stonebridge would never have embraced him at all, much less in front of the other men and with so much genuine emotion.

Kelly turned to Dansbury, who'd approached with one hand outstretched. They shook, and Dansbury said, "Welcome back."

Lady Beatryce stepped forward and reintroduced herself, to which he kissed her hand and replied, "Not Mrs. Churchmouse, then?" For the last time he'd seen her, she and Dansbury were at odds, on the run from assassins, and undercover as Mr. and Mrs. Churchmouse.

She smiled, then glanced to Dansbury. "Only on Tuesdays."

Like last time, the chemistry between those two fairly singed anyone standing in the nearby vicinity, and he immediately thought back to Freddie, abed at the Yellow Goose, and wanted nothing more than to return to her and beg her forgiveness. He clenched his fists, forcing himself not to rub at the ache stabbing him in his chest. He was happy for Dansbury, honestly.

MacLeod hung back, which was an improvement over a fist to the jaw or being tossed across the room, like last time, but his animosity was obvious.

Kelly nodded to the overly-large, giant of a man. "MacLeod."

MacLeod grunted in return and folded his arms. Kelly knew MacLeod would take time, but the thought didn't make it easier to swallow. He'd risked his life for—they'd been—

He cut off that train of thought; that way led to resentment. His relationship with MacLeod had always been different; they would work it out in the end. Once the giant forgave him his part in Amelia Chase's—he hesitated to use the word abduction—more like, extended stay in his carriage against her preferences, earlier in the year.

Besides, she'd handily punished him for his transgressions herself. In more than one way.

Stonebridge broke the strained silence. "We've been anxiously awaiting your arrival, I daresay. Ready to enlighten us? MacLeod," the duke nodded in the Scot's direction, "says you were to Wales, while not precisely under your own free will, but nonetheless, unconcerned about your ability to make it here in a month's time with evidence against the Society. And here you are, precisely on schedule."

Kelly flashed MacLeod a smile. "Glad you figured out my message. 'Twasn't exactly easy to come up with a coded message with any resemblance of sense under the circumstances."

MacLeod nodded but said nothing.

Kelly opened his traveling sack and pulled out the transcription Freddie had written out, the accounting pages, and the tapestry. He fingered the frayed edges of the embroidery, and once again, his mind, returned to Freddie. She'd risked it all for this. Everything. He clenched the fabric in his hand as is heart cracked wide open. He'd left her behind after she'd trusted him. She forgave him their long drawn-out past, whether or not there was anything to forgive. She never would have made love to him if she hadn't. His own betrayal turned on him, cutting him like a knife, but on the heels of that thought was the realization that he was in love with her. Desperately. He'd never stopped.

And he loved their son, Fionnán...hoped for a future he'd long since resigned to never find...a happy one, with both of them in it.

And yet, he may have ruined everything with his idiotic blindness to her needs and desires. His Neanderthal need to protect her. She'd said it more than once—hell, even Owain had said it—she didn't need his protection. She needed his support!

Kelly sucked in a breath and swallowed a curse. He needed to return to her. To grovel. But first—

He carded a hand through his hair and turned to Stonebridge. After clearing his throat, he said, "The entire ordeal is a significant and oftentimes unbelievable set of circumstances, which I will offer in a full debriefing later, but for now, the most important information is here. I have both credit and debit accounting pages from the Society, detailing the payments from various members of the aristocracy as well as several businessmen with fortunes at their availability. It's all laid out here, in the papers before you. But most importantly, I have learned that the leader of the Society, Lord Dawe, is holding a Society event, a masquerade, at his home in Cornwall in four days."

The men in the room and Lady Beatryce shifted, all looking to each other. This was news, indeed. Kelly pointed to the list of men with large donations to the Society. "While I can't verify the exact guest list, I do know that the majority of these men, if not all, will be in attendance. It's an opportunity on which we should capitalize."

"Indeed," replied the duke.

Kelly added, "Men initiated into the Society proper all bear a certain tattoo; the location varies by person. I've seen it and can readily identify the symbol."

Dansbury snorted. "Those imbeciles." Then, he glanced to Lady Beatryce. "Don't say it." Though there was no heat behind his remark.

Kelly couldn't help but wink and add, "Well, I for one, would love to hear it."

Dansbury snorted. "Don't get her started. She already knows she's superior to every single one of us."

Lady Beatryce laughed and patted her husband's cheek, "My dear, you are learning."

The two shared a look. Kelly sighed. "Good Lord, still in desperate need of that room, I see."

Dansbury never took his eyes from his woman and growled, "We have one. Right upstairs."

Stonebridge laughed, the change in him was really quite remarkable, "Later. Kelly. What do you know of this place in Cornwall?"

"I know it, though my information is about seven years out of date."

Stonebridge rubbed at his jaw. "Hmm. Risky. We could send a team to—"

Kelly shook his head. "We don't have time; we have to act now."

Stonebridge hesitated. "The confusion of the masquerade will be both a help and a hindrance. What we need—"

Suddenly, a new voice, a woman's confident and wise tones, entered into the conversation, "What you need is someone who knows the place."

The men turned in unison to see Lady Harriett Ross, Aunt Harriett to them all, cross the threshold to the duke's study; She was aunt in reality to Dansbury and called aunt as a signal of her familiar relationship by everyone else in the room.

Kelly replied with entirely too much cheek, ready to embrace the old dragon. "I know someone, but she's not an option." He offered up quick prayer: *Yet.*

The rest of the men groaned, and it was MacLeod who grumbled, "Och, of course, it's a woman."

Aunt Harriett marched straight over to Kelly, a fierce look in her eye, swatted away his outstretched arms, and from out of nowhere, brought out her umbrella and popped him upside the head with it. "Lucky for you, I stumbled upon the perfect *someone* for this occasion right out in the hall, you magnificent imbecile!"

The men around him winced in commiseration, all having felt the wrath of the Aunt Harriett's umbrella.

Lady Beatryce laughed.

Aunt Harriett argued, "But whose fault is it?" referring to his earlier remark about knowing someone who wasn't here.

But then all of the sudden, Freddie walked in, her eyes locked on his, and he nearly fell to his knees before her. "*His* fault," she said and nodded at him, "And *I* do. Know someone, that is. And it's odd to hear Kelly begging you all to act. The man never did have a sense of urgency about him, even a knock on the head didn't change that."

Kelly closed the distance between them in three strides. He wanted to hug her, but fear quickly replaced happiness, and instead, he grabbed her by the arm and marched her out of the room, never mind his earlier realizations. Yes, he loved her. Yes, he wanted to support her. But fear was a powerful deterrent to acting on those ideals.

Aunt Harriett called out, "Don't mess it up, Irish," then, "Do you need my umbrella, Frederica, dear?"

"No, ma'am" she called back. "I've got this."

Chapter Forty-One

They weren't five steps out into the hall, before Freddie shook off Kelly's grip. He didn't hesitate to release her, a point in his favor.

She rounded on him and backed him toward the wall, her finger poking him in the chest and punctuating her words. "The only reason I didn't punch you in the face in front of all those people is because I know how much you hold them in high regard. But if you ever think to leave me behind or manhandle me in that way again, I shall not be held responsible for my actions."

Kelly continued walking backward until he slammed against the wall. He appeared taken aback. *Good.* She would use the element of surprise to her advantage. This was serious. Though she had to work, and it wasn't easy, at not laughing when she glanced above his head and noticed that the pattern of the silk wallcovering behind him made it appear as if horns were sprouting out of his head.

She shook away the image and focused on his eyes, while stifling a smile. This was serious.

Kelly held up his hands. "Freddie—"

She brought her finger back up. "Don't. You will listen to me now.

No more charming smiles, or sugar-coated words. No more winks or passionate kisses. Definitely no kisses."

Surprisingly, he didn't reply with some sort of quip, like, 'Oh you find my smiles charming.' Instead, he dragged a hand down his face but nodded once; the fear and emotion in his eyes, which held no trace of true anger, was the only thing preventing her from punching him in the face anyway, now that they were semi-alone.

She rested her hands on her hips. "Were you listening when I told you about my time in St. Giles?"

Kelly nodded, but smartly, remained silent. It seemed one could teach an old man new tricks.

Once again, she held up a finger. "I'm serious, Kelly. Listen and understand. I don't need your protection or protecting, though I appreciate your desire to do so. Somewhat. It's endearing. Kind of." She shook her head, maybe she shouldn't reward him with too much honesty. "What I need is your support. Don't you understand? Even Owain understood that, in his own way. Eventually."

Kelly had the good grace to wince. And the good sense to remain silent.

She continued, "Everything I have been through has led me here. To this moment. All of it has made me who I am today, a woman I admire. A woman who is no longer helpless. A woman who—"

She cut off what she was about to say, a woman who loved him, for fear that he would dig in his heels and do everything, including lock her away, to prevent her participation in their take down of the Society. It would kill her should he go to such lengths.

It would kill *them*.

Kelly finally smiled, then shook his head. When she would speak, he wrapped her in his arms and whispered, "Ah, *mo ghrá*, you are remarkable. Do you know that? But don't ask me to like it." He twisted his lips then. "Well, actually, I do like it, a lot. But—oh, hell, it's all so perverted."

While they weren't precisely the words she would prefer to hear, for now, they would do. She pulled back, and added, "And Kelly, don't ever think to leave me behind like that again, do you hear? I mean it.

We have to have trust and forgiveness, or we have nothing," She was being awfully presumptuous, assuming a future with him, but they could deal with that later, "And if you do ever leave me behind *for my own good* ever again, I will cut off your balls and feed them to General Llwyd with a side of root vegetables and a fine Irish stout." She glanced down. "I may still consider it; we already have one child."

Kelly smiled then. "General Llwyd would never. He loves me too much."

He wasn't the only one.

From inside Stonebridge's study, everyone started laughing, but above the chuckles and guffaws, they heard Aunt Harriett and Lady Beatryce shout out, "Huzzah!" in unison.

To Kelly, she added. "Now, let's go back in there and make a plan to capture those bastards once and for all."

KELLY FOLLOWED BEHIND FREDDIE, WATCHING WITH PRIDE AS THE woman he loved reentered the duke's study, her head held high and saying, "We have a change of plans, Ladies and Gentlemen. Thanks to inside information from my brother, who is working to help us, we know that Cornwall is a trap. The masquerade will be at the Abbey in Luton—"

The men shifted once more, "Christ," said someone.

"An abbey...," grumbled another.

The women smiled; their eyes sparkling with pleasure, presumably at Freddie's confidence and knowledge.

"Indeed," Freddie added, "but this one is small by comparison to the usual abbey."

MacLeod snorted.

Kelly couldn't blame him. Truth was, small was a relative term; abbeys were notoriously large. "How did you come about this information again?" He hadn't been paying attention, lost in thought as he was.

She spun around. "My brother. Duncan."

Kelly crossed his arms. "And you trust him? We saw the papers with the information for the masquerade with our own eyes."

She nodded. "We did, but did you ever stop and wonder if it had all happened a little too easily?"

She had him there. He had. He dipped his head. "True enough."

"We were meant to find those papers. Fortunately, you have me," Freddie rested her hands on her hips and walked a circle, eyeing each of the men in turn. "That's right. Had you not had me around, you all would have been walking into a trap. Rather than grumbling about the size of the abbey, what you should be saying is 'Why thank you, Freddie, you saved our lives...'" She said the last in her best imitation Irish accent.

Kelly *pfft*ed. "I don't sound like that."

Freddie whirled around once more. "I beg to differ."

And everyone laughed at that, including himself, despite hearing several 'You certainly do's.'

Kelly crossed the room, to stand beside his woman. At the same time, MacLeod approached.

Freddie spoke before the Scot said a word. "Sorry for hitting you over the head, MacLeod."

MacLeod was surprised. "That was you?" and he laughed, which was a unique surprise. "Och, weel, if I was ye facing me, I'd have done the same, aye?"

MacLeod turned to Kelly. "You."

Kelly nodded. "Me."

MacLeod held out a hand. Kelly accepted it and said, "I'm sorry, too. For Amelia. I would never have let her be harmed. I just—" What more could he say, truthfully. He'd been desperate.

MacLeod's smile froze, and for a moment, everyone seemed to collectively hold their breath, then MacLeod nodded and said, "Aye. Apologies accepted. But you'd best apologize to ma Amelia, no?"

Kelly nodded. "Of course."

MacLeod continued to grip his hand, tightly. "You on both your knees, begging, wouldn't go amiss, aye?"

Kelly nodded again. "Sure, MacLeod, sure."

Then, MacLeod pulled Kelly in close, and the Scot's voice dropped to a whisper. "And if you ever do that again, I will kill you, no questions asked. You hear me?"

Kelly laughed. "You can try, old friend. You can try. Though, if I ever get it in my head to do such again, I'll hand you the gun myself."

MacLeod laughed then, stunning them all. "Deal."

Chapter Forty-Two

Four Days Later: The Masquerade at Dawe Park, Luton: Part One

Lord Dawe paced around his study, every so often pausing to glare at the space where the family tapestry used to hang. He'd hardly taken a moment to greet his guests, rude to be sure, but he couldn't contain himself. He was that anxious to hear word of Ciaran Kelly's demise.

And Frederica's, the traitorous wench.

Lord Dawe dabbed at the spittle that flew from his lips, then blotted away the sweat beading on his brow.

He might not even receive word tonight, depending on where his men had planned their ambush, but that mattered not. He was staying put until he had word; he didn't want to miss it.

Lord Dawe stopped to stare at the painting of his father, which hung over the mantle of the hearth—soon to be replaced with the proclamations proclaiming Kelly and Frederica's order of execution!

He felt the urge to laugh out loud in triumph but stopped himself from celebrating prematurely. Anything could happen, incompetent fools, the lot of them.

Instead, he said, "I did it Father. With this, I'll have won. After

Kelly and Stonebridge, no one will take us down. Our power will be absolute!"

He raised a fist to the air in triumph.

Then, froze. "What's that you say? The Welsh? Oh, never fear. They'll be next. And those filthy Scots. We'll have them all at our mercy; then, out of our country."

A knock sounded and Lord Dawe spun towards the door. "Enter!"

Several of his men entered, grimy and dirty from a hard ride, hats in hand.

"Well—are they dead?"

One man stood forward, twisting his hat in his hands. "We 'avenna seen them, Lord D. We don't think they took the bait."

"What!?" Lord Dawe felt as if his head were going to explode. "Duncan!" he shouted. "Where's my son? Duncan! Get him in here."

A moment later, his worthless son walked in the door, calm as you please, not a single sense of the urgency of the situation about him.

"Where is Stonebridge? You told me Kelly took the bait...so, where are they? Kelly should be dead by now, along with that bitch. I refuse to say her name. Well?"

Duncan steepled his fingers. "I'll look into the matter."

Lord Duncan reached for a brass globe on his desk and threw it at his worthless progeny. "You'd better look into it! Make haste! Round up as many men as you can! They might be here!"

Chapter Forty-Three

The Masquerade: Part Two, Lady Beatryce

They'd needed to commandeer quite a few men to even attempt to pull off what was going to amount to the largest take down of criminal activity ever seen in English history, or at least, according to Frederica Glyndŵr's mind, the largest. It took an ingenious plan to get everyone here and in position without tipping off the villains too soon. Frederica momentarily wondered how long it would be before the villains realized they weren't on the road to Cornwall and hoped it was not too soon.

The abbey was a massive dwelling with numerous exit points, not counting the hidden escape tunnels, the servants bustling about, the shadowed alcoves, and not to mention the numerous guests in attendance, the majority of which were guilty to some extent, some more than others, clearly, quite all right with murder and torture.

They had eight portable gaols surrounding the place.

Dozens upon dozens of men, many ex-military, who were in want of work now that the war with France was winding down.

And a sizeable cache of weapons, just in case.

They set up camp in the woods surrounding Dawe Park Abbey, watching and waiting until even the fashionably late had arrived.

As they waited, the Duke of Stonebridge, Ciarán Kelly, and their respective teams were stationed north, covering the main entrance. MacLeod was to the west. Dansbury to the east. And Lady Beatryce and Frederica held steady in the woods to the south.

Dansbury and his team were responsible for ensuring nobody hovered in the unused rooms within the Abbey itself, and that everyone, particularly the 'bigger fish,' were accounted for as the more high-profile guests were taken. Kelly was responsible for Viscount Sharpe, which was an uncomfortable non-conversation between the pair of them, to be sure. Many things were left unspoken on that subject.

MacLeod and his team were responsible for capturing anyone trying to escape outside through more nontraditional routes, once the other teams were in position inside.

Freddie's brother and mother were somewhere inside; her brother doing his best to keep an eye on the major players, while keeping their mother safe.

No one was talking about Owain's part in all this, and she was unsettled at the thought of his presence here.

At precisely 11:24 p.m., they received the signal. Lady Beatryce and Freddie glanced at each other and donned their masks. It was still odd seeing Lady Beatryce with her hair darkened, but her icy blonde was too infamous for her not to attempt to disguise it.

And it was odder still, for Freddie to look down and see her own breasts, pushed high with a corset and showing to advantage with a low-cut gown. She'd not worn a dress in quite some time.

And so, too, had Freddie darkened her own red tresses, for though she may not know many members of the ton, her family would recognize her on the spot, red wasn't a common enough hair color.

"Good luck," said Freddie.

"Luck is a sentiment for the unprepared. I prefer Good Skill. Or Happy Hunting," replied Lady Beatyrce.

Now, *that* was a thought Freddie could get behind. Freddie dipped her head. "Happy Hunting, Lady Beatryce. Ready?"

Lady Bea nodded. "After you."

Bea signaled to the men gathered around, and everyone fanned out, Frederica guiding Lady Beatryce to the closest, rear entrance to where the main gathering could be found. Their goal was to seek out one of the principle architects of the Society, Lord Middlebury.

The duke had wanted to capture that one personally, they had a past, but Lady Beatryce argued for the pleasure, for she and Middlebury had a past, too, and the duke consented. Besides, the duke needed to locate her father, and Freddie needed to avoid running into the man herself, even in costume, if at all possible, until the time was right. Thus, their plan was sound.

Freddie and Lady Beatryce darted beneath soaring flying buttresses and entered through a pointed archway. The door, well-oiled, opened soundlessly, courtesy of her brother, Duncan.

Freddie peeked through and was relieved to find the way clear. She darted through the doorway, and she and Lady Bea began walking the length of the short hall as if they had every reason to be there, chatting about the recent weather and the local gossip making the rounds, which they completely made up for neither one of them had been up on the latest *on dits* in recent months.

They stepped outside once again into the cloister surrounding the central garden and began making their way to what was originally the main church, presumably the main location of tonight's festivities. Even from this distance, they could hear the musicians playing the recognizable strains of a well-known waltz.

Frederica's laughter trilled tightly, influenced by her anxiety, which ratcheted up a notch or three as they passed the old chapter-house, which was now her father's study. Two stern looking men stood sentry outside the familiar black door, and Frederica had a difficult time carrying on her charade with Lady Beatryce, who gave Freddie's arm a comforting, much-appreciated, squeeze in response.

When they entered the nave through a side door without any alarms being raised, Frederica finally breathed a sigh of relief.

But only for a moment.

Before her, hundreds of gaily dressed men and women twirled past in a sea of glorious color, glittering masks, sparkling gems, and gold-dusted hair. It was a quite a juxtaposition for what was once a well-respected monastery, now a decadent and obscene exhibition of wealth and gluttony on display. Tables were shoved against the walls, overloaded with all manner of food. And servants' trays overflowed with glasses of all manner of drink. Most of the attendees appeared to be well on their way to being fully inebriated. Dresses hung a little lower, cravats a little looser or missing entirely.

How would they ever find Lord Middlebury in all this?

Or Kelly or Duncan or Owain, for that matter.

It seemed an impossible feat.

Normally, she wasn't this nervous, this shaken. But far too much was at stake here. And her family was too intimately involved, at every level.

And luck was with them, finally.

Lady Beatryce nudged Freddie gently and jerked her head to the left. "Middlebury is there. By the table with the ice sculpture on the far side."

Freddie snatched a glass of champagne from a passing servant and glanced surreptitiously over Lady Bea's shoulder as she took a sip. "I see him."

He was leaning into a woman, who twisted her hands before her and seemed ready to bolt at the first opportunity.

Lady Beatryce squared her shoulders, lifted her chin, and set her pace, which was far from her usual, purposeful stride; rather, she employed one a mysterious woman promising untold delights would engage.

Lady Bea, who stood a good head taller than the startled woman being cornered by Lord Middlebury, tapped the young lady on the shoulder, but her bright blue eyes never left her quarry's. "Run along now, sweetie. This man requires something a little *stronger*."

Frederica stood nearby, pretending to watch the dancing couples as they swept by; her purpose to offer back up should Lady Beatryce require it, though neither woman believed for a moment the extra caution was necessary.

Lord Middlebury straightened and widened his smile, too overconfident and tied up in his own lust to notice Lady Beatryce's sultry smile did not reach her ice-blue eyes.

His speech slurred, Lord Middlebury said, "Well, well. What do we have here? A young goddess, ready to take on a God?"

Lady Beatryce chuckled, but Middlebury seemed completely oblivious to the sharp tone surrounding her laugh. "I might be. How about we take a little walk? I know a place we can go that is dark and infinitely more private." Lady Bea walked her fingers up Middlebury's velvet-clad arm. "Who knows what sort of delights we shall find there?"

Lord Middlebury bowed. "I am ever your servant. Lead the way, my luscious vixen."

Freddie rolled her eyes and shook her head. What an idiot. God save all womankind from the like.

Still, Freddie followed, keeping to the shadows, following quietly behind the couple as they left the party, crossed the cloister, and entered a hall, walking along amiably until they reached an odd little prayer nook built into the wall at the opposite end of the hall near where Freddie and Lady Bea had first entered the abbey.

Lady Beatryce propped her leg onto the built-in bench and began lifting her skirts, slowly, as if taunting the young lord, and Freddie almost burst out laughing as Lord Middlebury leapt and began undoing the buttons of his falls with comical haste.

When Beatryce had her dress up to her thigh, she reached beneath her leg, and quick as an adder strike, whipped out a pistol.

"You can stop right there, Lord Middlebury."

Middlebury froze with half his buttons freed, an idiotic look on his handsome face. "What is the meaning of this?" he sputtered in outrage.

Lady Beatryce whipped off her mask and smiled as Middlebury blanched. The woman happily explained, "You're to be taken in for your crimes against the crown." She leaned in. "That's treason, if you must know."

Lord Middlebury began to stammer, his face red with fury, and Lady Beatryce laughed in the face of his ire. "B-but. Do you know who you're dealing with!?"

Lady Beatryce ignored him. "Yes, I think I shall relish watching you be drawn and quartered." She rested her finger on her lips. "On second thought, I have much better things to do with my time."

Quite frankly, Lord Middlebury hardly put up a fight as Freddie stepped out of the shadows, and the two women marched the man out the rear exit and to their waiting gaol in the woods.

The entire thing went off without a single hitch, and Freddie was pleased and confidently impressed.

Perhaps, they could pull this off without a single injury, after all?

But first, it was time for her to move into position for phase two.

Chapter Forty-Four

Meanwhile: The Masquerade: Part Three, Owain

"Mr. Kelly, sir, we have a situation."

Even though the soldier sounded dreadfully serious, Kelly had to stifle a chuckle for nearly looking over his shoulder for this Mr. Kelly, sir, fellow. He hadn't been called anything close to that in far too long. He'd not been much higher than pond scum when he worked undercover for the Society.

"Captain." Kelly smothered his amusement and dipped his head in acknowledgment.

"A message from Lord Dansbury. It's Viscount Sharpe, sir. He hasn't been seen since he arrived several hours ago."

"Interesting." There was no way the man had left. Thanks to Freddie, they had every conceivable exit covered with soldiers. That left the wine cellars, which long ago her father had converted to dungeons. Dansbury was responsible for the above floor rooms. It was up to Kelly to make his way downstairs and capture their target.

Kelly turned to the men surrounding him. "Black, Smith, and Nelson. You're with me. The rest of you, stick to the plan."

"Oh, and Mr. Kelly, sir."

Kelly turned. "Yes, captain?"

"Stonebridge says to warn you that Lord Dawe is aware we didn't fall for the trap. Dawe is frantic with madness. Stonebridge says to be on guard."

"Shite." Kelly turned to his men. "You heard that. Be extra vigilant, but the mission is still a go. We're to the cellars after Viscount Sharpe."

Together, he and his men donned their masks and made their way to their designated entrance. From memory, he followed the map Freddie had drawn and followed along the west-side cloister, through the kitchens, and to the cellar entrance without trouble. The servants there couldn't care less about the guests in their midst.

It had been far too easy, which made his skin prickle in alarm.

The cellar area was quiet, and not for the thousandth time, Kelly wondered at whether or not Frederica's brother could be trusted. Shouldn't there be a guard or two posted, especially if Viscount Sharpe was being held below?

He rubbed at the back of his neck as he felt his way down a stone staircase into the cool, dry cellars. A torch was lit near the bottom, and Kelly stepped carefully so as not to alert anyone who happened to be on guard.

Regardless, he was several steps from the bottom when a familiar voice called out. "It's all right. There's no one here besides me."

It was Owain. And Kelly would be a fool to trust the man's word, regardless of his past support of Frederica. Too much was at stake.

He maintained his cautious descent. When he reached the floor below, Kelly looked around and, weapon raised, discovered Owain had been telling the truth.

Viscount Sharpe stood behind the door to his cell, his hands resting through the bars, his mask dangling from one hand, and smirked. "I don't blame you for being distrustful."

Kelly nodded to his men, Smith and Nelson, who spread out to check all the corners. He didn't think anyone else was hiding down here, but it never hurt to be sure. Black had remained upstairs to guard the door less they became trapped.

Kelly pulled up his mask, folded his arms, leaned against the wall across from Owain's cell, and smiled. "How does it feel to lose?"

Owain shook his head and chuckled. "I'll let you know if it happens."

Kelly crossed his booted feet, the epitome of unconcerned. "Face it, old man. She's mine."

Owain froze and looked him straight in the eye. "Not. Yet."

A warning, to be sure.

Nelson returned, then, Smith trailing him. "The place is secure. Nothing else but bottles of wine and champagne."

Kelly stood from the wall. "Which means we haven't a moment to lose, someone will be coming for refills."

It was a matter of minutes before Kelly had taken some tools from his bag and picked the lock to the cell.

Owain stepped out of his prison. "I thank you, kindly."

Kelly dusted the dirt from his knees. "Don't thank me, yet. You're still to be detained, though I suspect you will find *my* accommodations infinitely preferable to the Society's." Kelly began to turn away, then paused. "Oh, and Owain." When the man faced him, Kelly drew back his fist and punched Owain in the face. Not hard enough to knock him over, but hard enough to warrant a square of linen to staunch the flow of blood. "That's for hurting Freddie. I'd do worse, but you gave Freddie a safe place to get on her feet, and you helped protect our child. For that, I owe you."

Owain shrugged and replied, muffled though it was, "You could say thanks by letting me go."

Kelly shook his head. "Sorry, but I still have to arrest you. You're guilty as hell. At the very least, for impersonating a member of the aristocracy, and you know how those bastards love their fancy titles."

Owain chuckled. "Why Kelly, how positively treasonous. Does Stonebridge know?"

Kelly grabbed hold of Owain's arm. "Let's go."

But their exit was cut off after all.

"Hold!"

It was Duncan, Freddie's brother, and he wielded a pistol. Four of his men stood behind him, armed as well.

Not great odds, but he'd had worse. Kelly stepped in front of Owain, who was the only unarmed man of the bunch, and shook his head at Duncan. "Freddie is going to be so disappointed."

Duncan smiled, then. "Perhaps, but I highly doubt for the reason you imply."

Chapter Forty-Five

The Masquerade: Part Four, La Grande Finale

Freddie watched her father through an eyehole in the door concealing the priest hole in his study. Disgust churned her stomach. She wanted nothing more than to confront him now, but she'd promised to wait until Stonebridge and Kelly had arrived. Right about now, she was regretting every single promise she'd ever made, but most especially *that* one.

The priest hole was large enough for a small bed and a desk, she knew that from memory, but the room was still cramped and musty and pitch black, she daren't light a candle.

And she'd nearly sneezed twice, which likely would have revealed her concealment to her father and ruined everything.

God, she didn't even have enough room to pace, which increased her frustration.

Worse, the men were ten minutes late, and Freddie wondered for the millionth time if Kelly had successfully rescued and recaptured Owain, and if so, how she felt about that. Because she honestly didn't know. She had no fear that they'd been taken by the Society. Kelly was witty, wily, and ridiculously charming. He could charm a damn snake if he put his mind to it.

The only positive part of watching from her concealed position behind the wall was her ability to witness her father's agitation, which was readily apparent. His cravat was askew, his hair in complete disarray, and he paced the floor, constantly. Every so often, he paused to look at the clock and run a hand through his hair again.

His world was crumbling to pieces, and she suspected by now, he knew it. Men were in and out of his study, while he yelled and blathered about. They knew she and Kelly had not gone to Cornwall, and Father was livid.

There was an ingenious horn near the eye hole and through it, she could hear most of what was happening in the room beyond.

Every time Father's men left, he would begin grumbling to himself, generally talking utter nonsense. On occasion, he even appeared to be talking to Grandfather via his portrait on the wall over the mantel. Perhaps, Father had truly gone mad?

Just then, her father raised a fist to no one, and there was no doubt about it. He was absolutely crazed.

Still, despite everything, and there was a lot of everything, it hurt to hear the parts where he raged on about her, calling her worthless, a whore, a traitor, a bitch. The words stung. But they weren't nearly as bad as knowing her father wanted her dead.

Despite his crazed, frantic tone and her knowledge of his past, evil deeds, his wish for her death bit the most. No one wanted to know someone wished them dead with such vehemence, but especially one's own father.

Frederica figuratively and literally lifted her chin. She would not let the mutterings of a lunatic get her down, regardless of who he was.

A few moments later, there was a clear knock on the door, and at her father's summons, the door swung inward.

It was Kelly and Owain, followed by her brother, Duncan.

This was not part of the plan, and Freddie readied her gun, for both Kelly and Owain had their hands raised as if in surrender, and Owain's face was covered in blood, obviously from a break in his nose. Kelly seemed intact, thank God.

But clearly, her brother held a gun.

Freddie's heart shattered at the sight. Heartbreak for her brother, and his betrayal. Fear for Kelly—and Owain for that matter.

To be honest, she could hardly believe her eyes. How had this come about? She had been so sure of her brother's words...

Duncan closed the door behind himself and locked it; the sound of the key turning in the lock echoed loud and clear around the room with ominous finality.

Kelly tensed as Father began laughing like a man in want of a stay in Bedlam. Dammit, she had to *do* something. She had the element of surprised on her side, but what?

Freddie narrowed her eyes and studied the scene before her. Kelly seemed to be studiously avoiding looking in the direction of the priest hole, which made perfect sense. He knew she was there and would never want to give away her position. But he wasn't trying to warn her away, either.

She glanced to Owain while doing her best to ignore Father's screeching and maniacal laughter. Owain, on the other hand, watched her door intently, which was interesting. How could he possibly know she was here? Unless, Kelly had told him—

She looked to her brother, who was also watching the priest hole, and she could have sworn he just...winked.

Could it be?

It was then that she noticed her brother held his gun in his right hand, while she knew he had always been left-handed.

She looked to his left hand, which he held down by his side with all his fingers splayed wide. Five?

She watched as he curled one finger. Four?

After a moment, he very deliberately curled another. Three.

When he was down to one finger, she glanced at his face, and he winked again. She grinned. Then, when he dipped his head, yes, she threw open the door right as all hell broke loose.

Kelly and Owain both pulled out guns. Stonebridge burst through the door.

Spittle flew from Father's mouth as he spun around in time to see her step through the doorway, her own gun raised.

Eyes wild, he snarled, "You!"

Frederica nodded. "I needed you to know that *I* am one of the instruments of your demise."

Her father pulled at his hair, which was already awry in every direction. "I will have your mother in Bedlam for this betrayal! Did you think about that?"

Frederica shook her head. "Mother will be fine. You, however, won't be hurting anyone ever again. Your reign of terror is over."

"But, but...you are my daughter," he screeched as Duncan grabbed him from behind.

Frederica smiled then but only had eyes for Kelly, who she'd found amidst the chaos; her anchor in the storm. "No. I am my own woman."

She should never have taken her eyes from the immediate threat, she knew better, for in that split instance Father bucked, wrenched Duncan's pistol, and spun toward Kelly all the while more men flooded the room.

A single shot rang out amidst the melee, and Frederica screamed as Kelly went down.

She raced across the room, her mind zeroed in on the love of her life, rolling on the floor, and—laughing?

She knelt by his side. "Kelly. Kelly, look at me? Are you all right?"

He lifted his head, his bright eyes locking with hers, one hand clamped around his upper arm. "Aye, love. I'm fine. It's just a scratch. Surprised me is all."

He sat up, and she swung her fist into his uninjured side. "Jesus, you scared the hell out of me, Kelly!"

"Awe, love," he said, as she threw her arms around his neck in relief. "I'm that glad to know you're concerned for my welfare. I should get shot more often."

She snorted. "Ooh...like hell, you should."

Her father's voice faded in the distance, as Stonebridge hauled him away.

Then, a familiar voice sounded—one of the most wonderful voices a woman ever heard—her mother.

"Where's my daughter. Young man, let me through. Frederica? Where are you, darling? I said out of my way!"

Frederica stood, a laugh and a sob—both—fighting their way out. She lent Kelly a hand while searching the growing crowd of people for her mother's loving face. She stood on her toes and waved. "Mother, I'm here!"

Suddenly, the crowd parted, and her mother raced to close the distance.

Their embrace was everything. Oh God, she'd missed her mother so much, had sobbed for her in the night so many times—but she was here, now, and that was what mattered.

Her mother pulled back. "Oh darling, let me look at you." She immediately pulled Frederica back into a hug, her voice tear-filled and muffled as she added, "I've missed you so much."

"Me, too, mother. Me, too."

Chapter Forty-Six

The Next Day

Watching Kelly get shot felt like it stole about thirty years from the end of her life. Thank God, the wound was only superficial. Well, as much as a bullet through the shoulder could be superficial. Infection was still a danger, but it could have been so much worse.

Freddie settled herself on the edge of Kelly's bed in the Duke of Stonebridge's grand London mansion.

Kelly moaned and blinked awake, and Freddie marveled once again to see those silver orbs direct their gaze on her. She stuffed away what she was sure was the widely recognizable grin of a woman in love and began straightening his bed sheets. The entire scenario was familiar, but so very different.

Kelly reached out a hand. "Freddie."

Freddie collapsed in the chair and fought back a sob. She masked her discomfort by asking, "How are you?" Her throat ached as she choked out the words.

Kelly reached out and caressed her cheek with the tip of one finger. "Better now."

She ignored the heartfelt look in his eye and jumped up to pace. What was wrong with her? She should be happy—relieved. He was going to be all right. And so was she. But at the same time, it meant everything was over. And now that the threat was gone, what did it all mean for them? For their future? For their family?

She wanted to know the answer. But she wanted a certain answer, and only that answer.

And she feared what that answer would, in truth, be.

So, she changed the subject of a conversation they hadn't even started, like the coward she really was. Sure, she was hard on the outside, but completely soft on the inside.

She resettled herself in the nearby chair. "What's going to happen to him?"

Kelly ignored her and reached for her hand, attempting to pull her toward him.

She swatted his hand away. "Be serious, Kelly."

One corner of his mouth lifted in a sensual grin. "Oh, I am. Deadly serious." He reached for her again. "I've seven years to make up for..."

Again, she pushed him away. This was important. They needed to get this part of the conversation out of the way, at the very least.

When she didn't budge, he growled but obeyed her command. "Fine. Well, if found guilty of treason, and he will be, he'll be drawn and quartered." Freddie gasped, and Kelly added, "That's the usual punishment for sedition. I hope they put his head on a pike outside the tower as well. Justice for all those he's murdered."

Freddie realized then, that he was speaking of her father, which considering the lengthy list of his crimes, the punishment he spoked of was possible, warranted even. But that's not who she cared about. "No not him. Owain."

Kelly finally successfully manipulated her onto the bed and into his arms. She felt his laugh rumble in his chest beneath her. "So that is his final name, is it?"

She lightly punched him in the side, mindful that he'd still been shot. "That's his real name, and I know you know it."

Kelly laughed with an, "Ouch," though her punch didn't really hurt.

"I don't know about Owain. He's guilty of *something*—even if it's impersonating nobility."

She sighed, knowing that his answer would sound something like that. On a positive note, Owain was being held in a makeshift gaol in the duke's own house and hadn't been taken to the Tower or Newgate, but she did not know precisely what that all meant.

She traced the design on the bed cover lying across Kelly's chest and said, "You know our son calls him Uncle."

Kelly sighed then, the sound so serious, finally, and squeezed her affectionately. "I can't just let him go, Freddie. He played both sides, ruthlessly. He took matters into his own hands. He wasn't always on the right side of the law. I have to see him brought to justice."

She nodded. "You're right, I suppose."

He tried to look down and see her face, but she burrowed further into his arms, hiding it from him.

"That's how it's going to be, is it?" he asked, a hint of laughter behind his words.

Freddie smiled into his side, then wiped the grin from her face and pulled back, a look of pure innocence on her face. "Oh, Kelly—whatever do you mean?"

But he knew.

They both did.

Chapter Forty-Seven

That Night

Once again, the clang of a metal key sounded in Frederica's ears. She'd be quite happy to never see a set of bars again, nor hear that telltale metallic sound. Even if she'd never been locked behind them herself...by pure chance. The first time she'd freed a man, it had nearly wrecked her, emotionally. This time—

Her candlelight fell upon Owain, standing in the shadows, casually leaning against the rear wall of his cell. He hadn't been chained, thankfully, though it would have been nothing for her to pick the lock. Still, she was glad she didn't have to do so.

He wore a smirk, but she could sense the question in his eyes. "Are you here to rescue me?"

He'd said it with a hefty dose of innuendo, and Freddie rolled her eyes. "This isn't the first time I've stolen a man from jail. At least, *you* can walk out on your own two feet."

"Why, Frederica, are you impugning my reputation—"

She chuckled. "Since when have you ever concerned yourself with your reputation?"

He stopped beside her in the doorway and glanced down. "Love, I am always concerned about my reputation."

She supposed that was true. Even if his known repute was a total fabrication; he used it as accurately as Kelly could wield a sword or his wit. And just as deadly. Which meant, it took an intentional measure of cultivation to hone such a reputation as his.

She settled one hand on his arm and, on impulse, said. "Thank you. For everything."

He smirked. "Shouldn't I be thanking you?"

"Be serious, Owain. I mean it. You helped me when I was lost. Without you—"

Owain shook his head. "Don't sell yourself short, love. You're one remarkable and resourceful woman, and don't ever forget that."

She nodded. "You've been kind—"

He performed an exaggerated shudder, but with a growl argued, "Definitely don't tell anyone *that*." With all seriousness, he added, "I'm not kind."

It felt like a warning, a reminder. Then, like the flip of a switch, his good humor returned. He was certainly mercurial this evening, and his tone was filled with innuendo. "But, love, are you sure you don't want to—" He gestured toward the exit.

Once more, Freddie found herself rolling her eyes; she waved him away with her hand. "I'm sure."

He stood from the wall. "I could—"

Now, it was her turn to gesture toward the exit. "I'm *sure*."

Ignoring her, he glanced down and titled her head with the curve of one knuckle. "It'll be an adventure. All the whisky you can handle. Men. Villains. *Me*—"

She twisted her head away and shook it with a laugh. "Just go. Before I hang you myself."

And he did, but he paused at the exit. "Does Kelly know you're doing this?"

She folded her arms. "It's none of your business."

He glanced toward the stairs leading out. "Perhaps, I should just—"

"*Go!*" she growled.

He held up his hands in supplication "All right, all right. Take care of yourself. Don't—" She could have sworn she heard him swallow. "We could have—Bloody hell. Just—Give 'em hell, Fred—"

And he disappeared into the darkness.

Chapter Forty-Eight

Moments Later

Freddie leaned against the doorframe to Kelly's room, a fond smile on her face as she watched the two most important people in her life—Kelly and Fionnán—simply be.

Kelly was upright in bed, leaning against the headboard, reading a paper, one arm still encased in a sling. Their son, Fionnán, was curled up next to him, sound asleep. It had been the stuff of dreams to see Kelly and Fionnán bonding over the last few days; she was glad she'd sent for their son after talking with her brother at the Yellow Goose.

She must have sighed, for suddenly, Kelly glanced at her over the top of his paper, his reading glasses, which only emphasized his glorious, quick-silver eyes, slid down his nose as he peered at her from over the top of the frames.

He arched a brow and lowered the paper to his lap. "How'd the great escape go?"

Frederica stepped into the room. "Great escape? I have no idea what you're talking about."

Kelly snorted. "I'm sure what's his name—Spyder, Sharpe, Puppet

Master, Owain—whatever his name is, is half-way to fucking Wales by now."

Frederica frowned and darted a glance to their son to verify he still slept.

"Watch your language," she admonished Kelly.

Kelly snorted but looked down and brushed the fine baby hair off his son's brow, absolute love shining in his eyes, while Freddie crawled into bed with them both. She propped her head up with one hand. "Do you know how much I love you?"

Kelly lifted the paper from his lap and shook it, as if returning his attention to it, but replied, "Oh, you do now, do you..."

She tossed a pillow at him, and he laughed, allowing the paper and the pillow to slide to the floor.

Freddie sat up, and leaning over Fionnán, attempted to steal a kiss, but Kelly pulled away, staying her with his good hand. "Freddie, wait." He sighed and pinched the bridge of his nose. "Look. I'm... I'm going to need you to make an honest man out of me. Aunt Harriett won't abide my living in sin, the child's sensibilities you know. The people of this town are so unforgiving, you know how it is—"

Freddie searched his eyes for his usual teasing demeanor, but in his way, he was actually quite serious. Well, mostly. "Kelly, is—is that a proposal?"

"Well, of course it is, you ridiculous woman. Don't you know? I think I have feelings for you..."

Her shoulders shook with mirth. "You poor misguided fool."

"Ah, Freddie, I love you, don't you know?"

She said, "Not really, no. Why don't you tell me about it?"

"Come here." He held out his hands, and Frederica stood on the bed, cautious not to step on Fionnán. Fionnán rolled with her weight and let out a soft snore but remained asleep.

Frederica carefully settled astride Kelly and hung her arms on his shoulders but looked down to their son. "Yes, he's your son, all right. Sounds just like you when you're sleeping."

Kelly tickled her sides and said, "Oh, I do, do I?"

Freddie stayed his hands. "Stop," she whispered fiercely, "You'll wake Fionnán, and we won't be able to go to sleep for hours."

"All right," he acquiesced, and he touched his forehead to hers, his voice softening. "Hmm, where were we? Oh, yes. I love you and have for so very long. You carved a Freddie-sized whole in my heart and inserted yourself there approximately seven years ago. And with your notoriously hard-headed, stubborn," she growled a warning, "*fierce* will, stayed there. I couldn't oust you. Therefore, what's a man to do? How could I not love you? You are remarkable, practical, smart, beautiful, ingenious. You're the perfect woman for me, the perfect mother for our children—"

"Children?"

"Yes, children. Dozens. Maybe, more. But, Freddie, only if you make me an honest man. You don't know what it's like to feel the wrath of Aunt Harriet's umbrella...so, will you, *mo ghrá*? Will you marry me?"

"Of course, I will, you charming, idiotic, rake. But," she walked her fingers up his chest, "what will you tell Stonebridge?"

"The truth, of course. People will have to know. There's the church to reserve, the priest to secure, the—"

She swatted his bare chest. "Not about *that*...about the, er, other thing?" She meant about her freeing Owain, though she daren't say the words directly.

He wrapped his arms around her and pulled her tight to his chest. "I don't know, but the hunt sure will be fun."

She shook her head. *Sigh. Men.*

Kelly shrugged. "He needs to know that I won."

She punched him lightly in the gut. "Oh, he knows."

The End

About the Author

Amy Quinton writes humorous historicals...with heat from her home in Summerville, SC. She lives with her husband, two boys, three cats (George, Astrid, and Toothless), and one dog (Bear). In her spare time, she likes to read, go camping, crochet/knit, read, hike—oh, who is she kidding, what spare time?

http://amyquinton.net

Sign up for her newsletter at:
https://app.mailerlite.com/webforms/landing/u4s4j6

facebook.com/AmyElizabethQuinton

twitter.com/AmyQuinton

instagram.com/quintonamy

amazon.com/author/amyquinton

pinterest.com/amyquii

goodreads.com/amyquinton

bookbub.com/profile/amy-quinton

What the Duke Wants

Agents of Change, Book 1

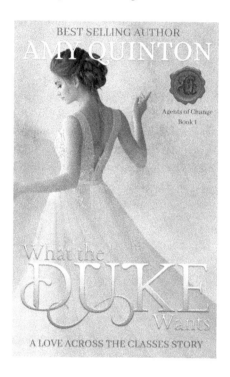

http://bit.ly/whatthedukewants

England, 1814: She is from trade. He is a duke and an agent for the crown with a name to restore and a mystery to solve.

Miss Grace (ha!) Radclyffe is an oftentimes hilariously clumsy, 20-year-old orphan biding her time living with her uncle until she is old enough to come into her small inheritance. Much to her aunt's chagrin, she isn't:

- Reserved—not with her shocking! tendency to befriend the servants...
- Sophisticated—highly overrated if one cannot run around

barefoot outside...

- Graceful—she once flung her dinner into a duke's face... on accident, of course.

But she is:

- Practical—owning a fashion house is in her future; unless someone foils her plans...
- In love... maybe... perhaps... possibly...

The Duke of Stonebridge is a man with a tragic past. His father died mysteriously when he was 12 years old amid speculation that the old duke was 'involved' with another man. He must restore his family name, but on the eve of his engagement to the perfect debutante, he meets his betrothed's cousin, and his world is turned inside out... No matter, he is always:

- Logical—men who follow their hearts and not their heads are foolish...
- Reserved—his private life is nobody's business but his own...

And he isn't:

- Impulsive—it always leads to trouble...
- Charming—that's his best friend, the Marquess of Dansbury's, area of expertise...
- In love... maybe... perhaps... possibly...

Can he have what he wants and remain respectable? Can she trust him to be the man she needs?

What the Marquess Sees

Agents of Change, Book 2

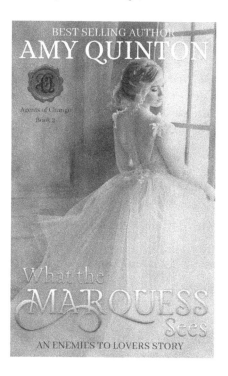

http://bit.ly/whatthemarquesssees

England, 1814: He is a marquess and a spy with a woman to protect and an assassin to thwart. She is...not nice.

The Marquess of Dansbury is a strong, charismatic man living a charmed life, despite interacting with the dregs of society as an agent for the crown. His past isn't without tragedy, but he is too amiable to allow misfortune to mar his positive outlook on life. Until now...when he finds himself tasked with protecting the one woman he actively disdains, Lady Beatryce Beckett, from a deadly and all too insane assassin. No matter, he is always:

- Charming—though perhaps not around a certain lady...

- Laid-back—again, maybe not around a certain lady...
- And strong—especially around a certain lady...

And he isn't:

- Irrational—ever. Even around a certain lady...generally speaking...usually...
- Or in love...with a certain lady. Especially not that. Honest...

Lady Beatryce Beckett is mean. She ruins other women on purpose. She lies. She cheats. She even steals. She's fast. And she takes particular pleasure in provoking a certain marquess. In short, she'll do anything to get what she wants: Freedom from her abusive father. Much to everyone's vexation, she isn't:

- Reserved—with anyone, but especially with a certain marquess...
- Trusting—with anyone. Ever. Even with a certain charming marquess...
- Or a coward—especially around a certain marquess.

But she is:

- Strong—she's had to be...particularly around... need she really explain?
- Worthy... of love. Possibly.
- And in love...Wait, what?

It will take a special man to see the true woman beneath the surface...and a strong woman to allow him that glimpse. Can she teach him that his ruthless drive to seek justice isn't all that different from her determination to be free?

What the Scot Hears

Agents of Change, Book 3

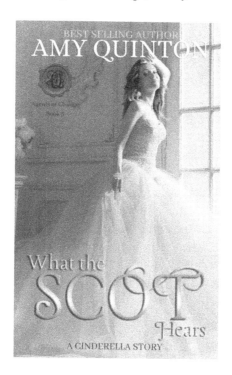

http://bit.ly/whatthescothears

England 1814: *Reticent Scottish Lord pursues Mouthy, Independent, American Woman...* She is an outspoken American orphan with a questionable past and a dubious purpose. He is a man of few words on the lookout for a traitor. How could they NOT get along?

Mrs. Amelia Chase is a highly-opinionated, 23-year-old woman from America on the run from her past with a penchant for self-preservation and a healthy love for Shakespearean insults. Much to a certain Scotsman's dismay:

She isn't:

- Quiet – not with her tendency to talk to everyone about anything...
- Demure – highly overrated if one cannot wear red and show off one's curves...
- Equine-savvy – she once fled some currish, toad-spotted, coxcombs – er, villains – in a stolen carriage at a pace slower than a meandering walk. Oh, and mistook a common mule for a thoroughbred. But other than that...

And she is:

- Brave – Smart, Loyal, Witty. Er, charming. Plus, Modest, Lonely, Secretive – Um, forget that last part...
- And In love – with a distrustful Highlander of all things...

Lord Alaistair MacLeod is an agent for the Crown and a man with secrets. He doesn't speak of them, he doesn't dwell on them, and he certainly doesn't let them define his future. Much. One thing is for certain, he definitely doesn't share his confidences with a peery, outspoken American woman who is obviously trouble, acts highly suspicious, and is far too nosy for her own good... No matter:

He is always:

- Focused – men who cannot stay to task are foolish...
- Pointed and Reserved – enough said...

And he isn't:

- Cheeky – like a certain American firebrand...
- Led by his... ahem...even when following on the heels of a curvy, red-wearing... ahem
- Or In love... especially not with a Troublesome, Meddlesome, so-called Independent American Woman...

Can he trust enough to embrace such an enigmatic woman? Can she awaken the passions of such an intensely private man?

Also by Amy Quinton

How to Take Revenge on a Disloyal Scot

An Agents of Change short story

Love is... revenge? Because what else's a girl supposed to do when she learns the man she loves has found himself a bride?

The Umbrella Chronicles: George & Dorothea's Story *A short story, part of Never Too Late, A Bluestocking Belles Collection

St. Vincent's days as a bachelor in good standing are numbered.

The Umbrella Chronicles: James & Annie's Story *A short story, part of Follow Your Star Home, A Bluestocking Belles Holiday Collection

Prodigal duke seeks professional matchmaker for matrimonial assistance. Prefers foolproof plans

in 10 parts. Magical solutions accepted. Missteps likely.

The Umbrella Chronicles: John & Emma's Story *A short story, part of Valentines from Bath, A Bluestocking Belles Valentine's Day Collection

A serious-minded, scientific man of learning seeks a complex and chaotic practitioner of all things superstitious who will upend his well-ordered life.

Hoodwinked for the Holidays *A short story, part of the Love in the Lowcountry: A Winter Holiday Collection, Volume 1

Wanted: Ghost with good reviews for special holiday tour. Team Player a must. Matchmaking skills NOT required.

Coming February 2020:

The Umbrella Chronicles: Chester & Artemis's Story *A short story, part of Fire & Frost, a Bluestocking Belles Collection

Beastly duke seeks confident any woman who doesn't faint at the sight of his scars. Prefers not to leave the house to find her.